Somewhere Between Bitter and Sweet

Somewhere Between Bitter and Sweet

LAEKAN ZEA KEMP

LITTLE, BROWN AND COMPANY
NEW YORK   BOSTON

Little, Brown and Company
Hachette Book Group
1290 Avenue of the Americas, New York, NY 10104
Visit us at LBYR.com

First Edition: April 2021

Little, Brown and Company is a division of Hachette Book Group, Inc. The Little, Brown name and logo are trademarks of Hachette Book Group, Inc.

The publisher is not responsible for websites (or their content) that are not owned by the publisher.

Library of Congress Cataloging-in-Publication Data
Names: Kemp, Laekan Zea, author.
Title: Somewhere between bitter and sweet / by Laekan Zea Kemp.
Description: New York : Little, Brown and Company, 2021. | Audience: Ages 12+. | Summary: Told in two voices, Pen, whose dream of taking over her family's restaurant has been destroyed, and Xander, a new, undocumented, employee seeking his father, form a bond.
Identifiers: LCCN 2020012182 | ISBN 9780316460279 (hardcover) | ISBN 9780316460316 (ebook) | ISBN 9780316460323 (ebook other)
Subjects: CYAC: Restaurants—Fiction. | Cooking, Mexican—Fiction. | Fathers—Fiction. | Family life—Fiction. | Illegal aliens—Fiction. | Mexican Americans—Fiction.
Classification: LCC PZ7.1.K463 Som 2021 | DDC [Fic]—dc23
LC record available at https://lccn.loc.gov/2020012182

ISBNs: 978-0-316-46027-9 (hardcover), 978-0-316-46031-6 (ebook)

Printed in the United States of America

LSC-C

Printing 1, 2021

For my father, you were better than us all

1

Pen

GREASE HISSES AND POPS beneath the staccato drums ticking from the speaker above my brother Angel's head. The song fades beneath the clank of metal and the sound of his voice calling orders across the kitchen.

"Adobada. Mole verde. Guiso de flor."

I hear him through the crack in the back door of the restaurant, my forehead pressed to the cold metal as I count my breaths, the beats in between. *Go inside. The restaurant is descending into chaos. You don't have time to fall apart.*

But the voice in my head isn't alone. There's another voice, biting and cold and cruel.

You're a mess, Pen. You're just going to make a mess.

I call it a liar, I pray that it is. Then I grit my teeth and yank the door open.

In the kitchen, glass bowls full of garlic, cilantro, and

guajillos slide across the counter, crashing against the faded Spanish labels pressed to jars of canela, anise, and comino. The glass jar of cumin tumbles, exploding against the concrete floor like a flash of orange gunpowder.

The impact ignites a thousand memories. My father's pipe speaking in tobacco apparitions. The knock and twist of the molcajete, the slap of my mother's bare feet on the kitchen floor. "Volver Volver" low and stretched like dough as my father hums it over the sound of the radio. Even when they're not here, their love is still the heartbeat of the place.

"Comin' in hot!" Angel slams a slab of meat down on the cutting board. "I need runners!" He slaps the counter, summoning the waiters who are dripping in sweat and trying to remember to smile.

But that's hard to do when you're slammed and short-staffed. Not to mention the fact that the number of free meals my father's been doling out has nearly doubled, which means fewer tips but twice the work.

Glass shatters and I rush into the dining room. Gabby, the new girl I spent six hours training this week, is on all fours. When she sees me, she cowers. I don't just forget to smile. When I'm at the restaurant my face is physically incapable.

She scrambles to scrape up the broken plate and slices her hand. She winces, but I'm not sure if the tears are from the pain or my proximity.

My other half, Chloe, abandons the hostess stand and steps between us. "Try using a broom next time." She helps Gabby to her feet before trading her hand for the broom.

While Gabby cleans up the mess, Chloe pulls me aside. "It was an accident," she says, reminding me that these kinds of things do indeed happen and that I should defer to her in moments requiring human compassion since she is much better equipped for them. Which also reminds me why she's my best friend. "Besides, half the people in here are so drunk they didn't even notice."

Chloe's right. We've reached that point in the night when we're slinging more drinks than tacos, and the Frankenstein monsters on our menu—which I'd created specifically for the inebriated—are flooding the line. There's the fried egg pork carnitas perfect for a pounding headache, and the barbacoa with bacon and refried beans that soaks up alcohol like a sponge. I watch as one of the waitresses carries out a stack of corn tortillas filled with tripas and potatoes smothered in queso blanco—the holy grail of hangover remedies.

Chloe pushes up her glasses, using her shirt to dry the bridge of her nose. "You okay?"

Beneath the buzz, her voice sounds far away. It still stings. But just because Chloe can sense something's off with me doesn't mean anyone else can.

Seeing my anxiety grow fangs is a privilege reserved for exactly one person (and only when we're spoon-deep in a carton of Amy's Mexican vanilla ice cream and there's no one else around to see me cry).

"I just took a quick break," I say, eyes trying to steal back more questions. "I'll be fine." I'm not exactly sure what *fine* even means, but it's good enough for her to let me walk away. For now.

On my way back to the kitchen I'm stopped by one of

our neighbors, Mr. Cantu. His baseball cap is covered in paint, and that's when I notice the spray can in each hand.

"Pen, is your father here?"

"He'll be back in the morning. Is there something I can help you with?"

He deflates. "I'm here to paint the sidewalk. He said he'd pay me fifty bucks."

I look from him to the crowd outside the entrance. The sidewalk's full of people. "Tonight?"

"Well, tomorrow morning. But it's just that I could really use the money now." He motions to the parking lot. "My wife's right outside. She already had the stencils made. We can get started right away."

Mrs. Cantu can draw almost anything—caricatures, animals, flowers. She turns her sketches into stencils and her husband paints them into custom house numbers. I didn't know my father had commissioned them to paint the sidewalk outside the restaurant, but it doesn't surprise me. There's someone doing odd jobs around here almost every day, not because we need the help but because they do.

"We're really busy tonight, Mr. Cantu...."

"I can set up cones. I can work around the crowd. Just give him a call," he pleads.

I lead him back toward the entrance. "I'm sorry, but he'll meet you in the morning. Like he promised."

He stops. "Then an advance. You pay me now, and I'll get to work as soon as the sun comes up." He's got a death grip on both paint cans, his eyes red like he hasn't slept in days. "Please, I have to have the money tonight."

I lower my voice. "Or what?"

He lowers his too, glancing at the faces nearby. "Or he'll take something else."

The look in Mr. Cantu's eyes spurs my pulse, then my feet. I make my way to the bar, knocking on the counter where Java, one of the bartenders, is flirting with some girls from a bachelorette party waiting to be seated.

"I need fifty from the cash register." I motion toward Mr. Cantu. "Another side job."

"What about when I come up short tonight?"

I sigh, taking the cash. "I'll figure it out."

He nods, relieved. Because I always do.

That's who I have to be when I'm here. Pragmatic. A problem-solver. Even when my brain is quicksand and no amount of medication can drag me out.

You're a mess, Pen.

Everything is a mess.

I find Mr. Cantu and hand over the money. "And you'll be here first thing in the morning."

"Yes, yes, of course." He shakes my hand. "Thank you, Pen. Tell your father thank you."

On my way back to the kitchen, the burn in my knees finally registers. Somehow, my five-hour shift has stretched into seven. I take the place of one of the platers, my thoughts silenced the moment my signature desserts start coming up the line. For the first time all night, the clenched fist around my lungs lets go. I adorn cakes and pastries with mint leaves and powdered sugar, cinnamon and drizzled cajeta. I suck the Mexican caramel from my thumb. Nothing hurts anymore.

Someone knocks into me from behind, my chest

smearing the coconut icing on the piece of cake I just plated. The cake I bake from scratch every single day.

I can hear Struggles, resident dish boy, wheezing behind me, his shoes squeaking as he tries to tiptoe back to the dish pit. I spin, my ponytail whipping him in the face as he raises his hands in surrender.

"I'm s-sorry. . . . I was just—"

I grab him by the shirt collar, waiting for everyone else to turn and look. I prefer an audience when I bite someone's head off. Not because I like the attention, but because I like the insurance. The scarier I am on the outside, the less likely they are to see what's underneath.

"Bring me another piece." Struggles takes a step and I yank him back. "If you so much as breathe on it, I will hurt you."

He scampers away just as another crash ignites from the dining room. I scan the floor for Gabby. Instead, two guys are wrestling by the bar, their bodies knocking drinks off the countertop.

As I wind back through the dining tables, the other bartender, Solana, claws at the arm of one of the drunkards until it's twisted behind his back. Java ducks behind the bar, groaning as he searches the shelves. I find what he's looking for before he does, and I poise the air horn between the two brutes. Then I squeeze. They hold their ears, rolling like insects until Solana and a few of our regulars drag them outside.

I call out to Java, "Disaster tax, stat!"

It's his cue to bump up the price of alcohol for the rest of the night. It's almost 1:00 AM, which means that everyone left in the bar will be too drunk to care. We'll make back what's currently stuck to the floor and then some.

Chloe already has a mop in hand, and I whistle for Struggles to roll out the bucket. He lathers the floor. Gabby grabs a tray of food. She takes one step into the soapsuds and busts.

I find Angel through the order window. He rakes a hand down his face, calculations racing behind his eyes of every broken glass and plate, every spoiled piece of food.

I can see that he's about to lose his shit, but the chaos of the restaurant is nothing compared to what's thrashing inside my own head. The voice I've been trying to ignore all night sinks its hooks in me.

Just collapse, Pen.

Let it all collapse.

The sound is a tsunami. But this—the mess, the money we've lost, the money we've been hemorrhaging for months—is more like a Category 5 hurricane, grainy and muted in a black-and-white photo. The worst of it still looming in the distance. Moving so fast it's practically still.

I can navigate that kind of stillness. Which is why Angel is always the one who gets to lose his shit while I'm the one who cleans up the mess.

As he hurls a string of expletives at anyone within earshot, I shove away the voice for the millionth time tonight, find a pair of gloves, and get to work.

By closing time, I reek of tequila and onions. There are only four hours until my father and the morning crew will get breakfast started. But I know he's already awake. From where I'm scrubbing tables in the center of the dining room, I see his headlights creep up the mural on the back wall of the restaurant, settling over the guitar-playing skeletons as he puts his truck in park.

Java strips off his shirt on his way to the back door. "Sol, you're still covering my shift tomorrow, right?"

She looks back at Angel. "I can't pour drinks and plate at the same time."

"New guy's starting tomorrow, so we won't need you in the kitchen."

"But we just got Gabby," I say.

"Yeah, and we all know how that worked out," Solana huffs.

"What's with all the new hires?" Java asks.

I want to ask the same question, and more specifically, why our father hasn't said anything about it to me.

"Struggles…" Angel slaps the dumpster out back. Struggles is halfway inside. "What the hell are you doing?"

Struggles climbs back out holding a crate of canned tomatoes. When he notices our looks of disgust, he says, "They're still good."

"You mean they expired three days ago." Angel tries to yank the crate from his grasp.

I step between them. "Which means they're still good enough for Struggles." I push the crate back into his arms and he races down the steps to his ride.

We wait for everyone to pull out of the parking lot and then we walk back around to our father's truck. Angel pulls the door open, letting me slide in first before he slumps down next to me with a sigh.

My back hurts, my legs burn, sweat painting my neck. I scrape my hair out of my face and find pieces of lettuce and dried enchilada sauce. Angel is just as filthy, the hours stuck to us in layers of grease while time has burrowed even deeper into my father's skin.

He's been waking up before the sun every morning for the past fifteen years. Cooking migas and tamales and carne asada. Cleaning up broken glass and spilled drinks and half-eaten food. Hiring cooks and bartenders and dish washers; firing them too. Wondering if people are going to show up that day, if they're going to like the food, if they're going to pay what it's worth. And going to bed every night hoping that it was enough. To pay the bills. To raise four kids. To open the doors another day.

I can see those worries on his face. But even covered in filth, in food my father used to love, in sweat I can't wait to wash off, there's nothing I want more than to wear the same worry he does, to wake up with the same freedom.

"You smell like shit," my father says.

"You mean I smell like money," Angel corrects him.

My father almost laughs, but then his eyes track to the neon glow of the restaurant sign stamped against the hood of the truck. There's something on his mind that can't quite make it to his lips.

"Mr. Cantu asked for an advance on the sidewalk," I say.

He sighs. "Did you give it to him?"

I nod.

"Good," he says, backing out onto the street.

"He seemed scared," I add, some of that fear still clinging to me.

This gets his attention, and it's just a flicker, his eyes quickly returning to the road, but I swear there was something like fear in them too.

"What's going on?" I ask.

Angel jumps in. "Did he take money from *you-know-who*?"

"Mind your own business," my father says.

Angel huffs. "Well, if he did, he's a fool. Especially after what happened to—"

My father slams on the brakes. Angel and I are thrown forward as the truck idles in the middle of the empty street.

My father looks right at us and says, "Never judge another man for how he tries to feed his family. We're no better than him. We're no better than anyone."

On the rest of the drive home, our father is quiet, Angel and I so still we're both close to dozing off. Suddenly, I feel my father reach an arm around me, letting me use his shoulder as a pillow. With the same hand he musses Angel's hair, and even though I know this is all we'll ever get, that his tenderness toward us will always be confined to the dark, I curl as close to him as I can and wish with everything in me that someday I'll grow into the parts of him that are better than us all.

2

Pen

Cocoa powder
Cinnamon
Condensed milk
Whipping cream
Strawberries
Blood

ONE DROP FALLS ON the strawberries I'm slicing up, another trying to fold itself into the whipping cream. I'm not sure where I heard that getting blood in the pancake batter is bad luck, but I know it's an omen the moment I see it.

I reach for the dishrag hanging over the sink, still soapy. Then I toss out the batter, starting from scratch with my one good hand.

"Did you cut yourself?" My little brother, Hugo, comes to stand next to me, tugging on the towel.

"It's just a scratch," I say, pulling away.

He grabs my elbow instead, and that's when I realize the loud thumping sound isn't my pulse but the whisk against the side of the bowl.

"Are you okay?" He cocks an eyebrow the way our father does, nose wrinkled as if he's trying to sniff out the truth.

But I don't tell the truth these days, so I just shrug and say, "Fine."

"Pen, can't we just have Froot Loops?" My little sister, Lola, has her head in her hands. "Please?"

"I'm sorry, but did you just say you'd rather have Froot Loops?"

She whines, still clutching her chubby cheeks. "Everything you make takes too long."

I move back to flip the cakes on the griddle. "Maybe because what I make is *real* food and not from a box."

"But I don't want that." Her bare feet slap the legs of her chair. "I want Froot Loops."

I grip the sides of the counter before taking a few deep breaths. Then I wave over my shoulder. "Fine. Do whatever you want."

The room goes quiet, the only sound the sizzle of the batter as I pour the rest onto the griddle.

"Did you just say what I think you said?" Hugo asks.

"What?" I glance back at them. "Yeah. She can have whatever she wants."

Lola jumps down from her chair and rushes over to the pantry, keeping one eye on me as she reaches for the box of cereal. She hugs it to her chest, taking slow steps around the kitchen as she grabs the milk and a bowl. She's still staring at me as she begins to pour, slowly at first, testing me. When I don't say a word, she pours the entire box into her bowl and smiles.

I lean over her. "And you better eat *every* last bite."

When the pancakes are finished, I wrap them up and carry them over to our neighbor, Mrs. Nguyen, with Lola and Hugo following behind me. Her son, Sang, has worked at the restaurant almost as long as I have. He's saving up to transfer to some fancy university, and as a thanks for hiring him, Mrs. Nguyen watches Lola and Hugo on Saturday mornings when both of my parents are at the restaurant. And when I'm supposed to be at the community college.

I've been watching them for the past few weeks, but now that winter break is over, it's time for things to go back to normal, which as far as my parents are concerned means that I'll be attending labs every Saturday morning— something they believe I've been doing since the start of the fall semester.

But today's a new day. A fresh start.

Who knows? Maybe this time I'll actually make it inside the building.

"Pen, what have you got for me today?" Mrs. Nguyen is already sitting on her porch, a steaming cup of coffee in her hand.

"Pancakes."

"The ones with chocolate and strawberries?" she asks.

I nod and she takes them, already peeling back the foil so she can tear off a bite.

"I just love these." She pats my hand. "Have you

convinced your father to start selling them at the restaurant yet?"

"Thanks. And not yet."

Compliments usually make me uncomfortable—I'd rather watch the way my food makes people feel—but Mrs. Nguyen has been my official taste tester since I was in elementary school. In fact, she was my first customer, spending twenty bucks on pralines every time I opened up a lemonade stand. At eighteen years old, I've finally come to accept her enthusiasm. Unfortunately, that enthusiasm hasn't quite rubbed off on my father. He's let me tweak the menu at the restaurant, but when it comes to my desire to take over the place, or even to open up one of my own, he hasn't exactly been supportive.

"You tell him he's losing a fortune," she says.

I shrug my backpack onto the opposite shoulder, letting the weight of all those unopened textbooks drag me to the car. "Thank you for watching Lola and Hugo today. I better get going, you know...to class."

"Oh yes, yes, *Em*. Have a nice day."

The parking lot hasn't changed; the science building looks the same as it did that first day of school five months ago. But as I sit in my car, watching girls I met during orientation skip up the steps, excited to play nurse, I try to convince myself that something inside *me* has changed. That today I'll actually go inside. That today I'll stop lying and be the person they want me to be.

Class starts in approximately seven minutes—the class I should have taken and passed last semester, moving me one step closer to a degree in nursing.

Six minutes.

I sit in the parking lot, watching the clock tick down. The car is in park, but I can't bring myself to turn off the engine.

What's the point?

I turn off the car, reminding myself how much I've already spent on tuition and books.

You're a failure, Pen. A liar. A waste.

I reach for my bag, trying to stuff down the voice, begging myself to get. Out. Of. The. Car.

It's too late. It's too late. It's too late.

And then I can't breathe.

My mother's shoes.

All I can think about are my mother's shoes.

How they've sat in the same spot by the door for almost twenty years. Scuffed and cracked, the shadow of her foot pressed to the leather even when the laces are loose. I imagine every hallway they've ever walked down, every mess they've ever stepped in, every second they've held her up when all she wanted was to collapse. Because one of her patients couldn't remember her face or their daughter's name or how to speak.

When she lost one, I'd wake to the knock of the rolling pin and the smell of dough warming on the comal. Sometimes I'd try to take the pin from her, but I think there was something about the rhythm that reminded her how to breathe. We'd work in silence. Three dozen tortillas later, she'd wrap them in foil and drive them to the family that only visited once a month. That would accept my mother's food without acknowledging she was more family to the deceased than they were.

And then the next day, she would go back to work.

For almost twenty years. She went back.

If I step out of this car, if I walk up those steps, if I sit at that desk and pretend...how long will I be sitting there before I realize I'm trapped?

I stare down at my hands gripping the steering wheel, following where the sunlight lands against my forearms. I trace the lines, remembering all of the times I tried to cut through invisible binds before. All of the times it only summoned new demons instead of snuffing out the old ones. I feel that familiar itch to climb out of my skin. Instead, I imagine myself in a cocoon, tugging it tight around me, trying to ground myself in the here and now.

I list what I had for breakfast.

I whisper the ingredients for my signature coconut cake.

I take a deep breath, the scents of a thousand shifts at the restaurant tucked into the fabric of the front seat. I start listing them too: mango and cilantro and epazote, tomatillos and roasted pepitas and tortillas.

The truth is, I can't sleep without those smells tangled in my hair.

So I have to decide what's scarier: living a life that doesn't belong to me, or losing the one I love. If the truth breaks my father's heart, I know he'll take it from me. But if it doesn't, if he understands, if I can *make* him understand, I can be free.

I weigh each option, simmering in the anxiety they provoke, in the hope. Because I have to do what scares me. Because, somehow, stepping into my fears is the only remedy I've found to ward off that feeling of helplessness. To stay in control. I always have to be in control.

Which means that today is not the day I go inside.

My stomach drops, my hand reaching to put the car in drive again.

Today is the day I tell them the truth.

———————

My shift at the restaurant doesn't start until five, but I know my parents will both be in the back having their monthly expenses meeting. Probably not the best time to disturb them, but it's rare for them to be in the same place at the same time. My dad is always at the restaurant, and my mom works nights at the nursing home.

When I walk inside, the place is just starting to pick up, tables topped with textbooks and mugs of Mexican coffee. After a long night of partying, the college students at the University of Texas drag themselves here in droves.

On Thursdays, they come here for the best palomas in town, thanks to my substitution of Jamaican tangelos and blood limes for the traditional grapefruit. And on Fridays, they come for half-price pork carnitas, legendary thanks to my addition of sweetened condensed milk, which caramelizes the meat with a sweet coating.

All I have to do is think about the flavors, and I taste them on my tongue. But beneath the salt of grease and gristle, I can also taste the lie. The one I've been telling for five months. To my parents. To Angel. And I can taste the truth. The truth I'm about to tell, whether my family likes it or not.

But telling them where I've been will be the easy part.

Telling my father why will be almost impossible. I already know what he'll say. That I'm supposed to be the one. Not Angel. Not him or my mother. I'm supposed to be the one untethered. Free. Because that's what he's always wanted. For himself—and when it didn't happen—for me.

And now you're going to break his heart.

The voice inside my head pins me to the doorway. I don't want to disappoint him or make him feel like a failure. But isn't that what I'll be if I don't fight for what I want? If I don't tell him the truth? Unless...telling the truth will unravel everything. What if he hates me? What if this is the last time I walk through these doors? The last time I come home...

And what if, untethered from the one thing that matters to me most, I start to spiral again? What if I can't stop it this time?

Hammered into the doorframe next to the entrance is an old prayer card, the guardian angel's mint green gown faded from where it's been brushed by countless fingertips. She's supposed to be on a bridge, sheltering two children as they pass in the middle of a storm. Crossing this threshold feels just as dangerous, and I graze what's left of the image, hoping some good luck rubs off on me. Praying for safe passage. For strength.

I told you. It's too late.

"Pen!" Chloe's long blond ponytail whips around the corner. "Are you okay? I thought your shift didn't start until five."

"Oh." I blink, the room coming into focus again. "Yeah. It doesn't...."

"Well…?"

"Well…"

I scan the restaurant, looking for my parents or Angel. My father just made him manager, despite the fact that he's a total flake. Despite the fact that I wanted the job and could have done it better.

"Well, what are you doing here?"

"Have you seen my parents?"

Chloe freezes. "Wait, aren't you supposed to be in class right now?" She lowers her voice, pulling me out of the breezeway. "Pen… are you actually going to tell them?"

Chloe isn't just the only person who knows about the voice in my head. She's also the only person who knows all of the things it's made me do. Like skipping out on an entire semester's worth of classes and then lying about it.

A long breath stutters out. "It's time."

"Pen…" She shakes her head. "What if you try again tomorrow? Double up on classes in the summer to make up for all that lost time. You can do this."

"I won't." Being firm with Chloe is my first test. Because I haven't just decided to stop lying to my parents, I've decided to stop lying to myself too.

"Have you thought about this? I mean, really thought it through?"

"What do you mean?" She's making me nervous. "Of course I've thought it through. Dad's always said that I'm the smart one, the responsible one. But then last week he suddenly decides to give Angel the manager's position just because I'm the one in school."

"But you're not in school."

"Exactly. Which is why I should be manager."

"Or why you shouldn't."

"What is that supposed to mean?"

Chloe's voice softens. "It means you *were* the responsible one. Past tense. Once they find out you've been lying, do you really think they're going to reward you with a promotion and a raise?"

"It's not about that anymore. I just want them to take me seriously. To see that I really want this. That school just isn't for me."

"They're not going to like that."

"I know, but I can't keep lying to them. It's making me sick."

Chloe pauses at the word *sick*. Then she reaches for my hand like it's something delicate. She looks me up and down as if searching for wounds beneath my clothes, in my voice, and all of the other places they like to hide. I let my eyes well up. I let her see. And it's such a relief to not have to hide the scars in front of her, to know that she doesn't judge me for giving them to myself in the first place.

"Whatever happens," Chloe says, "it's going to be okay."

"You really think so?"

She grips me tighter. "Whatever happens, we're going to *make* it okay." She looks me up and down again before reaching for a napkin. "Here…" Then she traces my bottom lip. "It was smudged."

"Thanks."

"Good luck."

I find my parents sitting around the table in one of the storage closets that has now become a makeshift office.

They're thumbing through receipts, my mom's hair in a frizzy mess on top of her head and my father's reading glasses slipping on the perspiration painting his nose. They look stressed.

I linger in the doorway, almost taking their ignorance as a sign that I should leave. That maybe the universe is giving me a second chance and I have approximately five seconds of invisibility left to run out of the restaurant and back to my car.

But then my mom says, "Pen, you're here early," and my heart starts to race. She looks up at me. "Is everything okay? Are Lola and Hugo—?"

"They're fine. I dropped them off at Mrs. Nguyen's."

"Shouldn't you be in class right now?" My father doesn't even look up from the receipt he's holding.

"Class. Right." My hands are slick and I stuff them into the back pockets of my jeans. "Well, I..."

"Was it canceled today?"

More like indefinitely.

"Or maybe Pen's playing a little hooky." Angel squeezes into the doorway next to me, bright yellow earbuds hanging over his shoulder, the faint sound of an electric guitar floating in the air like a gnat.

He looks exactly like our mother, every inch of him stretched and pressed.

"You're the only delinquent in this family," my mother teases him. "So, Pen, did you need something?"

Oh God.

I swallow. "I just wanted to talk to you..."

"About what?" My mother blows a strand of hair out of

her face, still examining the receipts on the table in front of her.

I wait for her to look at me, for both of them to look at me. For them to use their parental superpowers to see the lie all over my face so I don't have to say it.

Suddenly, the noise of the kitchen grows louder: the scuff of shoes, knives on cutting boards, laughter bubbling beneath the overhead vents.

"Pen." My mother waves a hand.

"Sorry."

The doorway shrinks another inch, Angel eyeing me.

"You wanted to talk," she says, nodding.

"I...I did. I..."

Angel nudges me. "Spit it out, Pen."

I shoot him a look. I mean it to be snarling and terrifying, but I can see by his reaction that it's more pathetic and panicked. I brace myself for what's coming next, and so does he.

"I wanted to talk to you and Dad about school."

"Is that why you missed class today?" she asks.

"Sort of." *Stop lying.* "No. I mean..." *Deep breath.* "I didn't just miss class today."

My father finally looks up. His eyes settle on my face, unblinking and impatient.

"What do you mean you didn't just miss class *today?*" my mother asks.

"I've missed a few," I say, voice quaking. *You're doing it again.* "No. Mom, Dad, I've missed more than a few. The truth is, I haven't been going to school. At all. And—"

"No." My father's voice is low and drawn and knocks the air from my lungs.

He crumples the receipt in his fist as if forcing down a yell. But my father doesn't yell. Instead, he guts you with all of the things he doesn't say, with sighs and silence. With shaking his head and kneading his hands and making you stew there in your own fear.

My father takes off his reading glasses. I stew.

"Since when?" he finally says.

"Since…never."

"But last semester…" My mother shakes her head, confused.

"I didn't go."

"But you said—"

My father looks at my mother. "She lied." Then he looks at me. "You lied."

"I did. But…I'm…"

He stands, pushing past my brother and I before heading for a shelf across the kitchen. He carries back an apron, handing it to me without looking. "There's a rush."

"Dad."

"No!" He slams his hands down on the table, the metal legs squealing. "Tonight's your last night."

"What?" I absorb his rage, shaking. "But, no, you can't do that."

"Pen…" Angel tries to pull me from the doorway.

"Dad, please. Mom…"

She bites her lip, staring down at her hands.

"Please, Dad. I'm sorry." *You're unraveling. Everything's unraveling.* "Please. Just let me ex—"

My father lifts a hand. "Take your sister."

But Angel doesn't reach for me. He doesn't have to. I

tuck the apron under my arm, deflated and on fire, and then I march through the kitchen for the last time.

Angel tries to catch up to me. "Pen, are you okay...?"

I brush past him and find Chloe by the hostess stand, assigning sections and rolling silverware. When she sees me, the fork she's holding clamors to the table.

"What happened?"

I stop. Numb.

She spins me so that we're shielded by a wall, sensing my tears before I do.

I bite them back.

"Pen?"

If I open my mouth, I'll break. I try to breathe instead. *In and out.* But all I want is to crawl into the corner. To walk straight into traffic. To stop this feeling even if it stops me.

Stop. Stop. Stop.

I can't let them see the cracks. Widening. Splintering into a million pieces. I can't let them see me in pieces.

"Pen, you're scaring me."

Not as much as I'm scaring myself.

"He said..." I try to steady my voice. "He said tonight's my last night."

Chloe slumps down in a chair. "Maybe..." She shakes her head. "Maybe he just needs to cool down. Maybe later you might catch him in a good mood and..."

"My dad's not like that. He's not fickle, and he's never in a good mood."

"He'll change his mind."

"He won't."

She grips my shoulders, cheeks red too. "He will."

"And if he doesn't?"

The squeak of rubber soles pulls my gaze. "Hey, Pen..." Struggles.

Chloe crinkles her eyes into her *get the hell away from me* stare and says, "She's a little busy."

"Sorry, Pen." He shudders. "I just thought you'd want to know that the new guy's supposed to start tonight and we can't find any more TACOS T-shirts in the back."

I bury my face in my hands. "He can have mine."

His eyes widen. "Whoa, you're quitting?"

"No." Chloe pushes out of her chair. "Pen is not quitting, and you better not say anything to anyone, you got it?"

He nods.

"Pen is still your boss."

He nods again, taking a slow step back.

"Who's your boss?"

"Pen is..."

She stares down at him.

"And you," he adds.

"Good. Now run along."

He kneads his hands. "But the shirts...?"

"Check in the freezer," I say. "Second shelf to the right."

Struggles runs for the kitchen.

"The freezer?" Chloe asks.

"Three summers ago the air-conditioning went out. We put the shirts in the freezer and then slipped them on in the afternoons to stay cool."

"Let me guess, Angel's idea?" Chloe rolls her eyes, but

there's just a hint of admiration in her voice. She's been in love with my older brother since we were thirteen and he was a sophomore.

"Who else?" I force myself to stand, zipping on my signature scowl before word of my firing makes it around to the other employees. "How's my face?"

She pinches both of my cheeks. "You've got a nice blush. Don't worry, looks very natural. Although, you might want to touch up the lip."

"Again?" I reach for my tube of Brava lipstick.

"Hey, you're the one who keeps chewing on them."

I purse my lips, checking my reflection in one of the windows until the girl staring back is more bitch than breakable. Then I tie my hair into a high ponytail behind my red bandana as any trace of my almost-tears evaporates.

Chloe finds my reflection too. "We're going to make this okay," she says again.

I lean against her, hoping she's right.

Chloe leads the way back through the kitchen, waving me forward when she sees that the office is empty. My parents' car isn't parked out back anymore, and I'm relieved. Unfortunately, that doesn't save me from being interrogated.

"What the hell was that about?" Angel says.

I don't answer him, just turn on my heel and head in the opposite direction.

"Hey." He grabs me by the wrist, pulling me back into the office/storage closet before slamming the door closed. Then he paces. "Pen." He says my name slow, careful. "What's going on?"

"I told you. I'm not going to school."

"Yeah, but why the hell not?"

"You know the answer to that."

He hangs his head back, sighing, because he does. "But you should know by now, Pen. Dad doesn't care about what we want."

I take a step closer, searching him for wounds the same way Chloe searched me. "You didn't have to listen to him, you know. You could have listened to your heart instead."

He rolls his eyes before lowering his voice. "Dad sees the way the army screwed up Tío Ramón, and he thinks the same thing will happen to me. I can't convince him otherwise, and I can't leave home with him hating me."

"So you hate him instead."

He shakes his head. "I hate this place." He points between my ribs. "The place that you love but that he is never in a million years going to let you have. You making a different choice doesn't have to mean he wins."

I look him in the eyes. "But it means *I* lose."

"You lost because you lied." He exhales. "Why did you have to lie about it, Pen?"

I know he really wants to say *to me. Why did you lie about it to me?*

"I don't know."

"That's not good enough, Pen."

He's past being confused and has run through angry straight to hurt.

"They wanted it for me," I say. "They wanted it for me so much."

"I know."

"So I lied. I didn't want to hurt them." I look up at him. "I didn't want to hurt you."

"And now?" Angel searches my eyes, earnest, almost afraid. "You didn't want to hurt anyone...but now?"

"I guess I couldn't take it anymore."

The words dredge up memories like shards of glass. That's how I remember the last time it happened—in fragments. I know Angel remembers it too, the shades drawn, my closed bedroom door, the invisible bruises left behind by their voices and the bedsheets and the sun. Back when everything used to hurt. Breathing. *Being.*

But I've been on medication for almost two years now, the darkness barely lapping at me, waves always receding just in time. Until today. But, unlike with Chloe, I don't let Angel see that I'm breaking. He wants me to be fine, and as he searches my eyes, I let him find what he needs, his fear evaporating.

He looks down, eyes settling on his new name tag instead. "You couldn't take it anymore...because he made me manager...and not you."

My cheeks burn.

"Shit, Pen." He exhales, gripping his scalp. "What am I going to do around here without you? Huh? Why did you have to get yourself fired? From our father's restaurant."

"I think you know that's the last thing I wanted to do."

I love my father's restaurant. Even though beneath his owner's smile I can see that he's grown to hate it. And even more that he hates me being here, following in his footsteps. But I can't help it. I love my father's name on the sign and the murals on the wall that my grandfather painted before he died. I love being swaddled in the scents of my childhood. I love the scars and calluses and burn marks. My friends. My home. That's what it is to me. Everything.

"Maybe..." I sigh, eyes pleading. "Maybe you could talk to him."

"Me." His voice is sharp, amused. "Yeah, right."

"Think about it. Inventory's coming up. Payroll. Another audit from the IRS. Dad made you manager, but we both know who really keeps everything together when he's not here."

He rolls his eyes. "Oh, come on. You think I can't take care of things?"

I cross my arms. "Can you?"

He chews on the inside of his cheek. "Fine, I'll talk to him."

3

Xander

THE MOUTHWASH SLOSHES BETWEEN my cheeks until my eyes burn. I spit it out, flecks of blood swirling near the bottom of the sink. I've been grinding my teeth in my sleep again.

"Xan?"

I hear the squeak of the bottom stair and race down before my abuelo can attempt the second one.

"I'm coming." I round the corner. "I'm right here."

"Oh good." He stops to cough into his handkerchief. "I didn't want you to be late."

"It's just down the street. Nacho's. You remember."

I lead him back to his armchair, pulling the coffee table with the remote and his glass of tea within reach.

"Nacho's. I remember that boy, Ignacio. Used to run a real Mexican restaurant. But that was before..." He stops to cough again. "Before he turned it into a strip joint."

I hand him the remote. "It's not a strip joint, Abuelo. It's a bar." I spot the tacos de papa still sitting at the kitchen table. "Have you eaten?"

"It's four in the afternoon. I wasn't hungry."

"I know, but you will be later and I won't be here."

"For Christ's sake. I'm not an invalid. I'll fix myself a sandwich or something."

"I'll get out the—"

He shoos me away. "I can get the bread. Now you go. You don't want to be late for your first day."

I put the tacos in the fridge before pulling the bread down onto the counter.

"I'll be back late," I remind him.

He lifts a finger and I draw closer. Then he pats the top of my head. "You'll do good."

⸻

The keys jangle in my back pocket. I could have taken the car, but the restaurant is only a few blocks away and I like the sun. It sizzles up from the sidewalk, heat waves flexing like snakes and reminding me of the way I used to chase their tails all the way to the mercado. Back when I still lived with my mother in Mexico. When she used to make menudo every weekend and I was the only one who could pick out the best meat. I'd sit at the kitchen table, picking the hair off the tripe while she started the broth. It would simmer all night, and I'd wake up to the smell of onions and freshly sliced lemons.

One day when I was nine, I set out to finally catch a handful of the sun. I wanted to hold the glimmer in the palm of my hand. So I ran. Shoes kicking up dirt, sweat dripping down my back. I'd stopped to catch my breath, hands slumping to my knees. Up ahead, blurry behind the sun, I could see two men walking. That day I limped home with a bloody nose and my pockets empty.

My mother looked me up and down like she was seeing me for the first time. A few days later, she began to pack my things, her eyes never settling on my face as she said, "If I knew how to be your mother, I would. But I don't want my heart outside my chest. Outside where anyone can stomp on it." She turned her back on me. "You're going to live with your abuelo." Then, under her breath, "Because his own son didn't ruin him enough the first time."

It's been almost ten years since she found another family, but I'll never stop wondering what would have happened if I'd made it to the mercado that day.

Light reflects off the tinted windows of the restaurant, reminding me that I'm a thousand miles away. When I step into the breezeway, there's already a line, people holding drinks and watching the big TV screens behind the bar while they wait for a table.

Nacho's is somewhere between a dive and a taqueria. One side of the restaurant is covered in a traditional mural, vaqueros on horseback and folklórico dancers leaning over the patrons as they eat. But on the other side, the wall lining the bar is covered in old photographs, posters of local bands, and vintage ticket stubs.

It's become somewhat of an attraction for the college crowd lately, but the people in my neighborhood have been tithing to the taco gods as long as I've lived here. You've got the flu? Order Nacho's famous caldo de res. You need some money? Ask him if you can wash dishes. You're missing home? Order his bread pudding. And if you're trying to start over, ask him for a job.

No one knows how he keeps the lights on with so many handouts, but as that neon sign buzzes late into the night, you can't help but sense something supernatural about the place.

I sense it now, the smells of my childhood waking my lungs.

When I finally manage to push my way toward the hostess stand, I'm greeted by a girl with dirty-blond hair and thick hipster glasses.

"How many?" she asks.

"I don't need a table. Tonight's my first night."

"Ahh..." She narrows her eyes. "New guy. Follow me."

She leads me past the bar and beneath a sign that reads EMPLOYEES ONLY. We pass a row of lockers, a few employees changing out of their shirts. The tile grows slick, and a small lanky kid almost slips trying to push past me. I brace myself against the wall.

"Careful." The girl in the glasses looks back. "You don't want to trip on your first day."

She stops in front of a tall guy with arms like licorice. He's beating his tongs on the edge of his grill, bright yellow headphones tucked in his ears.

"Angel." She clears her throat, nudging him. "Angel!"

He smiles, goofy and so wide that his headphones fall out. "New guy, right?"

"Yeah." I reach out a hand. "Xander. Xander Amaro..."

"Xander..." He lets the first letter buzz against his

teeth. "Hey! Everybody!" He beats against his grill until the kitchen is quiet. Then he hangs an arm around my shoulder. "Everyone, this is Xander. He's the new guy."

At least ten pairs of eyes are glued to my face. They blink, a few people cross their arms. And then they all erupt into laughter.

I turn to Angel. "What'd I do?"

He smiles. "Nothing yet." He gives the girl with glasses a nod. "I can take it from here, Chloe."

She calls back, "I sure hope so."

Angel wriggles his eyebrows. "Let's get you a shirt, shall we?"

I follow Angel through the kitchen, people parting like a wave. The lanky kid who almost busted earlier licks his lips, braces sparkling. The girl with the frizzy topknot next to him . . . growls. Or at least I'm pretty sure it's a growl.

Angel bends down to dig in a box full of NACHO'S TACOS T-shirts before pulling one out and handing it to me. It's frozen, the sleeves unfolding with a crack.

He cocks his head. "Qué raro."

"Is there a bathroom?" I ask. "Somewhere I can change?"

"Aw, new guy's a little shy. . . ." I hear over my shoulder.

I know they're just busting my balls, but the word *shy* makes me bristle.

It's what my mother's friends used to call me when I'd choose to help them in the kitchen instead of wrestling with their sons over a busted soccer ball. It's what my American teachers used to say about me when I wouldn't speak, couldn't because I was too busy chasing words like flies, trying to make sense of the voices buzzing around me. I always felt like I was surrounded by a pack of wolves, jaws ready to snap the second I did something wrong.

I scan the faces around me and I know that on my first day with a new pack of wolves, I can't cower and retreat. I can't let them eat me alive.

So in the midst of kissing sounds and baby voices, Angel trying to nudge me out of the flames, I make the decision to plant myself. Then I strip out of my shirt, in front of everyone, letting them take a long, hard look.

The sounds evaporate, and for a second I wonder if the eyes have too, but then I hear something glass slip off the counter, cracking just as I yank the NACHO'S TACOS shirt down over my head.

I face Angel. "Now, about that bathroom."

He points to a door up ahead.

It's heavy and strangely narrow. I yank it open, hinges squealing, and suddenly my toes are hanging over nothing. I catch hold of the doorframe before I slip off the edge and fall headfirst into the dumpster. A hand grabs the collar of my shirt, yanking me back inside.

I spin. "What the hell?"

The girl with the frizzy topknot yells, "I guess you won't be needing that bathroom after all," and everyone starts laughing again, this time doubled over, hands slapping knees.

"Sorry, man." Angel lets go of my shirt. "But you know how this goes." He turns me in the other direction. "And the real bathroom's that way."

I keep glancing back the entire way. Even when I reach

a door marked with the words EMPLOYEE BATHROOM, I kick it open with my foot first just to be sure.

When I see the stalls, I step inside, but I'm not alone. A girl stands over the sink, long ponytail slipping over her shoulder, flyaways held back by a red bandana she's folded into a headband.

"Sorry..." I reach for the door again.

She looks up, nose freckled and eyes wet. Lips as red as her bandana as she says, "You look like you almost died."

For some reason, my tongue is dry and three inches thicker. She presses a finger to the corner of her eye, mascara smearing. She sniffs.

"I...think I almost just did," I finally manage to say.

"Did they try to get you to fall in the dumpster?"

"Yeah."

"Don't worry, the hazing doesn't last long. Usually, just until the next new person starts."

"When will that be?"

"Who knows?" She shrugs, chewing on her lip. "Actually, probably tomorrow." She heads for the door.

Just as I'm washing my hands, it pushes open again.

"Oh good," Angel says. "We thought you'd run away or something."

A guy half Angel's size with a pathetic excuse for a mustache follows behind him. He's wearing a bright green bandana and a tool belt slung over his hips that's full of various utensils and plastic containers filled with different colored sauces.

"Xander, this is Lucas. You're gonna hang with him today."

He holds out a hand and I shake it, my own coming back sticky.

"I'll just leave you two to get acquainted."

Lucas looks me up and down for a good thirty seconds, then smiles. "Listen, I like you. I think you've got a real future here, and if you stick with me, you'll be just fine." He leads me back toward the kitchen. "There's just a few things you need to know first. Now," he lowers his voice, "the big doof that introduced us, that's the boss's oldest son, aka our manager."

"Manager?" I stop. "Seriously?"

Lucas rolls his eyes. "Yeah, don't get me started on that one. The good thing is he doesn't give you shit when you're late."

Lucas leads me around to the prepping stations. He points out two guys with the same black hair, both chopping onions with the same methodical crunch and swipe.

"The Medranos. Completely identical except for Aarón's... Well, let's just say he got electrocuted when he was still just a dish boy and he's never been the same since. Idiot was trying to plug in the radio after scrubbing down a plate. Whole place lost power."

We move past the prep station to the washroom, a small alcove with four sinks, two of them already piled high with dishes. The scrawny kid with braces snaps on some gloves. He reaches for one of the plates, and Lucas pulls me back behind the wall so he can't see us. Then we both watch him pick off some old food and toss it into his mouth. My stomach turns.

"And how many times has *he* been electrocuted?" I ask.

Lucas sighs. "Who knows? That's Struggles."

My brow furrows. "Struggles?"

"Yeah, because he always looks like he's struggling to live."

Struggles takes another bite off the dirty plate.

Or struggling to die.

Lucas waves me forward. "That's Chelo." He points out the girl with the frizzy topknot.

"I think she growled at me earlier."

"Oh, don't worry about her. She growls at everybody. Partly why she doesn't work front of house anymore."

"Partly?" I ask. "What's the other part?"

Lucas looks me dead in the eye. "You don't want to know." He nods to the tall guy next to her. "That's Sang. Been here so long he's practically a Prado. Their families are tight, and Sang will snitch you out in a heartbeat to prove it, so don't get on his bad side." Two pretty girls walk by, stealing Lucas's focus. "Andrea and Mari," he says, his voice low. "Both waitresses and both total bitches."

I want to ask why, but I sort of suspect it's probably just because they won't sleep with him, which has bruised his outrageously inflated ego. I could tell Lucas was sort of a creep from the moment I met him, and the side-eye he's getting from Andrea and Mari only confirms my suspicions.

He slides over to them, gross smirk on his face. "Ladies, have you met my friend here? Uh," he leans toward me, "what's your name again?"

"Xander."

"Right. Xander. New guy."

"Yeah," Andrea says, unamused. "We saw him."

There's an awkward pause, the girls waiting for Lucas to say something worth their time and Lucas probably waiting for me to do the same.

"Oh well, then...I guess we'll catch you later...." Lucas pulls me around the corner. "Christ, man, I thought a guy like you would have some kind of game."

"A guy like me?"

"Yeah, you know," he waves his hands, "pretty." He shakes his head. "Forget it." He starts toward the kitchen and then immediately throws himself back against the wall. "Oh shit."

"What is it?"

"Pen." He peers around the corner again. "Oh no, and she's got her *Rosie the Retributioner* face on."

I remember the girl in the bathroom with her red bandana.

"Who's Pen?"

"Pen, also known as Penelope Prado, also known as Nacho's oldest daughter, also known as Head Bitch in Charge."

"I thought you said Angel was the manager."

"Yeah, and who do you think manages him?"

I remember the quake in her voice, the tears on her face. "Come on, she can't be that scary."

Lucas is still clutching the wall, fingernails digging into the grout as he watches Pen from across the room.

I nudge him. "Can she?"

"Sometimes she can be...almost pleasant," he forces out. "But tonight's her last night. The old man fired her this morning."

"His own daughter?"

"Apparently she lied to them about going to school. For an entire semester." He averts his gaze. "Shit. Here she comes."

Pen rounds the corner, those bright-red lips leading the way. She purses them, eyeing Lucas and me, and it reminds me of the sweet seam along a cherry. Until she opens her mouth.

"For fuck's sake, Lucas. We've got thirty new orders. Where the hell have you been?"

"Just showing the new guy around...." He takes one long step out of reach. "That's all."

"His shift started half an hour ago. I'm pretty sure you've covered it by now."

"Yeah, yeah." He throws up his hands. "We're going."

She crosses her arms in response, watching us the entire way back to Lucas's station. Lucas turns to me, about to say something, when a horn blares. I reach for my ears and see a guy with blond hair gripping an air horn.

"That's Java," Lucas yells.

"Let me guess," I yell back. "Deaf?"

"Only in his right ear."

The drumming of Angel's tongs clashes with the horn and then everyone is yelling. Angel races around the kitchen in this strange half gallop, half dance, banging on equipment, slapping people on the back of the head.

"You know what that means, fuckers! We've got a rush!"

He finally makes it back to the grill, the rest of the room in a flurry. People run back and forth from their stations, grabbing bowls and rags and spices. Angel switches on the stereo, and in all the chaos I can hear the first line of "Suavemente," Elvis Crespo wailing about besos and wanting to feel sus labios.

Suddenly, every instrument has a culinary utensil equivalent. Angel takes care of the drums while Chelo, who I hadn't realized could manage more than a growl, takes care of vocals. She screams into her spoon, switching between the one in the refried beans and the one in the mole verde. Lucas plays some strange version of the xylophone on the condiments strapped to his waist, and the guy with the air horn does a power slide straight into Pen's legs. He puckers his lips at her and she swats him with a wet rag.

"Ready for your crash course?" Lucas asks.

I strain over the music. "Ready as I'll ever be, I guess."

Lucas winks and hands me a pair of tongs. "Angel grills, we plate. Basically, we're two rungs above Struggles over there."

Steaming meat slides in our direction, Lucas leading it onto a plate before glancing up at the ticket. He reaches for his belt, covering the meat in some orange sauce and then using his gloved hands to load it with toppings from the trays in front of us. There's cilantro, onions, lime wedges, corn salsa, avocados, and chili peppers. Ten different kinds of salsa, all marked with different colored tape that read either PUSSIES, NIÑOS, BADASS MOFOS, or LOCO. I assume they're heat indexes, and when Lucas tells me to fill some plastic cups with a few *milds*, I reach for the salsa marked PUSSIES.

"Whoa, careful." Lucas points to a bottle out of sight.

I pull it to the front and it reads GABACHOS.

"Pen..." Lucas taps the salsa I reached for first. "Took offense to the labels. Now Pussies is the hottest salsa we have." He dares to glance at her.

She's chucking a plate of enchiladas into the trash and spewing something hateful in Angel's direction.

"What did you mean by two rungs?" I ask.

Lucas nods around the kitchen. "Well, you've got your dish boys, like Struggles, who are last in the pecking order." He gestures to the identical twins. "Then you've got veggie prep. Then you've got platers, like us." He points to the burners next to the grills, each one topped with a huge steaming pot. "Right there's your special teams, and then on the grills you've got your starting lineup. Fish, then pork, then poultry." He points at three guys to the right of Angel, their heads shaved, tattoos bleeding out from their buzz cuts. "And Angel's the quarterback. He takes care of the most important food group—the red meat."

"Nice analogy."

He smiles, stopping to wipe his nose on his sleeve.

I notice Pen breaking off some fresh cilantro into one of the pots on the stovetop.

"And what's Pen do?" I ask.

"Everything. Almost the entire menu is from that big, bossy, beautiful head of hers."

She shoves Angel to the side and checks the meat on his grill. She says something about an order coming back too well-done and he just sighs, elbowing her out of the way.

"And they're still firing her?"

"I give it two weeks. Tops," Lucas says. "They'll beg her

to come back. Or maybe she'll just sue her dad for, I don't know, copyright infringement for all of her recipes, and then they'll have to close the place down and none of us will have to step foot in this godforsaken dive ever again."

"You don't like working here?" I worry for a second about what exactly I've gotten myself into.

"I don't really like work in general." He laughs.

"Then why do it?"

He nods to the stack of plates to my left and I reach for one.

"Got to. I've got three younger sisters and...well, my dad can't exactly work"—his voice is suddenly flat—"since he's sort of dead."

Porcelain shatters, cutting through every sound in the entire kitchen. People stop what they're doing, turning to stare, and I know that my show of confidence earlier in the night has officially been erased. This is who they'll remember.

I kneel, scooping the pieces into the hem of my shirt. "I'm sorry." I don't know if I'm apologizing for the plate or for what Lucas just said. Maybe both.

A pair of bright-red Vans step into my field of vision. I look up and Pen is holding a broom. She hands me the dustpan.

"I got it. Thanks." I scrape up the last pieces and feel a sting.

"Shit." Pen scans the room. "Can somebody get a towel?"

Lucas hands her the rag hanging from his waist.

She rolls her eyes. "A clean one?"

Angel hands her a blue towel and some hydrogen peroxide. I dump the broken plate in the trash and try not to drip on the tile as Pen leads me back to the employee bathroom. She holds my hand over the sink and then she pours the peroxide over the wound.

"Sting?"

I shake my head and she pours some more, wound fizzing.

"Wait here," she says, the door shutting behind her.

I try not to look at myself in the mirror, but after a few seconds I have to. My heavy breaths smear the glass, and I wait for Lucas's words to rise up through the fog. A premonition. The answer to a question I used to be too afraid to ask. A question that has consumed me for the past six months, ever since I finally felt strong enough, angry enough to start looking again. For my father's new life. For his body.

My mother wasn't the only one who disappeared. He left us first when I was just barely old enough to remember. To miss him. Hearing my mother say goodbye had cauterized those wounds. But the ones my father left behind were still wide open. Festering.

And in that festering, my fears told a story with only two possible endings—that my father was alive and wanted nothing to do with me, or that he was dead and the past decade of searching didn't matter.

Pen pushes back through the door. "Here." She presses a bandage over the cut, blood already showing dark through the padding. She puts the gauze between her teeth, ripping it, and then she leads it around my palm, twisting until it's tight.

I don't realize I'm not blinking until everything blurs, smearing her face and mouth, which is just inches from my skin, her breath brushing the tips of my fingers. She lets go of me and seems to pause too, her eyes somewhere between expectant and hesitant.

"Thanks."

I linger. I should get back to Lucas and his plates and his toppings bar. But I don't want to go. And it isn't just because once I do I'll look like a total jackass.

"You should, I mean, we should get back." Pen throws the door open without looking at me, and then she's lost in the shuffle of the kitchen, her carefulness suddenly gone as she shoves one of the buzz cuts out of the way and tears the tongs out of his hand.

I reach for the apron closest to me, tying it around my waist.

"The rush is finally dying down," Lucas says, not acknowledging what just happened. I'm relieved. "We have some time to run through a few of these dishes a little slower if you want."

Lucas pulls down a plate, loading it up with some refried beans and rice before showing me how much meat to load into each taco.

I try to pay attention, to memorize the measurements, the placement of the food. But I keep glancing over my shoulder. I keep looking for Pen. Because I'm still not sure which version is the real one—the girl in the bathroom who wrapped my bleeding hand or the girl who makes the special teams shudder every time she walks by.

She orbits the room, checking orders, tasting the food, breathing down people's necks, casting strange looks in my direction. I focus back on the plate in front of me.

"You got that?" Lucas eyes me, waiting.

"Yeah."

He narrows his gaze over my shoulder. Pen is looking back. She scratches at her arm before heading out to the front.

Lucas faces me again. "Oh no."

I ignore him, fumbling with the tortilla I'm holding.

"Oh, hell no."

"What?" I keep my voice low, hoping he'll do the same.

"Don't go there, man."

"Go where?"

"You know where. Trust me on this one. You do not want to mess with Pen."

"I'm just," I keep my voice cool, "making tacos."

"Yeah." He slams another tortilla into my hand. "And you keep making those tacos."

By the end of the night I make one hundred and twenty-six tacos, my fingertips blistered from the heat of the comal. Then I walk home on numb legs, every step on that empty street making my ears ring.

Halfway down the block, lights swell behind me. I spot the side of the police cruiser, every muscle stunned. The window clicks, rolling down slowly.

"First day done." Officer Solis smiles. "Need a ride home?"

It takes me a moment to shake off the fear.

He sees it too. "I didn't mean to sneak up on you."

I open the door, sliding inside. "It's okay. I'm just exhausted."

He laughs. "That's what I like to hear. So, tell me all about it. Was it what you expected?"

I look down at my food-stained clothes, sweat sticking the grime to my skin. "Uh, not exactly."

"Let me guess." He cocks his head. "Better?"

I remember the cut on my hand, the wound making it stiff. Then I remember Pen.

"Definitely better," I say.

"That's good." He turns down my street.

"Thank you. . . ." I stare into the floorboard. "Again."

He pulls into the driveway. "Don't mention it."

There are a million things Officer Solis has told me not to mention. Like the time he pulled me out of a scuffle during gym class when he was still the student resource officer at my high school. Or the time he dropped a few dollars on the floor at the convenience store and pretended like they were mine. Then there was the month he drove my abuelo back and forth from his doctor's appointments because his bronchitis was getting bad and I wasn't old enough to drive. He used to buy me lunch in the hospital cafeteria while we waited.

He's kept a close eye on me ever since he found out from one of the counselors at the school that I was undocumented. His parents used to be undocumented too, until he sponsored them and they became legal citizens. Because of some stupid rule—something called a *derivative*—my abuelo can't do the same for me, and I don't exactly have any "immediate relative relationships" to speak of at the moment.

But Officer Solis has always treated me like family.

"You know, I really think this is going to be good for you, Xander. A chance to finally feel settled here."

In return for all that he's done for me, all he's ever wanted was for me to feel like I belong. But I've been undocumented for so long, it's hard to shake the feeling that I'm not always welcome. Or safe.

Officer Solis puts the car in park, dims the lights so they don't wake up my abuelo. Then he pulls a business card from his shirt pocket. "Have you told him that you're looking again?" He doesn't hand it to me, waiting for an answer.

"Not yet."

"But you will."

I swallow, trying to imagine that conversation causing my abuelo anything but pain.

"It's his son, Xander."

"And he's *my* father."

Officer Solis exhales. "You're right, but their history's much longer." He nods to the front door. "And that man's raised you like his own. You owe him the truth for that reason if nothing else." He hands me the card. "Just...do this the right way."

"Is there one?"

He looks at me. "Always."

4

Pen

MY MOTHER IS WAITING for me in the kitchen when I wake up. Just like I knew she'd be.

My last shift at the restaurant ended at 2:00 AM, but I stayed late, helping Angel get things ready for the morning. Something I would have saved for the next day if there were going to be a next day. But there won't be.

I sit down across from my mother, still in my pajamas and smelling like tacos. She smells like gardenia and hairspray—the essence of practicality, which is exactly what my parents want me to be. They want me in a pair of scrubs, studying dental assisting or nursing, and they want me to smell like gardenias and hairspray. But I don't want that. I want this. Sour garlic and all.

"How was work?" She takes a sip of her coffee.

In just those three words, I know she's angry. My mother is usually careful and considerate—mandatory in her line of work. But instead, she asks me about the one place I'm never allowed to see again, proving that she's so upset my feelings no longer matter. I no longer matter. Because now all that matters is the lie.

"Busy." I try to keep the conversation neutral for as long as possible. Which is approximately five more seconds.

Then my mother grips her coffee cup, staring down into the steam as she says, "We're going to give you a choice."

"A choice?" And then my stomach sinks.

She keeps her eyes down. "You can either stay in school and live at home or..."

"Or what?" Suddenly I'm standing. "You're kicking me out?"

"No, Pen. It's—"

"It's what? Dad's idea, right? He can't stand the sight of me so he's kicking out his own daughter."

She finally looks back, eyes wet. "His eighteen-year-old daughter."

"I didn't realize I had an expiration date. I can find another job. I can come up with the money you and Dad used to take out of my check for rent. I'll—"

"It's not about the money, Pen."

I sit down again, leaning toward her. "Then don't let him do this." I can feel my pulse in my ears. I'm shaking with it. "Please. Mom, I'm not..." My voice catches and I feel like a child. I wish she'd see me that way one last time. "I'm not ready."

"Oh, Pen." She frowns. "You've been ready since you were five years old."

I pinch my eyes shut. Running away with a My Little

Pony suitcase full of socks and donuts is not the same as being ready. Being bullheaded isn't the same as being an adult. And I'm not. I have no idea what I'm supposed to do next. And not just the next month or the next day, but the next minute. Doesn't she know that? Doesn't she know that I hadn't meant to unravel my entire life? Doesn't she know that I'm sorry?

"Please. Mom."

My mother is supposed to be the understanding one. The one who forgives you just so she can sleep, who can't stand being angry because it makes her feel guilty. The one who can take my father's hand and reverse the tornado inside him.

"No." Her voice is strange and hard. "I've always been easy on you, Pen. But I was easy on you because I trusted you. Because I trusted that you'd always do the right thing. But you lied to me, Pen. To me."

She sounds like Angel. Not hurt by my decision, but by the fact that I made it alone. That's when I realize the real reason they're making me leave. Not to punish me, but to give me exactly what I asked for.

"Pen..." She exhales. "What were you thinking?"

I feel the answer in my gut, but I can't tell her the truth. That it was her life I was running from.

"I'm sorry."

I search for something stronger, less hollow, but there's nothing to combat the emptiness. Between my ribs. In her eyes. I'm so afraid of it swelling, filling me from the inside. And I can't help but wonder why she's not as afraid of me relapsing as Angel was. But then I remember that this isn't the first lie I've ever told her. The first—*I'm okay*. I've been saying it for years, and on a day when it couldn't be further from the truth, she finally decides to believe me.

"I know you're sorry, Pen. So I'm going to let you decide. Are you going back to school...or not?"

I grit my teeth, that same sick feeling that kept me from getting out of the car now keeping me from telling her what she wants to hear.

"You've been in this neighborhood, in that restaurant all your life, Pen. You know how hard it is, how people have to claw and climb for any kind of opportunity. And you've got one." She shakes her head, anger turning to desperation. "You think your father and I work ourselves to death so you can grow up and do the same? You think I give up putting my own children to bed at night because I'm living my dream?" She quakes. "You are my dream, Pen. You going to school, getting out of this neighborhood, and making something of yourself. That's my dream."

For a few seconds I can't breathe, the sight of my mother's armor slipping off, piece by piece, making me fall apart just as fast. Because I can't give her what she wants. Even if it *is* her dream.

My voice breaks as I say, "But it isn't mine."

She looks away, waiting for me to change my mind. I wait too, for the strength to keep pretending. But there's nothing left.

She stands, face fallen. "Then I'm sorry too." She carries her coffee into the bedroom and closes the door behind her.

I sit in the kitchen for a long time. Until the smell of

the citrus-cleaned countertops is replaced by the smell of cinnamon and green bell peppers and my father's favorite rum. Until I can hear the sound of stone striking stone; my father's voice summoning the past.

"This was my great-great-grandmother's metate."

The ground corn looks like a bed of snow, my father grinding it by hand on a slab of stone. I touch the craters and flecks of rock and it feels like something ancient. Something magical.

"Can I have it?" I ask.

My father laughs. "Someday it'll be yours." He winks. "But not until I'm dead." He scoops up the ground corn and places it in a bowl. "Now we're going to mix everything together. Are your hands ready?"

I wriggle my fingers, ready.

My father pours the saltwater while I scrunch the mixture like Play-Doh. Only this kind, you can actually eat. The masa begins to take shape like a moon slowly rising.

"You know what I like to do when I'm having a bad day?" my father asks.

"What?"

He makes two fists, an exaggerated scowl on his face that reminds me of the Tasmanian Devil from Saturday morning cartoons. Then he pounds those fists into the masa, hard and fast. He karate-chops the dough, and I laugh so hard I almost fall off the stool I'm standing on.

"Whoa, keep your balance." My father pushes me upright. "Cooking is all about balance. Remember that, Penelope." He scoops up a small handful of dough and plops it into my open

hands. "Roll it like this." He works the dough into a ball, perfectly round.

My hands move much slower, the shape coming out lopsided.

"Perfecto," he says.

Then he takes the dough and places it on the countertop, instructing me to do the same.

"Now we make them flat." While he uses one hand to spin the tortilla in a circle, he uses the heel of his other hand to flatten the dough.

I try to copy him, but my hands are still too slow, jerking the dough and almost tearing it in half. He's pressed three tortillas in the time it takes me to do one.

"Why don't you just grind and press the masa at the restaurant?" I ask, impatient.

He begins tossing tortillas onto the comal, flipping them three times before they puff up like little clouds.

"At the restaurant, we're in a hurry. We need to cook fast so people leave happy." He wipes the sweat from his brow. "But at home, we cook to remember."

"Remember what?" I ask.

"Where we come from." He pinches the finished tortillas with his fingers and moves them to the tortillero de palma to keep them warm. "We cook to remember the people who came before us." He places my misshapen tortillas on the comal next. "But most importantly, we cook to remember what love tastes like. That's why we grind the masa and roll it out by hand. So that when your brother and mother sit down to eat, they'll taste the time we spent and how much we care for them in every bite."

As we gather around the table for dinner later that night, I can't wait for my mother and Angel to take that first bite.

"Try mine." I push one of my misshapen tortillas onto my mother's plate.

Angel takes one too. Then my father.

"Should we count to three?" my mother says.

Angel sits on his knees, almost as excited as I am. "One."

My mother smiles. "Two."

My father winks again like the two of us are in on a secret. "Three."

We all take a bite, but I'm not looking at my mother or Angel. I'm looking at my father, who is savoring my imperfect creation as if it's the best thing he's ever eaten. He opens his eyes and there is a light in them that warms me from the inside out. Because he tasted the love. Because he showed me how to put it there.

———

The memory rips to shreds, along with every smell, every taste, every laugh, and every word. Every second I spent in this kitchen growing up. And even though I don't want it to be over, even though I didn't think it ever would be, I finally stand, walking out of my mother's kitchen, through my father's front door, and into the blistering afternoon sun.

———

When I pull into Chloe's driveway, I just sit there for a long time, clutching the wheel until she taps on my window. I can't move. She frowns before walking around to climb into the passenger seat.

"You can stay with me as long as you need to," she says.

"Thanks." I try to keep my voice from shaking. "Maybe just while I look for a place."

Chloe still lives at home too, although, since she's actually going to school to study graphic design, and therefore doing something productive with her life, it's perfectly acceptable. I know her mom will let me stay. It's just the two of them, and for almost every Saturday since I was twelve, just the three of us.

"Your dad asked me to give this to you." Chloe slides over my last paycheck.

I take it, fingers brushing the ink, and it feels like something dead. Final. Like he never wants to see me again.

"Gee," I mumble, snark hiding the pain underneath, "how nice of him. Maybe now I won't starve."

Chloe rolls her eyes. "Come on, you've only been homeless for, like, a day. And you're not even really homeless. It's not like they threw all of your stuff out on the front lawn."

"They might as well have. Pretty soon I'll be one of those bums digging cigarette butts out of a convenience store ashtray." I bury my face in my hands. "Or worse."

Chloe laughs. "What's worse than that?"

"I don't know. Smoking them?"

Her smile fades. She pokes me in the side with her index finger. "Hey, look at me."

I groan, spreading my fingers just wide enough to see her eyes.

"What did I say before?" She pulls my hands away from my face. "We're going to make this okay."

"How?" My voice breaks, the tears hot at the back of my throat.

"The same way we always do. Together." She wraps her arms around me. "If anyone can make it on their own, it's you, Pen."

I try to let her words sink in, but the worries have already hardened into a thick shell.

What if I can't find another job? What if I can't find a decent place to live that I can actually afford?

What if I don't want to?

"You're stronger than you think you are, Pen. You always have been."

I search her voice for even an ounce of inauthenticity. There is none. She believes what she's saying.

"And you don't have to do it alone." She takes my hand. "Promise me you won't try to do it alone."

"I won't."

She searches my voice for the same inauthenticity. I search too. For the truth, or maybe another lie. Maybe the only difference is what I choose to believe. And I want to believe that I'm as strong as Chloe says, as strong as everyone at the restaurant believes me to be. I tell myself that if I just keep doing the things that scare me, I will be. And this is definitely the scariest of all.

5

Pen

THE FIRST APARTMENT COMPLEX is just a few blocks from the restaurant. The rents aren't listed online, but it doesn't look too high-end. There are plastic pink flamingos around the pool, for Christ's sake.

"We do have a one-bedroom available with a great view overlooking the pool. There's a microwave, and a washer-and-dryer unit. Plus, a great walk-in closet."

Chloe gives me an excited nudge as we follow the leasing agent up a set of stairs to the model unit. She leads us into a spacious living room that opens into a small kitchen. There's a shiny white stove, and enough counter space to ice two sheet cakes at once. I don't even need to see the rest.

"How soon could I move in?" I ask.

"It would take a couple of days for all of the paperwork

to go through. But if everything checks out, I'd say you could move in by next week."

"I'll do it."

Chloe shoots me a look.

"It's perfect," I say, shooting one back.

"Well, then, if you'll follow me downstairs, we can get started on that paperwork I mentioned."

We follow the leasing agent back to the main office, every step making me feel more like a grown-up. We sit across from her as she prints the contract.

"Pen?" Chloe clears her throat and pushes the top sheet closer to me.

"Is this the...?" I'm not sure what it is. Surely not the...

"Price," the leasing agent finishes.

"Of the apartment?" I'm sweating.

"Yes." Her voice drops. She knows I'm broke.

"And this is the cheapest you have available?"

She nods.

"And there aren't any promotions going on right now? No student discounts or anything?"

Chloe digs a finger into my side, but I ignore her. I lied about being a student before and I can do it again. If it means getting my dream apartment, I will.

"No."

The walk back to my car feels like a mile long. I wrench the door open and throw myself inside.

"It's the first place we've looked," Chloe tries to reassure me.

I press my forehead against the hot steering wheel until it burns. "But it was perfect."

"Obviously not." Chloe tosses her cell phone into my lap. "Where to now?"

I scan the web page for our next destination. "Golden Oaks."

"Hey, that sounds fancy."

It isn't fancy. Golden Oaks is a series of efficiencies facing the Strip, which is a busy highway lined with liquor stores. There is a man standing on the corner with a sign that says:

NO BULLSHIT HERE
I JUST WANT A BEER

"At least they're honest folk around here," Chloe says.

I pull into the parking lot, which is really just a patch of oil-stained dirt in front of a small office building. We idle for a few minutes before a plump woman opens the door and spots us. She waves a hand, trying to lure us out of the car.

"Listen," Chloe starts, "at this point I feel like you should just face the reality of the situation, and if this is the type of place available in your price range, you should at least see it."

The first unit we see has four walls. That's it.

The woman hacks up something wicked and says, "Definitely a great starter place."

Chloe huffs. "Yeah, you can start with a toilet."

Luckily, the second unit has a toilet, plus a sink and a microwave. All lining the same wall.

Chloe shrugs. "At least you won't have far to go when—"

I swat her. "Don't even finish that sentence."

The third and final unit has a toilet, a sink, a stove and microwave, and a man sleeping in a roll of carpet.

The woman closes the door, backs away. "That one's still being cleaned." She clasps her hands. "So, should we head back to the office and crunch some numbers?"

The next apartment complex is a little farther north, which means that on a good day, the Austin traffic will only be slightly apocalyptic. We pull up to a tall concrete building with bars over the windows.

"At least you know it's safe," Chloe says.

"You know, your sarcastic optimism might just get you strangled."

"I'm just trying to help."

A man wearing a green tie greets us in the main office. He smells like tanning oil and peppermints. "Now, we do have a small waiting list for some of the bigger units, but our apartments on the higher floors are all vacant."

The elevator doors open and it's like stepping into a sauna. My shoulders are touching both the leasing manager and Chloe at the same time, and it takes approximately two seconds before I'm pouring sweat.

When the doors finally ding open we all spill out, the leasing manager leading the way to a tall red door. He fiddles with the key before pushing the door open.

The space is empty, but it's clean. The floors are

concrete, spinning a draft from one end of the room to the other that actually offers a little relief. The kitchen is a relief too. There's a working oven and a small porcelain sink. Someone has even left a cute paisley hand towel draped over the side.

"And the bathroom's just through here."

We're led across the narrow living area and through a door at the far end of the room. It's the only door in the entire apartment. I expect to see an empty bedroom first, but there's just a toilet and a shower.

"I thought this was a one-bedroom," I say.

"This is a flat," he corrects me.

"Wait, so there're no one-bedroom units available?" Chloe asks.

"Walls are extra," he says. "This is our cheapest unit."

"How much?"

"Six hundred a month, but utilities are included."

It's barely in my price range, but since losing my dream apartment, it's also the first unit we've come across that doesn't seem to have something else already living in it.

My phone rings and when I look down, it's my mother. There's a pang in my chest, and for half a second I wonder if she's calling to beg me to come back. But then I remember that it probably wasn't even her decision in the first place.

I snuff out the hope and silence the ring, my thumb hovering over the MESSAGE button. I have this urge to tell her it's only taken a mere nine hours for me to find somewhere new to live. For me to stop needing her.

Apartment hunting with Chloe. Can't talk now. Looking over a contract.

I push SEND.

"Now, if you'd like to follow me back downstairs, we can discuss leasing options."

Back on the first floor my phone rings again, but this time when I look down it's the restaurant.

"Would you excuse me for a minute?" I step into the hall as Chloe unleashes a string of questions about the price and the neighborhood and the other tenants. I press the phone to my ear, expecting it to be Angel. "Hello?"

"Pen."

For a minute I can't speak. I'm too scared.

My father clears his throat. "Hello?"

"I'm here," I say.

"Good. Listen, your brother is out on a catering job and he took the keys to the safe. Do you still have your set?"

I swallow, dreading a face-to-face encounter this soon. "Yes."

"I need you to come unlock it."

It isn't even a question. As if I would actually be in the mood to do him a favor. I clamp my jaw, filtering my thoughts, searching for something that isn't profanity. But then it occurs to me that my mother might have told him where I am, that he knows I'm this close to signing a lease.

My father is direct when he's giving an order, but never when it comes to his emotions. If he's had a change of heart, he'd never say it out loud. Instead, he'd ask me to come to the restaurant for something business-related and then say something about seeing me tonight at dinner—as if the whole thing had never happened.

All I want is to pretend like the whole thing never happened. Maybe if I do this, he'll forgive me. Or maybe he already has.

The longest my father has ever stayed mad at me was when I told him he should let Angel join the military and live his own life. He didn't speak to me for almost three days, my job at the restaurant the only chance I got to hear his voice. He would tell me to make this or clean that or ask so-and-so if they wanted to pick up an extra shift. Every time I would linger, trying to make him see me, and in the meantime, I was the model employee, trying to show him that even though Angel didn't want to follow in his footsteps, I did.

Maybe it was seeing himself in me that finally ended our feud. Or maybe it was seeing himself in me that started it. Once it became clear that he didn't want me to take over the restaurant, I stopped being his little girl and started being his shadow. We stopped talking the way we used to. We stopped joking. We stopped cooking together. But if he lets me come home, at least I'll know I never stopped being his daughter.

"When do you need me to come?" I finally say.

"Now."

I leave the leasing application unsigned, thank the manager for the tour, and jump in my car. After dropping Chloe off, it takes me less than ten minutes to get to the restaurant, my foot barely coming off the gas pedal as if my father's forgiveness is merely sand inside an hourglass.

When I walk inside he's standing in the doorway leading to the kitchen, too far for me to read his expression.

Silently, I follow him through the kitchen. It's Sunday, which means the Medrano brothers are already juicing the Jamaican tangelos and blood limes for tonight's palomas. *My* famous palomas. The citrus hits my nose, making my eyes water before my father has even said one word to me. I dry the tears before he sees them.

When we reach the safe, I hand over my key. He unlocks the door and pulls out three thick envelopes stuffed with cash. The safe usually only houses a few hundred dollars in case the registers are short, and a small supply of Cometa Chicxulub hot sauce—a rare blend that's over a hundred dollars a bottle and named after the crater made by the asteroid that supposedly killed the dinosaurs.

"What is that?" I ask.

He ignores me, pocketing the money and my key.

"You're keeping it?"

"You don't work here anymore."

Every hope that's been propelling me forward dissipates in an instant. My father didn't ask me here to make amends. He asked me here to prove a point—that he's the one in control.

Desperation pushes me into his path before he can walk away. "But I thought…" I clench my fists. "I thought that maybe you'd asked me to come by so we could talk or something. I thought that—"

His voice is flat. "I asked you to come by because I needed your key to the safe."

"That's really it? You still can't even speak to me?"

He won't look me in the eye, but I'm watching his. They're still angry, but then he blinks, takes a breath, and for just the slightest moment, they soften. Like maybe he's considering.

But then he says, "I can speak to you, Pen. But I won't. Not about the restaurant."

"But, Dad..."

He doesn't look at me as he turns and walks away, and as I head back out to my car, I've never felt so invisible. Until my mother sees me. She's in the parking lot, dressed for her shift at the nursing home. I think about getting in my car and speeding off, but our eyes meet and I can't move.

"Pen, I've been calling." She shades her eyes from the sun, trying to read my face.

"I've been busy." I look down, fiddling with my key ring, now one key short. "You know, looking for somewhere new to live."

"You were really looking at apartments?" There's actually a hint of pride in her voice, but all I can focus on is the underlying surprise, and it only makes me angrier.

"Yeah, remember, you kind of kicked me out?"

"We didn't kick you out."

"You did."

She sighs. "We just want what's best for you, Pen. We just want you to learn to stand on your own two feet."

"Well, I am."

"Well...I hope so, Pen."

There's that surprise again. Like I'm incapable of

finding my own place. Like she can't believe an entire day has gone by without me needing her help.

I think about that last apartment, those four concrete walls. I imagine being alone there in the dark—the sounds, the shadows, the emptiness. I concentrate on that feeling until the fear swells and I know I have to step straight into it. Because making it real is the only way to take back control.

"Actually, I'm just on my way to sign a contract."

"Where? How much is it? Do you need your father and I to come take a look at it?"

"I've got everything taken care of."

"But we could come see it. We could help you go over the contract."

She has no idea how badly I want to say yes. How badly I wish it were her who'd driven around with me all day instead of Chloe, who was telling me what to do now. I *just* want her to tell me what to *do*.

But she can't come with me, and she can't tell me what to do. I have to make my own decisions. I have to grow up. I have to prove to them and to myself that I can.

"I don't need help," I finally say. "But I should head back before the office closes."

As I drive away, my mother watches from the parking lot. I think she'll go inside once I reach the end of the street, but she just keeps standing there. My father comes out and then I make my turn onto the next street, glad they're confined to my rearview mirror.

I'm even more glad that they can't see me. The dread of what I'm about to do, of how everything is about to change, laps at my insides. Rising, rising. I stop at a red light and grip the steering wheel.

Just sink, Pen.

Let yourself sink.

This time the voice is a siren song.

The light in front of me turns green, but I can't move.

Horns blare behind me, windows down as people shout. A man a few cars back leans out, flashing me the middle finger. I try to tell myself to ease off the brake, to push down on the gas. *To breathe.*

It isn't until I see someone approaching the car in my side mirror that I realize I've been holding my breath.

The man bangs on my window and I tense, his expression wild. Angry. I catch sight of my own reflection in the rearview mirror, the breaths finally coming slow and shallow the longer I stare into those eyes. I wait for that familiar face to form over my own—the one I wear at the restaurant. The one that keeps me safe.

That's what I have to remember. That no one else can save me. Not my parents. Not Chloe. On days like this, in…moments like this, the only one who can save me is myself.

I scrape the lining of my purse, snatching the pill bottle before tapping one into my open hand. I toss it back.

"Move the fuck out of the way, lady!" The man raps on the window again.

Only this time I don't flinch.

"Fuck you!" I yell and then I gun it, the back tire almost catching his foot.

I take a deep breath. Then another.

Up ahead, the apartment building comes into view again. I put the car in park, an ache forming in my throat, and I'm not sure if it's because I'm afraid or sad or both. I'm certainly not excited.

Because I'm not ready.

But I guess none of that matters now.

6

Xander

WHEN I HEAD FOR the door, Abuelo is already sitting on the porch with our neighbor, Mr. Daly. He's a massive hoarder, and he and my abuelo play cards in the afternoon, betting on things that don't even belong to them. Like the washer and dryer that's been sitting in the McDermotts' yard for almost three months, or Mr. Martinez's cattle trough–turned–aboveground pool that you can just make out through the holes in the fence.

Abuelo coughs into his handkerchief, gesturing with the other hand. "I'll bet you this old ashtray and raise you that lawn mower across the street."

Mr. Daly straightens. "Oh yeah? Well, I'll call your bluff and raise you that lawn mower *and* that little Speedster in the driveway next to it."

It's pointless, and whoever wins gets absolutely nothing

except the satisfaction of pretending to steal the neighbors' stuff.

"I'm heading to work, Abuelo. There's sausage and eggs in the fridge if you get hungry."

Mr. Daly removes his hat, forearm wiping the sweat from his brow. "Hold on there, boy, where you workin' at?"

"Nacho's Tacos down the street."

"Nacho's? You mean that strip joint?"

Abuelo throws up his hands. "That's what I said."

"It's not a strip club."

Mr. Daly gestures for me to come closer. Then he tucks something in the pocket of my shirt and whispers, "Those aren't even their real names, you know."

I don't glance down at Mr. Daly's parting gift until I reach the mailbox, and there, glinting in gold foil, is an extra-large, hypoallergenic condom.

I let it tumble out of my pocket before kicking it into the gutter. Then I open the mailbox, sifting through newspaper ads and flyers for cable television before my fingers graze an envelope with my name on it. I stuff it into the back pocket of my jeans before Abuelo sees, and then I head to work.

When I reach the kitchen, the mariachi music is already in full swing.

"Hey, you're back!" Lucas slaps me on the shoulder. "Listen, we're working a catering tonight with Angel. Biggest one of the year, so we need all hands on deck."

Foil pans line the plating station, where Lucas and I load them with fajitas, refried beans and rice, and Mexican

71

wedding cookies. I stack them three at a time before following the flickering lights above the alley to the back of the truck.

After we finish loading everything up, Lucas and I cram into the front seat next to Angel while Struggles and Java crawl in the back. As soon as we pull up to the event, I can feel the bass from the music rattling under the truck. The parking lot is full, silhouettes already swaying near the windows even though we're half an hour early.

Lucas kneads his hands. "Check it out." He nods to one of the silhouettes writhing on the other side of the window. Long, thin, with big boobs. "Well, gentlemen, looks like I'll be catching another ride home tonight."

Angel rolls his eyes. "Not after she finds out you need one."

"I just so happen to ride the bus because I'm environmentally friendly, and it just so happens that girls find that sexy."

"You know what else they find sexy?" Angel asks.

"What?"

He hands him a tray of food. "Men who work."

Lucas is the first to push through the back doors of the convention center. We follow the swirling lights into the main ballroom, the music pulsing, and then we stop, Angel almost losing his grip on the cake.

Women with cotton-candy hair and men in Velcro shoes wander in circles around the dance floor.

Lucas frowns. "Fuck!"

We set up the food along the far wall, each of us

manning three trays and serving the people who come by with plates.

An elderly woman with a strange blue tint to her hair points to the fried potatoes. "Are these real potatoes?"

I nod.

She points to the corn salsa. "Is this real corn?"

"Yes." Lucas leans over the trays. "It's all real, ma'am. Everything but that ridiculous blue poodle on your head." He mumbles that last part under his breath.

Java laughs, his accent bold, maybe Slavic. "Damn, Lucas, what's gotten into you? That's no way to speak to a lady." He nudges him. "So much for you getting laid tonight."

Lucas bristles. "Fuck off."

"Oh, I will. You're the one who doesn't have any plans."

After an hour of watching the most obscene dance moves of the 1930s, Lucas convinces Struggles to steal some wine coolers, and they each take turns crouching behind the serving station to chug them.

"You sure you're good?" Lucas tries to offer me a swig.

"Yeah, actually, I'm gonna find a bathroom. I'll be back in a minute."

I sidestep past banquet tables, following the strobe lights to the hallway. In the bathroom, I disappear into a stall and shut the door behind me. I reach into my pocket, feeling the envelope but not able to pull it out. My thumb grazes the ink on the front as if I'm about to toss an old coin into a fountain. I don't let myself make a wish.

My fingers finally slip into the corner where the

adhesive hasn't quite stuck, the faint tear so loud in the empty bathroom. My hand grows still. I lean against the stall. *Just do it already.* I rip it open in one swipe before plucking out the letter.

> *Dear Mr. Amaro,*
> *Our records do not indicate the detainment*
> *or deportation of the named, Victor Amaro,*
> *within the last 60 days. Our department will*
> *be unable to fulfill your request.*

There's no signature. Just another generic response. Another dead end. I've received five of these letters in the past year, but every sixty days I keep checking.

Once, I was so fed up I tried contacting an immigration lawyer instead. But three installments later, the guy was $800 richer and I was still at square one. I went to his office one day to confront him only to discover that he'd disappeared. No gold plaque outside the door. No fake diploma from an Ivy League law school on the wall.

The money I'd used to pay the lawyer had been from my abuelo. Gifts from every birthday and Christmas since I'd gone to live with him. Money he'd begged me to save for college, for my future. Instead, I squandered it on the past.

When I step back into the ballroom, Angel, Lucas, and the other employees are suddenly standing at attention, their gazes pinned to where Mr. Prado stands on the other side of the serving table. He isn't alone.

A man holding a glass of whiskey, lip stretched with tobacco, narrows his eyes as I approach.

"And who's this young man?" The stranger's voice is honeyed, like he's some kind of performer and we're his expectant audience.

I duck behind Lucas, something about the attention making me itch.

The honey reaches the man's eyes as he reaches out a hand. "The name's J. P."

I swallow. "X-Xander."

Mr. Prado steps between us before I can reach back.

"The kids are working," he says, and then a little lower, "and this is between us."

The man wags a finger, one eye pinched shut like he's examining us through a scope. "Nacho, what have you been telling these kids about me? They all look like they're afraid I'll bite." He raises a hand to his mouth and says conspiratorially, "Don't worry. My bark's much bigger."

"J. P...." Mr. Prado tries to lead him away.

The twinkle in the man's eye disappears. "You're right. I didn't just come here to celebrate the Johnsons' fiftieth wedding anniversary. I also came here to see an old friend and to find out how his business is doing." He nods to us. "Seems like you've got quite a few people on payroll. Business must be good."

Mr. Prado is so stoic I can't tell if he's breathing.

"Or maybe it's just your heart of gold getting in the way again.... You sure do like picking up strays." J. P. finds my face again and winks. "I heard it's dangerous running around out here without tags."

My insides tie themselves into a knot.

Everyone in Monte Vista knows Mr. Prado hires undocumented people. But this man isn't from Monte Vista. I can tell. And not just because he looks like a stranger, but because he's glaring at us like we're strangers too.

My hands sweat and I stuff them in my pockets. Maybe he's just heard rumors. Maybe he's just trying to get a rise out of Mr. Prado.

Maybe I'm still safe.

Mr. Prado forces J. P. back, some of his whiskey spilling out of his glass.

"We're not old friends." Mr. Prado seethes. "And you're not welcome here."

J. P. takes a step back, a hand raised. "That's okay." Then he nods to a table in the far corner of the room. It's surrounded by men in uniform, the strobe lights reflecting off their police badges. "I've got plenty of other friends."

J. P. disappears behind the people spinning in circles on the dance floor. While Mr. Prado shoots daggers at him.

While Angel clenches his fists.

While my heart races.

I look down at my Nacho's shirt, wondering if in this neighborhood, it's not a disguise, but a giant red flag. Maybe it doesn't matter what I wear. Maybe people like that can tell I'm undocumented just by looking at me; at the color of my skin, at all of the ways my body doesn't belong.

Angel growls, "Everyone get back to work."

We shut everything down early, packing up in silence.

The quiet follows us all the way back to the restaurant.

Until Angel puts the truck in park and Lucas asks, "What the hell was that about?"

Angel's still gripping the steering wheel. He's quiet for a long time, jaw clenched like he's wrestling with something. Then he says, "I don't know." And I can tell he means it.

Back at the restaurant, the place is packed, the sound of the dining hall like a vortex. Waitresses run plates in and out. Solana is behind the bar, sliding drinks back and forth. Chloe's at the hostess stand, perched on a chair and yelling over the crowd in the doorway.

Lucas hands me an apron, both of us frantically tying them around our waists. "Do you think he was telling the truth?"

"About the cops?" I swallow, thinking he means J. P. and his thinly veiled threat.

Lucas slides three plates over to the pickup window. "No, Angel. Do you think he's telling the truth about not knowing what that was all about?"

I glance over at the grill. Angel already has his headphones in—no crazy dance moves or even a bob of his head, the tongs in his hand the only thing moving.

"He seemed as confused as we were."

Lucas shrugs. "Yeah, I just hope..." He pauses. "Never mind."

"Do you know who that guy was?" I ask.

Angel finally breaks out of his daze and slams his hand down over the order bell. "We need some runners over here!"

Lucas loads up another plate. "People call him El Martillo, and he's the reason a lot of businesses in Monte Vista have closed down. My aunt took a loan from him once. A neighbor told her J. P. was a good guy, not like the other loan sharks who charge an arm and a leg in interest. They said he cared about helping undocumented people. We found out that wasn't true the day they boarded up the windows to her salon. A few weeks later, they knocked the whole thing down and built some apartment buildings." He shakes his head. "I can name a dozen other businesses tied up in his bullshit."

"And Mr. Prado?"

"He's basically Batman to El Martillo's Joker. Except without the justice."

"Is J. P. a criminal?"

Lucas shrugs. "What else do you call someone who uses blackmail and intimidation to extort people out of their hard-earned money? But apparently he can do whatever he wants...."

I think back to his uniformed posse watching us from the corner of the room. "Because he's got the right friends?"

"Exactly, which means we can't do anything that might put us in J. P.'s crosshairs. Because he'll always win."

I didn't think Mr. Prado was afraid of anyone. What does it mean if he is?

Chloe looks back from the hostess stand and sends a few waitresses to run plates. Gabby works her way up to four, wobbling a moment before finding her stride.

She slides between a guy and a girl breaking out of an embrace, barely missing the girl's big sparkly handbag.

"Oh shit." Lucas holds his breath. "This is not going to be good."

A few tortilla chips tumble to the floor.

"No." I shake my head. "Definitely not."

The crowd by the door is ready to burst at the seams, a guy who is obviously already wasted trying to push through. Chloe chases him into the dining area and then he stops. Right in front of Gabby. Then she slams into him, all of the food she's carrying crashing to the floor.

Lucas hangs his head. A moment later, Angel is in the dining room, his manager tag askew. The drunk guy jams his finger into Angel's chest. I don't even see who throws the first punch, but all of a sudden they're tangled and falling into the table of six that Gabby was on her way to serve.

The trusty air horn blares, and the place is a zoo. People rush the entrance, trying to squeeze through the front door in one rumbling stampede.

When it finally empties, the last of us stand in the middle of the restaurant, staring down at the mess of food and silverware and melting ice. It looks like some invisible hand has come down and spun the restaurant like a top.

Chloe rushes to Angel's side, kneeling next to him. She whispers something, her voice firm, but when he looks up I can't tell if he's reassured or terrified. But then the bell above the restaurant entrance chimes and his father steps inside. And there is no question. Angel is scared for his life.

So are the rest of us.

I wait for Mr. Prado to yell or drag Angel outside. But he just looks around; one sweep of the restaurant is all it takes before he raises a finger and Angel follows him into the parking lot.

Everyone runs for the windows, trying to get a front row seat.

"Get the hell away from there!" Chloe summons everyone to the center of the room. "That is none of your business." She hands out trash bags. "This mess is."

There are a few groans, people kicking at chairs.

"Hey!" Chloe yells. "You want to get paid or not?"

She hands me a trash bag before pulling all the shades down and planting herself between us and the door. Then we have no choice, a barrage of moans and murmurs and various curse words filling the dining room as we all get back to work.

After we've been at it for about an hour, Chloe dismisses the staff in chunks, Gabby and Mari high-fiving when they're the first to leave. Java and Solana are next, followed fifteen minutes later by Lucas and Struggles. Lucas makes a celebratory foul gesture on his way out the door, Chloe kicking him in the rear.

"You okay to stay a little longer?" Chloe asks me. "You're the only one who hasn't been bugging me to leave."

"Yeah, sure."

"Great!" She heaves a tub of cleaning supplies into my arms. "Supply closet. Thanks."

I make my way back to the supply closet, but when I crack the door I'm not alone. Pen's examining one of the shelves, a few spice bottles already tucked into her bag. She presses a finger to her lips before pulling the door closed behind me.

I set down the tub of cleaning supplies.

"So, I'm guessing you heard that I'm not exactly supposed to be here right now." She fiddles with one of the glass bottles, puts it back on the shelf. "Or ever."

I'm not sure what to say, still surprised to see her.

"I just needed a few things."

I raise an eyebrow. "Things you can't get at the supermarket?"

Pen shrugs, staring up at the ceiling. "I may have held onto my spare key. I just...I wanted to be here. That's all."

I nod. "I'm sorry about what happened. And about you and your dad."

"Yeah, well, he's..." She runs a hand through her hair. "He and I have always butted heads about everything."

"Maybe you're too much alike."

She huffs. "You speaking from experience?"

I stuff my hands in my pockets. "No, not really."

She notices the disappointment in my voice and I wish I hadn't opened my mouth.

She examines me more closely as she says, "What's your dad like?"

"He's..." My throat's dry and I swallow. "I don't know...."

She realizes she's staring too close, backs away. "I'm sorry."

I lean against the wall. "It was a long time ago."

The words feel like a lie. It's been more than a decade since I watched him drive away, but every time I follow a new lead and it amounts to absolutely nothing, that sting is brand-new.

Because time doesn't heal wounds. It makes them evolve, more durable and more potent. The sting of being left never goes away, it just disguises itself, erupting in fights after school and empty shot glasses that are numbing one second and gasoline the next.

Pen doesn't see the memories behind my eyes and I'm afraid to bring them up, shattering whatever this quiet moment is. Because I need the quiet and whatever feigned safety exists in this space between us.

She moves to the wall, slumping down at my feet. "What about your mom?"

It's almost three in the morning and I'm exhausted. But something forces me to join her on the floor.

"She left too," I say.

The air trips over Pen's lips. "After...? How could she do that?"

I shake my head. It feels strange that she's angry, that she cares at all.

"That's so shitty," she says. "I'm sorry that happened to you." I wait for an uncomfortable silence, but Pen chases it away. "Some people just aren't meant to be parents."

"Yours seem pretty great."

Pen's shoulders slump. "They're not so bad, they're just..." She hugs her knees. "Stubborn. Neither of them went to college, so it's just such a big deal to them, and I get that, but it's not for me. I tried it, I really did, but..."

"You would rather be here."

"They groomed me for this, whether they realize it or not. Even when I was just a kid, my dad would let me wrap the silverware, and then it wasn't long before I started tweaking the menu here and there. He knew I was like him. He knew that given the choice, I would choose this. So he took it away." Pen stares at the walls like they're closing in on us. "I could do it, you know. I could fix this. If he'd just let me try."

"The restaurant?" I ask.

"Everything."

The lull I've been waiting for finally slips over us, and I know it's my turn to chase it away.

"What would you change?" I ask.

Pen looks up at me.

"If this was your restaurant, what would you do?"

Her face is hard again, thinking. But then she smiles. "Can I show you?"

When I crack the door, I don't hear any footsteps. The parking lot out front is finally empty—Mr. Prado's truck gone—but I know Angel and Chloe are still here. Pen slips out first, waving me over to the back door. Through the window we can see Angel and Chloe sitting on the back steps, their shoulders touching.

Pen leads me to the kitchen before flipping on the lights. She circles the room. "First, I'd knock out this entire wall." She steps through to the dining area. "And then I'd put a long display case filled with pastries and candies. Maybe we could even open a drive-through window leading out into the alley so people could take their food to go." Pen makes her way to the window, tapping the glass. "I'd extend the patio area, maybe put in a big pergola with some of those hanging lights. We could rip out all of those weeds back there and have live music on the weekends."

"So is that what you really want? Not your father's restaurant, but your own?"

Pen sinks down into one of the booths, scratching at her thumbnail. I sit down across from her.

"I...If I could do anything, I'd own my own bakery."

She looks around as if someone might overhear, but it's just the two of us, and suddenly that fact is making my hands sweat. I duck them under the table, accidentally grazing her knee.

"Pen, what the hell are you doing here? Are you out of your mind?" Angel's spotted us, the terror returned to his face.

She stands, rolling her eyes. "I just needed a few things."

He pokes at her overstuffed bag. "A few things. You're stealing. After you were just fired!"

"I'm not stealing. I'm simply borrowing these until Dad changes his mind, and then I'll bring them back."

"Give her a break, Angel." Chloe pushes Pen toward the entrance. "She's going."

"She better be."

I try to catch Pen's eye one last time, but she and Chloe are whispering about something on their way out.

Angel hangs his head. "Jesus, being manager is going to kill me." The almost-laugh catches in his throat. "Shit. Can you believe the day we've had?"

"You mean this isn't typical?" I try to smile.

"It wasn't." He sighs. "But now...?" Then, in a voice much smaller than he is, "Maybe everyone's right. Maybe I'm not cut out for this."

"I don't believe that." The truth is, I'm not sure. This is

only my second shift and I can already tell that Pen was the glue holding this place together. I *am* sure that's not what Angel needs to hear right now.

He slings an arm around me and it's as unexpected as finding Pen alone in that storage closet. "You're all right," he says. Then he checks the time on his phone. "Jesus. It's past three and you're still here? Thank God there's at least one person I can rely on."

The pang is practically invisible. Not because of Angel's praise, but because it means I get to come back. That he wants me to come back.

"Are you going to be okay?" I ask.

Angel grows still, thinking. Then he exhales. "I'm fine. Let's lock up and get the hell out of here."

7

Xander

THE LAWYER'S OFFICE IS downtown in a small brick building that looks abandoned. The windows are blacked out, the walls a raw pink that reminds me of a doctor's office. It kind of smells like one too. Stale and sad and sick.

The first thing I do is seek out signs of permanence. There's a water dispenser in the corner, an indoor plant, a few of the leaves browning. One of the drawers of the receptionist's desk is half-open and full of empty candy wrappers, and six photos of her children line the wall behind her. The phone rings and when she goes to answer it, I notice that a few of the buttons are faded, her fingers finding the correct extension by memory.

These relics, combined with the fact that it was Officer Solis who gave me the address, encourage me to finally take a deep breath.

When they call me back, a redheaded woman with green eyes greets me in Spanish. "¿Cómo puedo ayudarle?"

I reach in my pocket, pulling out the only document I have containing my father's information—a petition for child support that my mother filed after he left. I always wondered what would have happened if he'd responded, if he'd kept sending her money like he'd promised. Something to shelter us, to keep her heart from being so easily bruised. Sometimes I like to think it would have made a difference. That she would have kept me if she could. That she would have wanted me....Maybe they both would have wanted me.

"I'm looking for someone," I say. "A man named Victor Amaro." I point to his name on the scanned document. "He came on a work visa fifteen years ago."

"How old are you?" she asks.

"I'm eighteen."

She lays the paper flat. "In the case of an outstanding custody or child support issue, the federal government can only assist *children* who are legal citizens. You're an adult." She hands me back the slip of paper. "I'm sorry."

"I'm not seeking child support. I'm just trying to find out where he is."

I think about all the old phone numbers and addresses stuffed in the shoebox under my bed. Thin scraps of paper and faded photographs, corners bent from all the nights I've spent staring, searching every inch for clues.

I know my father's twenty-year-old face better than I know my own—the dimples, the crooked bottom teeth, the five-o'clock shadow with hints of red. In every picture he's smiling. Sometimes if I stare long enough—long enough for my bedroom outside the frame to dissipate, long enough for the light to catch his eyes, to make it look like they're staring back—I can feel myself smiling too.

But then I remember. His face becomes static again and I'm just as stuck. After a decade of searching, I can relay every detail about those photographs, about the places he's been. I can recall the cadence of every stranger who's answered one of his old phone numbers. But I don't know where he is. I don't know *who* he is. And without that, I don't know who I am. And I need to.

I *need* to know.

The woman leans forward and that's when I realize my eyes are wet.

"When did he leave?" she asks.

"When I was four." I swallow. "He said he'd come back for us, but he never did."

Her head tilts, expression soft. "And now you need to find out why."

I nod.

She leans back, thinking. "You've checked with the consulate?"

"Several times."

"So there's no record of him becoming a permanent resident or having been deported in the past fifteen years?"

"No."

She pauses. "And what about you?"

I'm quiet.

"Are you a permanent resident?"

I don't answer, but she doesn't push me.

"You know, I see some cases where a person travels alone to the States to find work." She treads carefully. "At first they stay in touch, calling home, wiring money just as often. But then the calls become more infrequent. The money disappears, and then so do they." She pauses. "They realize they can have a fresh start. Reinvent themselves." She twists a paper clip between her fingers until it's a straight line. "What I'm trying to say is…they become someone else and sometimes that new person just doesn't want to be found."

I stare at my shoes, speckled with grease from the restaurant. "I know he might not want to see me."

"And you're prepared for that?"

I nod again. Even though I'm not sure. Time has dulled the memory of him walking out that door, the years that have passed fueling the questions instead. That's the fire that needs putting out first, even if it ignites something else.

She slides a business card to me. "When they have the funds, I refer a lot of my clients to a private investigator I know. He's honest, thorough. If you're serious about finding your father, give him a call."

I tuck the card in my pocket. "I will."

When I reach the door, she stops me. "What was your name again?"

I look back. "Xander."

"Ah." She nods. "Alejandro."

I shake my head. "Just Xander."

She smiles. "Well, good luck, Xander."

———

As I step out of the office my phone rings. Nacho's. It's my first day off since I started, but when Angel asks me to come in for a few hours, I'm actually relieved. I don't want to go home, for my abuelo to ask where I've been.

A few weeks after I came to live with him, I finally mustered up the courage to ask about my father. His son. He was quiet for a long time, staring into his cup of coffee. Then he got up from the kitchen table and walked away. He stayed in his room the rest of the day and I stayed at the table, afraid of moving, of making a sound. I didn't want him to leave me too, so I never spoke of my father again.

He didn't either. But he knew I still had questions. And yet, every time one of my father's photographs went missing from the photo album he kept at the bottom of his closet, he never said a word. He never tried to stop me. But that was probably only because he thought the photographs were all I wanted. Or all I'd be able to find. What I'm doing now isn't quite as harmless. Which is why, despite what Officer Solis thinks, I just can't bring myself to tell him.

When I get to the restaurant I find Lucas and a few others in the back alley, all climbing into Angel's truck.

"Another catering?" I ask.

"Not exactly," Lucas says. "In my experience, when Angel takes us on these little excursions outside the restaurant, it's never good."

"What do you mean?"

Struggles pushes past us, climbing into the back seat. "He means that if it was anything worth doing, Angel wouldn't be keeping it a secret."

We pull up to a tall residential building just off the highway. A girl steps out from behind a box truck. Pen.

"Oh, hell no!" Lucas groans. "She better live on the first fucking floor."

"Shut the hell up," Angel snaps. "You're all getting paid for this shit so just suck it up and do it."

Chloe heaves a couple of boxes into Lucas's arms and then she hangs her head back, staring up at the building.

"She doesn't live on the first floor, does she?" he asks.

Angel reaches for a box, sighing. "Try the sixth."

Pen is already directing the others and telling them which boxes contain breakables and which ones we aren't allowed to touch.

I take my place in line, Pen handing me a box of cookbooks. "Trying to get in good with the manager?"

"According to the others, I was tricked."

She loads another box on top of the one I'm holding. "That's probably true."

Pen stares at me and I stare back. When my arms start burning I realize I've been standing there too long.

She realizes it too. "Well?" She puts her hands on her hips and I remember that there are five floors between me and her new apartment.

I turn to follow the others, relieved when I spot the elevator. Struggles is still huffing and puffing by the time we reach the sixth floor. He drops the box marked CLOTHES in front of Pen's door and I kick it the rest of the way inside before setting down my own.

"Can you believe Pen's moving into this place?" Lucas leans over the sink, funneling water into his mouth. He wipes his face with his forearm. "It's like a concrete box."

I step around the room, but I don't see four concrete walls. I see *space*. I don't have very much of it living with my abuelo. When I first moved in, the house was already full of memories: trinkets and old mismatched furniture, Western figurines, vintage beer bottles, and his giant coin collection. There wasn't much room for anything new, especially not me, and I felt it every year I grew an inch taller, that small house pressing in on me.

It takes six trips to get all of Pen's stuff into her new apartment. After carrying in her mattress we all collapse on the floor, the cold concrete suddenly a welcome amenity.

Pen flops down too, she and Chloe back-to-back as they try to hold themselves up. Sweat trickles from under her bandana, one drop making it all the way down the slope of her neck and beneath her shirt.

"Jesus, Pen, you better be making us some dinner after all this."

She shoots Angel a look, then smiles. "Fair." She slides a few box cutters across the floor. "But only after you guys help me unpack."

Lucas stabs one of the boxes, splitting the tape. "Then there better be cake too."

"Ask Angel," Pen says, "he's the one paying."

Angel kicks one of the empty boxes. "Me? What do you mean I'm paying?"

"After seventy dollars for the moving truck and another two hundred for the deposit, I have enough for exactly one month's rent."

Lucas falls onto his back. "Shit. You mean we're gonna be moving all this stuff again in a month?"

"No." Pen looks down. "I'm not going back. I'll figure it out...." She makes doe eyes at Angel. "But today—"

"Today I'll pay for groceries." Angel sighs. "Just tell us where you want everything before you go."

Pen kicks a few boxes over to Struggles. "These four go in the dresser against the wall."

He unfolds the flaps on the box in front of him, jumps back. "What the hell? I'm not touching these."

Pen rolls her eyes. "It's underwear. And you're on the clock."

"It's *your* underwear."

"Yeah, Struggles." Lucas plucks something black and lacy from the box and yanks it down over Struggles's head. "It's just Pen's underwear."

Struggles swats at it like he's walked straight into a spider-web. Lucas shoots another in his direction and Struggles fires one back, both of them aiming lace and thongs like arrows.

One lands against my knee, a pair of plain cotton pant-ies, and I freeze. Before I can even move, Pen stomps by and scoops them up.

She grips them in her fist. "If you shoot one more I will

break your fucking fingers and make you eat cake with your feet."

They shudder.

"Now, put together this furniture while Chloe and I run to the supermarket."

They both nod, getting to work as she disappears out the door.

I'm on bookshelf duty and after I finally get it to stand up straight, I start ripping into the boxes at my feet. The first one is the cookbooks I carried. They smell like sugar and garlic, and I line them up on a middle shelf, using a jewelry box as a bookend.

I feel like a kid again, snooping through my grandfather's keepsakes, trying to make the puzzle pieces fit. Pen's a puzzle too. There are photo collages of her and Chloe from when they were younger, and small plastic trophies from soccer tournaments and track meets. There are framed photos of family vacations, wooden scraps covered in doodles, a mannequin head draped with tangled necklaces.

I wind up an old carousel, paint-chipped horses slowly moving in a circle, and I wonder what kinds of things I'd put on my own bookshelf, what proof of my existence I've collected over the years. The clothes I brought with me, I've outgrown. There aren't any baby pictures of me, no Christmas cards or favorite toys. No memories in three-dimension. No proof that I'm even here or that I belong to something bigger. A family.

That's what I see when I look at Pen's past, what I feel

when I hold it in my hands. The kind of love that anchors. That binds. And even though Pen and her father are fighting, I can see in Pen's memories that this is a family that belongs to one another. Always.

My gaze drifts down to a small mirror on one of the shelves, and my reflection catches me like a snare. Buried deep in my eyes, folded in the scrunch of my brow, I see my abuelo. I see the parts of him he passed down to my father, the parts of my father that were passed down to me. Right there. In three-dimension. They aren't my memories, but maybe they're still proof. That even though I don't have a bookshelf full of mementos, I am still here. I am still rooted in something.

By the time Pen and Chloe are back from the market and getting started on dinner, the rest of her stuff already unpacked, I'm still standing in front of the bookcase holding a ceramic lizard and trying to decide where to put it. I finally slide the lizard next to the mannequin head, and when I step back to admire my collage, I bump right into Pen.

My face warms as she takes a step toward one of the shelves, reaching for a small wooden flute. "I forgot about this." She presses it to her lips, a laugh coming through faint and high-pitched. "My dad made it for me. I played it every day that summer and drove everyone crazy. I was pretty terrible." Her eyes float up to the rest of the shelves. "Jesus, I haven't seen some of this stuff in so long. It must have been trapped in the back of my closet somewhere."

"I got a little carried away," I admit.

She shakes her head. "It's perfect." She puts the flute back on the shelf. "Thank you."

"Uh, Pen, I think something's burning." Chloe stands over the open oven door, fanning the smoke with a rag.

"Oh shit!" Pen slips on an oven mitt and yanks out the pan. The cake is charred. "Who the hell knocked my timer onto the floor?" She scrapes at the top layer, the one underneath still golden. "Thank God." She tucks a strand of hair behind her ear. "Nothing a little icing won't fix."

After letting the cake cool, Pen pulls the icing from the fridge and slathers it on in long strokes, her eyes inches from the surface as she switches to a spoon and carves little waves. She rinses a handful of raspberries before lining them up like tiny houses, their curved edges fitting perfectly within each scallop. She tosses one into her mouth before reaching for the sifter, powdered sugar falling onto the raspberry houses like fresh snow. She blows at the spots that are too heavy, the snow windswept and glittering.

Lucas's stomach growls, everyone watching Pen impatiently.

She glares at him, reaching for a few mint leaves and tying the stem into a tiny knot. She perches it in the center, completing her winter scene. As she dims the burners and pulls the other dishes from the oven, she doctors them with the same care—stirring and scooping and tasting and shaping. She steps away from her masterpiece, smile cutting into her flaming cheeks as she wipes her brow with a small hand towel. Then it's time to eat.

We circle up, using empty boxes as a makeshift table

while we eat arroz con pollo and Pen's raspberry cake off Styrofoam plates. Struggles belches something fierce after his second piece and Chloe throws a roll of socks at his face.

Angel shakes his head, laughs. "Not again."

"Not another underwear fight?" Lucas says. "Or not another Sock Hop 2019?"

Angel rolls onto his back. "Shit, I forgot about that."

"Yeah," Lucas says, "your dad used to be so into those team-building exercises. Remember when he made us do that Cake Walk of Death and everyone who lost had to jump off that platform blindfolded?"

Pen scoffs. "You mean that two-foot ledge into the neighborhood swimming pool?"

"Hey, that shit was scary," Lucas argues. "No one knew how high up we were until Struggles jumped and we heard the splash."

Struggles glares at him. "You mean until I was pushed."

Angel pats him on the back. "Hey, you came out on top once. Remember, when you won that hard-boiled-egg-eating contest?"

Struggles loads his plate with two more slices of cake.

Lucas raises an eyebrow. "You know you're not actually competing in a contest right now, right?"

"Can you blame him? That cake is a Penelope Prado original." Pen smiles. "Almost as good as my famous coconut cake." She licks the back of her fork. "But not quite."

"Yeah." Lucas stabs his fork into the raspberry filling. "It sucks that they're taking it off the menu...."

Angel shoots daggers at Lucas.

Pen looks from Lucas to Angel. "What's he talking about?"

Angel fiddles with his fork. "Dad and I discussed it. . . ."

"Screw you." Pen shakes her head. "You know you can't take it off the menu."

"Actually," he lowers his voice, avoiding Pen's eyes, "we already did."

Pen grows still. "We?" Her cheeks redden and she looks like she's about to say something else. But then her eyes sweep across the room, registering the rest of us, and she stops herself.

Angel and Pen both stare at the floor. It doesn't take a genius to figure out that whatever relationship they have with their father is strained. He fired his own daughter from the family restaurant, after all, and he seems to be on Angel's case any chance he gets.

Still, after all the years I've spent looking for my own father, waiting for him to look for me too, I would take strained silence over nothing any day.

Angel stands. "We should probably head back to the restaurant." He musses Pen's hair on his way to grab a set of keys off the counter. "I'll drop off the box truck on the way back."

Angel heads into the hall and we file out after him. Chloe rushes out too, stopping Angel just before he reaches the elevator, talking to him in a voice that I recognize from the other night. She seems to be good at calming him down, and I wonder how long she's been doing it. I wonder if he'll ever notice.

"Shit, I left the box cutters." Lucas nudges me. "Can you run back in and grab them for me?"

I stare back down at Pen's door. "Me?"

He lowers his voice. "You saw her. She's emotional, and emotional Pen is scary Pen."

I roll my eyes at Lucas before heading back toward her apartment. When I reach the door, it's still slightly ajar. I push it open and spot her sitting on the floor.

"Pen?"

She stands, her back to me. She rubs at her eyes, hands coming back stained with mascara.

"Did you forget something?" Her voice is clipped, a warning to stay away.

But I'm already another step closer. "Are you okay?"

She takes a deep breath, holds on to it for a long time. I step into her line of sight, her tears stalled as she tries to hold on to them too.

"I'm fine." She hides her face, stepping to the window.

"You know . . . you don't have to be."

She glances at me, confused. Then she presses the heels of her hands to her eyes again. "He could have just fired me." She shakes her head. "He didn't have to erase me."

There's a faint tremble in her voice, and it feels like whatever threads have been holding her together are ready to snap. She senses it too, which is why she's trying so hard to not let me see, to not let anyone see.

The creak of the door pulls my gaze. Pen looks up too, tears drying on command.

"Did you find those box cutters?" Chloe asks. "They're all waiting downstairs."

I grab the box cutters off the floor and then I find Pen's reflection in the window one more time.

I want to tell her that I understand. What it's like to feel invisible, to feel like all you're good for is forgetting. But I don't say a word. She seeks my eyes within the glass and I'm silent. And then, even though leaving is the last thing I want to do, I turn and go.

8

Pen

I TWIST THE KNOB on the slow-moving carousel, bells tinkling, and it unlocks something in me. Memories, warm and then cold, until I'm crying so hard I can barely make out the photographs or Chloe's face as she comes to stand next to me.

She leads me to the bed, and then says, gently, "Scoot over."

I crawl under the blankets, still examining my life in fragments, the tears warping everything until it looks like one of those abstract paintings that people call genius even though it's just a bunch of lines and dots. Is that all my life is? Starts and stops and scribbles? Mistake after mistake?

"He hates me," I finally croak out.

Chloe strokes my hair, brushing it away from my face. "That's not true."

"Then what is?"

Chloe tilts my chin, leading my gaze back to the bookshelf. "You tell me...."

No matter where I look, I find something my father has touched. Soccer trophies from every summer between first and eighth grade line one of the shelves. The restaurant sponsored our neighborhood team and supplied everything from the jerseys to the equipment. My father would never cheer when I scored a goal, but on my way back up the field, he'd wait for me to look and then he'd wink.

On the shelf below that, jars filled with seashells from our yearly trip to the Gulf Coast. I remember how we used to sit in the shallows, his hand over mine as he slid it across the sand, teaching me how to search for sand dollars. It was then that I learned how to interpret my father's love not by his words but by his actions.

I try to interpret them now, but all I can remember is how angry he was, how he looked at me like I was a stranger.

"I don't understand why I'm not good enough." I squeeze my eyes shut. "I don't understand why I'll *never* be good enough."

Chloe reaches for a photograph of me and my father at the beach, holding it up. "Is that really what you see?"

I blink, trying to examine his expression past the tears. At first, it's stoic, his face as empty as it always is. But then I see the way the left side of his mouth turns up slightly. I see his hand as wide as a baseball mitt as he rests it on top of my wet hair. I see our matching suntanned skin. The way I'm hugging his knee like it's rooting me to the spot. My body just a branch, a permanent piece of him.

"That's not what I see," Chloe finally says. "But something's telling you to believe it. And it's that voice, the one only you can hear, that worries me most." She wraps her arms around me. "It's lying to you, Pen. That's all it's ever done."

"I know." I surprise myself, the response coming out like a kind of reflex. But there's a sense of resolve in it. Like this part of me that's been buried, that's been fighting to come to the surface, is finally starting to see the light.

But it also feels fragile and temporary, and I'm scared that any second it'll slip from my grasp.

"What's the voice telling you now?" Chloe says.

I pluck the thought like a poison berry and force it to my lips. "That I can't do this."

Chloe tightens her grip on me. "And what do you say back?"

Another thought blooms on my lips, the taste this time somewhere between bitter and sweet. "That I will."

I wince against the glow of my cell phone, checking the time. Six o'clock. Chloe just left to catch her 7:00 AM class, but not before making me promise to call her if I needed anything.

What I really need is a pair of earplugs to drown out the awful squealing sound coming from behind the wall. My next-door neighbor has decided to take a long shower in which he plans to sing every song from *West Side Story*. Including the instrumentals.

He butchers a high note and I throw my shoe against the wall. He coughs, goes quiet, and then I hear the shower shut off. The walls rattle, pipes probably purging the last of the hot water.

For a long time, I lie perfectly still, listening to the cars on the street, staring at the walls, at the barred windows, until the solitude is staring back. I wait for it to reach for me, to wrap me up.

I pull the blankets tighter and glance at my phone again. Nine o'clock.

I pinch my eyes shut and bury my face in my pillow.

Time starts to slip away from me and I let it. Along with everything else on my to-do list—the phone numbers and addresses of nearby restaurants, the number for the renters insurance company, the dirty dishes that need to be washed, the misplaced clothes and shoes and cooking supplies that the guys from the restaurant did their best to unpack but probably just stuffed into random cupboards.

The only one who didn't make a mess was Xander. Instead, he pulled out my childhood memories, one by one, brushed off the dust, and wove them into this mesmerizing patchwork, this haphazard portrait—revealing a life I hardly recognize anymore.

From where I lay, I carve out each piece, matching it to an age, a place, a feeling. My eleventh birthday party. *Fear.* The sound of my mother's voice. *Safety.* Hugo's favorite ice cream. *Joy.*

My cell phone is to my ear before I even realize I've dialed the number.

My mother answers. "Pen? Are—?"

"Let me talk to Hugo."

There's silence and then my little brother takes the

phone. My little sister's voice swirls around the mouth-piece too. She's crying.

"She forgot this morning when she woke up," Hugo says.

"Forgot what?" I ask.

"That you wouldn't be here." His voice is hard, so much like our father's.

"I'm sorry, Hugo. You know I didn't want to."

Something brushes the phone, like a hand over the mouthpiece.

"Pen?" It's my mother again.

She's the last person I want to talk to. Even though I can tell in her voice that she's hurting just as much as I am. Maybe I want her to. Because even though it's awful, sharing it is the only thing that makes it more bearable. "I have to go."

When the phone finally slips from my fingers, it's 5:00 PM. I'm concrete, each breath barely chipping away at the things that hold me down. But I *know* this feeling. I *miss* this feeling.

It used to sit in the corner of my room, watching me sleep, waiting for me to wrap myself in it like a warm blanket. It used to follow me home from school, reminding me that moving only made things worse. That I should be still. That I should disappear. It used to stare back at me from my vanity mirror, whispering *how*.

The doctor called it a chemical imbalance. All I needed was to tip the scales. But even though the medicine helps, the voice more like a nudge, a familiar tap on the shoulder, it hasn't gotten rid of it completely. I stare at the little white pills on the kitchen counter; imagine one resting on my tongue. And then I imagine what happens after I swallow—the loosening of the chains, the bruises they leave behind.

I remember the first time it happened, puberty inciting a war inside me that finally erupted the day after my abuelita died. I remember Lola's tiny hand on my shoulder, Hugo peering into my room through the crack in the door—both too young to see her death like a fog, to harbor the memory of me getting lost in it.

Angel pulled them away. Then my father sat next to me on the bed while my mother could barely watch from the hallway.

He took my hand, and in a voice that was both furious and afraid, he said, "We don't get to give up, Pen. You don't get to give up." He squeezed me harder. "Whatever's gotten into your head, you fight it." He shook me, tears welling up in his eyes. "Do you hear me, Penelope Rosario Ruiz Prado? You fight!"

I trembled and I cried and I fought. Because he told me to. Because when my father demanded strength, I had no choice but to become strong.

I reach, trying to remember *how*.

But all I hear is that voice like honey. Like thorns.

Close
your
eyes.
And

sink.

I feel the chains, but I don't let them tighten.

Instead, I remember that moment. The moment when he needed me to be unbreakable and I learned how to pretend. Ten seconds, thirty seconds, one minute at a time until I was someone new, the girl stuck in that bed an apparition whose hauntings I could keep at bay with cooking and those little white pills.

I stare at them across the room and then I drag myself out of bed, reigniting the resolve my father had forced me to find.

My knuckles ache, the bottle barely cracking open. I shake, pouring the pills into my open hand. They skitter, falling onto the counter. I scoop them up. Drop them on my tongue. Swallow. Deep breath.

9

Pen

A BEEPING SOUND PULLS my eyes open. It's morning again. I can hear someone pushing buttons, and then footsteps quickening into a run. I slam my pillow over my ears, trying to figure out how I didn't realize during the walkthrough that the walls were paper-thin, how I missed every burp and cough and sneeze that is suddenly so loud I barely hear the knock at the door.

When they knock again, louder, I startle before creeping to the peephole. When I look through, it's empty. But the moment I turn my back there it is again, so quick it's just a scratch and a thump. I look through the peephole again. Still nothing.

I turn my back and three hard bangs make the doorknob tremble. I wrench it open, the trill of laughter following two small children as they disappear at the end of the hall. And maybe it's because I'm sick of feeling like a victim, or maybe it's because I'm out of my mind, but suddenly I'm charging after them. I round the corner and spot two little boys in their pajamas hiding behind a fake potted plant.

I growl, "Where's your mother?"

They suddenly pale.

I snatch them by their shirtsleeves and drag them back to their apartment. Doors open on the way, people peering out at them kicking and crying. I relish the audience the same way I do at the restaurant. Better for my new neighbors to think I'm some kind of psychopath than a helpless little girl who lives alone.

The blond one wriggles. "Let go of me, lady!"

I bang on the door of their apartment.

"Shut up, doofus," the other one snaps. "She's gonna tell Mom."

A woman with a lit cigarette opens the door. Also still in her pajamas.

"These yours?" I say, and then I hurl them inside.

The woman doesn't say a word, just raises an eyebrow and takes a drag on her cigarette.

I march back to my apartment. Another door creaks open, a man in jogging clothes stepping out. He takes one look at me, his eyes wide, and then he bolts for the service stairs. That's when I remember that I'm still in my underwear.

I slam the door to my apartment closed, leaning against it. The breaths come fast, the realization that I'm out of bed, out of its grip, making me dizzy.

I check the dresser drawers for my sweatpants, but

some idiot, probably Struggles, has stuffed the first two with shoes. I finally find a pair of jeans in the trunk at the foot of my bed. They smell like sugar and have a small butterfly on the front left pocket. Lola's. They fold over my arm, my fingers picking at the holes.

Just get back in bed.

Crawl under the covers and close your eyes.

Instead of reaching for my pillow, I reach for my cell phone and plug it in. A flashing appointment reminder pops up as soon as it powers on.

10:00 AM–11:00 AM
INTERVIEW @ Tiers of Joy Bakery

My sense of self-preservation returns with a jolt and I'm dressed in a matter of seconds. The elevator ride takes longer than usual, my makeup dripping down my face by the time I make it to my car.

When I arrive, I'm five minutes late. My hands sweat against the steering wheel, and I rake them across the seat before finally heading to the door. The bakery is bigger than I expected, the parking lot already full. Women in big sunglasses carry pink boxes tied with bows out to their Lexuses and BMWs.

I pass a redhead juggling a Pomeranian, a Birkin bag, and a long box of gluten-free cupcakes on her way out the door. She gives me the once-over, unimpressed, and when I step inside the bakery to find young women in traditional white double-breasted jackets, long hair tied back with simple black ribbon, not a red lip in sight, I realize why.

I look down at my clothes, tight and loud and wrong. But there's no turning back now.

"Are you here for an interview?" a girl asks from behind the counter.

"Oh, uh, yes."

"Thought so," she says. "Didn't think you were a customer. Follow me."

I'm not sure if that was some kind of dig, but from the way she smiles I convince myself it wasn't.

"I'll go get Maureen and then we can start the test."

Test. My stomach drops. Tests were one of the many reasons why I spent last semester ditching school. I stand in front of one of the worktables, watching from across the kitchen as two girls meticulously ice cupcakes before balancing them on an elaborately tiered cake stand.

"Grab the girl an apron."

The employee who led me back tosses me a pink apron, and I yank it over my head just as a large woman reaches out to shake my hand.

"I'm Maureen, and your name is...?"

"Pen. Pen Prado."

"Nice to meet you, Pen. We've been looking for a new apprentice for a few weeks now. Spring is our busiest time of year. Tell me a little about your previous experience."

"Well..." I fumble with the strings on my apron, suddenly unable to move my hands and speak at the same time. I finally get the first bow done, wiping my forehead before she sees the sweat. "Well," I start again, "I spent my whole life working in my father's restaurant—Nacho's Tacos. I came up with most of the menu. The desserts are sort of my specialty. Everyone loves my white chocolate coconut cake."

"Family recipe?" Maureen asks.

"Something like that. But I do like to put my own twist on things. I've taken almost every classic Mexican recipe on the menu and—"

She cuts me off. "What are some of your other specialties?"

I swallow, searching her eyes as if they'll reveal the appropriate answer. "I can make empanadas, pan fino, cuernos de azucar, orejas, pan de huevo...."

She cuts me off again. "So, tell me, Pen, do you only have experience cooking Latin food?"

"Well"—if I could somehow score a point every time I started a sentence with *well*, I'd have this interview in the bag—"most of the things I make have some kind of European or North American equivalent. It's not that hard to make the leap. I mean, as long as I have a recipe I can cook almost anything."

She crosses her arms. "Anything..."

The smile on my face is so wide and fake it starts to hurt.

"Pen, do you mind if I ask you a personal question?"

"Sure."

"Tiers of Joy is an essential part of this local community. What do you know about this neighborhood or our customer base?"

All I know is what I observed upon arrival—the customers are mostly rich white women, the place is pet-friendly, the employees are robots.

She stops me before I even start. "I can hear your passion for Latin food. After all, you did grow up working in a Latin restaurant." She looks me up and down. "Indelibly, it's left a significant mark on not just your cooking style but your way of life. I'm just not sure if that"—her eyes crinkle into a condescendingly cheerful smile—"*style* will be a good fit here."

The anger is instant. I almost don't recognize it at first—it's been a long time since I was rejected in *this* way for *this* reason. But it's the type of rejection you never forget.

Like the time Michelle Smiley didn't invite me to her thirteenth birthday party. The next Monday at school she broke down and told me that her parents didn't want me sleeping over because they were afraid I would tell my father how many TVs they had or where her mother kept her nice jewelry.

Or like the time when I was seven and my father and I were pulled over on our way home from La Pulga. They made him get out of the car, and for three minutes I didn't breathe. They asked him for documentation—not even stopping to consider that he was born in this country—and when he went to reach for his wallet they slammed his face against the trunk of the car. Even though they'd told him to move. Even though he had a Texas driver's license and a United States birth certificate.

I tore out of my seat, flying at the policeman's knees. His partner wrenched me up by the arm, dragging me off the street while my little white Keds kicked up dirt and rocks. While I screamed and cried.

Instead of getting angry, my father started offering discounts to anyone in uniform. A few weeks later, he even served the two cops who had given him a bloody nose.

I was furious, and when I asked him why he did it, he said, "Because I'm not the only one in this neighborhood who might get stopped."

He wanted them to love our neighborhood, to see the human beings who lived there up close.

But I'm not in the mood to build bridges. Because Maureen's distaste for my *way of life* isn't just the kind of rejection that keeps you within a five-mile radius of home, speaking in another language when you're out in public, clinging to the sights and sounds and tastes of your native country even though, before you arrived, you were willing to trade it all in exchange for a one-way ticket. It's the kind of rejection that can get you killed.

Now I have a choice—*I always have a choice.* I can retreat and let this feeling fester. Let it follow me home and force me under the blankets again. Or I can snuff it out...by letting it explode.

"Give me a chance to bake you something," I plead.

"Something," her voice is stern, annoyed, "French." She narrows her eyes at me. "Mille-feuilles. I want it in an hour. I expect you can find your own way around the pantry." She glances at her wrist, sighs, and shakes her head. "The next interviewee should be on her way. Candice, will you go and see if she's waiting out front?"

But I'm not worried about the next interviewee. Because whoever she is, she won't be baking in this kitchen for the next twenty-four hours. No one will.

They leave me standing over a bowl of dry ingredients I pulled from the pantry that make absolutely no sense together. The other girls take turns watching me from where they stand, side-glances not even making me sweat.

Eventually, they lose interest, the other interview already starting—a wide-eyed blond being shown around the facility. She introduces herself before relaying the year she just spent at a culinary academy in Louisiana.

No one is watching me as I swap out a few traditional ingredients for a few *nontraditional* ones. I pour the final mixture into the pan, slam the oven door closed, crank it up to the highest heat, and then I walk out.

"A grody gordita?" Chloe is sprawled out on my bed, paralyzed in awe. "And then you just left?"

She gags and I almost do too, both of us remembering the infamous stink bomb created by a (still) unnamed source during last year's Nacho's Tacos Prank Wars. The recipe was found on a scrap of paper beneath a jar of pickled jalapeños, the writing barely legible. But I'll never forget the secret ingredient—human hair. Which I just so happen to have plenty of.

"Just walked out..." I fan the short strand of hair I sacrificed in my quest for revenge.

Chloe's laughter fades. "I'm sorry they were such assholes."

"Me too."

She wraps her arms around me. "I...did see an opening at El Pequeño Toro." *The Little Bull.*

I whip around. "A fast-food chain?"

She climbs off the bed. "I know that place is like a revolving door, but that's sort of the point. There's no way you won't get hired, and you can make some cash to hold you over until you find something better." She rummages through a pile of shoes, which I have not had time to correctly organize yet. "Boots or flats?" She places one on each foot.

"We're just going to Angel's."

She kicks off the boot and slips the flat back onto her bare foot. She looks nervous.

"Is something going on?"

"What do you mean?" She doesn't look up.

"Did something happen at the restaurant? I mean, you and Angel, you're not, like..." I can't even get the words out.

"No." She sighs.

"Well, good."

"Wow, thanks."

"I didn't mean it like that." I choose my next words carefully. "I meant good for you. Angel's not...He's just sort of a flake. You know that."

"He's not always like that."

I raise an eyebrow. "He's my brother. I think I would know."

"So, what if he's changed?"

"Has he?" I ask.

"He could." Her smile is faint. Hopeful.

"And Maureen could call any minute to offer me the job even though I probably almost burned down her bakery and everyone in it."

Chloe lets out an annoyed huff. "You'll find another job."

"And you'll find another boyfriend."

I grab my bag and head for the door when the pipes start wheezing again. They choke out a sneeze, water rushing between the walls.

Chloe looks up. "What's wrong with your apartment?"

I roll my eyes. "It's constipated."

10

Xander

WHEN I SHOW UP to the address Lucas gave me, the driveway is full of cars. I pull on my Nacho's shirt as I head up the sidewalk and notice the garage door is cracked a few feet, lights blinking across the concrete, something cracking like pool balls.

"Xan the man!" Angel grabs my shoulders and gives me the once-over. "Oh shit. Did you think you were working tonight?" He laughs. "Let me get you a beer."

The cold bottle stings my hand, and when he isn't looking I set it on a table next to the couch. There's a couple sitting on the lopsided arm, shoving their tongues down each other's throats. They finally come up for air and I recognize Mari and one of the Medrano brothers.

Angel beckons me into the garage. It's lit by a cheap disco ball, and there's a pool table in the center where

Lucas leans over, squaring up a shot. He spots me, or more specifically my shirt, and scratches.

"What the hell?" He guffaws. "You live in this thing or something?"

"I thought you were calling me in for another catering."

Angel rolls his eyes. "You didn't tell him it was a party?"

"I didn't think I had to." Lucas claps the chalk from his hands before gesturing around the room. "Xander, welcome to the annual Nacho's Tacos Purge."

My brow furrows. "Nacho's. Tacos. Purge?"

Angel slams another beer into my chest. "Yes. You see, tonight is about us sticking it to the man."

"And puking out twelve months' worth of tacos," Lucas adds.

"Sticking it to the man," I repeat, wary. "You mean your dad?"

"Details." Angel waves a hand before leading me from room to room where every Nacho's Tacos employee is either taking a shot or a toke, or eating a plate full of spaghetti.

"What's with the spaghetti?" I ask.

"It's the most anti-taco food there is," Angel says, matter-of-fact.

"So, if everyone from work is here, who's running the restaurant?"

"We close once a year for pest control or some shit. Anyway, the point is that tonight we're free and there isn't a goddamn taco in sight."

The garage door screeches open, landing against the

ceiling with a crash. Everyone crouches down, waving at the smoke to see who's just walked in.

Pen.

"Shit. What the hell is wrong with you?" Angel rushes over, yanking the garage door closed again, Chloe barely ducking inside in time.

"What?" Pen plants her hands on her hips. "There's puke all over your sidewalk. I'm not stepping in that."

I've never seen Pen out of her Rosie the Retributioner getup. Even the day we helped her move into her apartment she was wearing an old Nacho's T-shirt and her hair was pulled back in her signature red bandana. But tonight she's wearing these black shorts that climb above her waist and a dark blue tank top. A strand of her hair is caught under her bright pink bra strap. It's out of a ponytail for once, hanging long down her back.

She flips it over her shoulder, eyeing my shirt. "Angel didn't mention this was a party, did he?"

"Not exactly."

She purses her lips. They're darker this time, almost purple. "Want to grab me a drink?"

"What do you like?" I ask.

"Something sweet."

I feel her eyes on me all the way down the hall. When I finally find the kitchen, I pluck a drink from the ice-filled sink and pop the top against the counter.

Just then people pass me in a rush, Angel dragging a cooler through the back door. Everyone files out after him, the backyard small and mostly covered in concrete. Angel unstacks chairs while Lucas tries to get a fire to catch in a few of the aluminum trash cans near the fence.

Pen reaches for her drink.

"What's going on?" I ask.

"The Purge Olympics. It's a drinking game. Except there aren't really any rules or a way to win or..."

"Any point at all?"

"Other than to get shit-faced while attempting to humiliate each other?" She shrugs. "Not really."

"Okay, everybody take your positions!"

"Is it some kind of race?" I ask.

Chloe steps between Pen and me. "A race, a relay, a trivia contest."

"A little bit of truth or dare," Pen adds. "Oh, and an endurance test."

People form a line at both ends of a small card table. Pen grabs my wrist and pulls me in line behind her.

"Teams?" I ask.

"For now."

Sang and one of the Medrano brothers square up first, a beer between them. Miguel wipes a hand across his brow, Sang shaking out his arms like he's getting ready for a boxing match.

Lucas plucks a slip of paper from a baseball cap before slamming it down on the table. "Lyrics to 'Rocket Man.' Go!"

They both start screaming at the top of their lungs, fighting over each other and the chatter behind them. The first time Miguel flubs the words, everyone on our side of the table cheers. He flings up his hands, Sang pushing the beer in his direction. He downs it, slamming the bottle on the table. Then Lucas slides over another.

Chelo and Struggles are up next. She growls at him and he shivers.

Lucas slams down another slip of paper. "Spanish alphabet, backward, while standing on one leg. Go!"

Struggles flaps his arms, barely able to keep upright. Chelo presses her hands together, in what I assume is some type of yoga pose, perfectly centered.

When Chelo has already gotten through three letters and it becomes clear that Struggles is just repeating what she says, Lucas grabs him by the shirt and pours the drink down his throat. Struggles charges back to the end of the line, screaming like he's won while the rest of his team tries to kick his legs out from under him.

After two more rounds, it's Pen's turn. Java stands across from her.

Lucas crosses his arms, a strange smirk slowly inching into his mustache as he reads the instructions on the piece of paper. "Two-parter," he finally says. "Name every single employee at Nacho's Tacos and who slept with who."

Pen steps back, her hands on her hips as if to say *No way I'm losing this one*. I can tell Java knows it too. But then why does she look so uncomfortable?

Lucas pulls out a list, some kind of roster. "Chronological order will probably be easiest."

Pen and Java take turns ticking off names, people cheering and laughing every time they air someone's dirty laundry. Others stand off to the side, shaking their heads or blushing or trying to call them both liars.

"Java Juraeva," Pen says.

He clenches his fists on the other side of the table.

"Slept with Solana Reyes."

He throws up a hand. "That's fucking cold, Pen."

Her face is still. "Twice." She sighs. "Miguel Medrano." Her voice drops. "Slept with Mari Gomez. Last weekend."

Mari jabs a finger at Pen, already plastered. "Yeah, and what about you?" She throws her empty beer can at Lucas. "This game fucking sucks."

"It's the rules," Lucas says, facing Pen. "And she's right. You skipped yourself."

Pen glares at him. "You think I'm dumb enough to shit where I eat?"

"Fine." Java smirks. "I'm taking this thing home." He stares at Pen from across the table. "You may not be dumb enough to screw the help, but your brother sure is. I think you skipped him too. Let's see.... How about we start with the most recent? Or what about the most frequent?" He laughs to himself. "Actually, I think they're the same person."

She lunges for him and Angel holds her back, though he has the same murderous look in his eye.

Lucas's shoulders slump. "Java, why do you have to be such a dick when you drink?"

Java ignores him. "Angel Prado."

Chloe stiffens next to me.

"Slept with—"

And then Pen starts chugging. She slams the empty

bottle down and Java's team erupts in cheers. She wipes the foam from her chin as she wobbles to the back of the line. Chloe hooks her by the elbow, uneasy.

Pen just lifts a hand and mumbles something like "Don't."

My turn is an impromptu spelling bee, and I only win by default when my opponent, one of the buzz cuts (who is already so drunk he can barely stand), tries to argue that the word *propitious* starts with the letter *J*.

Even though I'm not the one who had to chug a beer, my stomach still turns when I see the next event.

Lucas sets out a pair of Hula-Hoops, two baseball bats, and a long braided rope.

"Rules!" he shouts. "Ten Hula-Hoops and ten spins around the bat before you can join your team at the tug of war. On my count..." Lucas counts down to one and then he blows a tiny whistle that makes my ears itch.

Struggles takes off running first, which is a horrible idea considering he'll have to hold the rope alone against Chelo, who is twice his size. When they both make it to the bats, they both slow down, their knees almost buckling under the nausea.

"Oh no." Chloe buries her face in Pen's back. "I can't watch this."

Both of them turn green as they scramble for the rope. I don't see who takes off next. When Chloe runs off to escape the sounds of dry heaving, Pen drags me behind a tree with low-hanging branches.

"Are we forfeiting?"

"On the contrary," she whispers conspiratorially. "We're actually winning." She parts the branches, groaning just as

Chelo pukes all over the rope. "Well, *will be* once the rest of these idiots exhaust themselves and pass out."

"Hose!" Lucas yells, Sang running over and spraying Chelo with water.

Pen lets the branches close on us again.

"So," I start, "I guess you're sort of an expert in people's dirty little secrets?"

"Only the humiliating kind." She exhales. "It was a shitty category. But with this crew, it's either bite or get bit."

After having been in their midst for a little over a week now, I say honestly, "They don't seem that dangerous."

Miguel has his forehead pressed to the bat, turning in slow circles. Sang comes up behind him and pantses him in front of everyone.

Pen snorts. "Yeah, I guess not."

"What else can you tell me about what I've gotten myself into?"

"What you've gotten yourself into"—she smiles, nostalgic—"is the most faithful and fucked-up family you will ever meet."

My chest tightens at the word. *Family.* As I look out on the Nacho's employees, laughing together, howling up at the moon like a pack of wolves...there's nothing I want more than to be a part of *this* dysfunction. A part of *something*.

Pen parts the branches again. Everyone is slipping in the mud as both teams wrestle the rope back and forth. With one more tug, Struggles's team loses their grip, flying forward.

They move on to some crude obstacle course, people hopping onto couch cushions and climbing chairs and footstools, avoiding the ground. I notice the group has thinned, everyone too sick sitting against the house, disqualified.

"You touch the grass, you take a shot," Pen says, marveling at the chaos. "Last year Lucas broke his arm trying to jump from the top of the doghouse onto a barstool." She laughs. "It's the reason he stole my trademark look. I used to tie that bright green bandana on him before every shift to keep the sweat out of his eyes."

She talks about him the same way she talks about her brother, and I wonder, "How long has Lucas worked at the restaurant?"

"Almost three years. But we've known him longer. His family used to come in at least once a week. But that was before..."

"Before his dad died?"

She nods, then stops, remembering something painful. "It was cancer. And it was...slow." She lowers her voice. "Lucas doesn't like to talk about it. But he's not the only one who's had it rough." She glances at Solana, sitting in filth, disqualified. "Solana and her mom left Guatemala when she was fifteen. En route, they were robbed. She ran but her mother was too exhausted. Who knows how long they'd gone without food or water?"

My heartbeat ticks up, remembering. "Bandits killed her mother?"

I traveled with a coyote, the fee my abuelo paid affording us the luxury of traveling by bus most of the way. But that didn't mean we were always safe.

"She made it the rest of the way alone and ended up

with her aunt, who lives just a few blocks from the restaurant." She lets out a long breath. "And then there's Mari, who takes care of her four younger siblings because her mom's diabetes has her in and out of the hospital, and Andrea, who had a baby when she was sixteen—the two of them lived in her car before moving to the shelter near the restaurant—and Java, who spent his first three years in the country living in a one-bedroom apartment with seven other refugees...."

She goes down the line, relaying every hang-up, every heartbreak any of them has ever experienced until it feels like I'm meeting them all for the first time.

"Your dad's helped a lot of people," I say.

She looks down. "I'm pretty sure it's the only reason he keeps the restaurant open."

"I'm sorry," I say, "I didn't mean to bring up—"

"It's okay." Beneath the moonlight streaming through the leaves, shadows hiding her eyes, she's much harder to read than the last time I saw her. Then she finally says, "I guess it just reminds me what I'm fighting for. Not just the restaurant. But what it means." She meets my eyes. "To all of us."

Before I can respond, Chloe finds our hiding spot, hissing between the branches. "Finish line's this way."

Back in the living room, everyone circles around the coffee table, which is covered in a towering pyramid of shot glasses, Angel pouring tequila down over the top.

"Final round," he says. "Good old-fashioned truth, dare, or drink. The last person standing wins."

Lucas motions to Java and Struggles. "Okay, you guys are up first."

They both look like shit, Java barely able to stand while Struggles's hair is plastered straight up with peanut butter from one of the obstacles from the previous event. He smells even worse, and Lucas has to hold his nose as he flips the coin, Java gagging as Struggles calls heads. It's tails, which means Java is up first.

Struggles smirks. "Okay, Java, truth or dare?"

"Dare."

"Figures. I dare you to play the rest of this game completely naked."

Java doesn't even flinch. He strips out of his clothes, everyone taking a few steps back to avoid skin-on-skin contact.

"Damn, Java." Lucas laughs. "I didn't know you were smuggling Vienna Sausages in there."

"It's the fucking alcohol," Java spits back.

"The alcohol you drank tonight or the alcohol your mom drank when she was pregnant with you?" Lucas says.

Java lunges for him, putting him in a headlock. "Need to see it up close?"

They break apart, the room erupting in laughter.

Java jams a finger in Struggles's chest. "Your turn, dick face. Truth or dare?"

"Dare."

"Okay." Java's eyes water. "I dare you to eat every drop of peanut butter on you."

There's a collective groan, Struggles staring down at the sopping mess mixed with mud and blades of grass.

"Come on, Struggles," Lucas begs, "just take the shot."

It's the easiest choice, the most obvious. But Struggles

isn't the sharpest tool in the shed, and, frankly, I've seen him eat worse out of the dish pit.

He narrows his eyes at Java. "I accept."

Another collective groan morphs into hacking and gagging as he lifts his hand and takes the first bite.

"Shit, Lucas." Angel waves a hand. "Don't make us stand here and watch this."

"Rules," Lucas says, his eyes watering too.

"We'll be here all night!" Pen yells.

But she's wrong.

Struggles opens his mouth to take another bite and then he hurls all over himself.

"What the hell?" Angel pushes him back outside, Struggles still gagging.

Lucas and Java run out after them. I hold my breath, trying to block out the sound of their retching.

Chloe wipes tears from her eyes. "Killed four birds with one stone."

Pen tries to give her a high five, but their hands fall limp.

There are only three of us left. Pen steps up to the table across from Miguel Medrano, still scorned after Pen revealed that he'd slept with Mari.

Pen wins the coin toss and gets him to admit that he was the one who clogged the employee bathroom one summer, causing the pipes to explode. Apparently, this was during one of Mr. Prado's now infamous team-building exercises, which included a taco-eating contest where Miguel found out that ghost chilies don't exactly agree with him.

"Truth or dare?" he says when it's Pen's turn.

She stares down at the shot glass in front of her. "Truth."

"Okay…" He hesitates. "The truth." He doesn't look at her as he speaks. "Where'd you really get those scars on your arms?"

Everyone who's still conscious holds their breath, and my eyes can't help but wander to her forearms. I never noticed them before, the faint white lines. They look delicate, like string, like maybe underneath those dark lips and that angry stare, that's all she's really made of.

Angel pushes the shot glass in front of his sister. "Drink, Pen."

Her fingers curl around the glass, but she doesn't pick it up.

"Fucking just drink." Angel fumes, his muscles itching to reach for Miguel and strangle him.

I wait for Pen to transform again—into the girl who was crying alone in her apartment, or into the girl who strikes fear in the heart of every Nacho's Tacos employee. I don't know who she'll choose to be in this moment, and from the way she stares straight ahead, almost numb, I'm not sure if she knows either.

But then she lets go of the glass, looking right at Miguel as she says, "I did it."

In an instant she looks like she did when I found her in her apartment. And I hate it. I hate watching Pen fill a room with her voice and her stare, bigger than anything, and then three words making her shrink. I don't want to watch her shrink.

Before I can muster up the courage to ask if she's okay,

light explodes against the back windows, glass charred black.

"What the hell?" Angel runs for the backyard. "I told you no fires in the trash cans!"

The room empties until there's no one left but a few people snoring. Pen stays put too, standing across from me, her expression stoic.

"Should we call it a tie?" I say.

She slides a shot glass over to me. "There's no such thing."

"Okay…" I reach for the coin. "Call it."

She calls heads. She wins.

I try to steady my voice. "Go easy on me."

"Truth or dare?"

"Truth." It's the only game I want to play with her.

"Okay. Where are you from?"

I sigh, relieved. "Puebla. I came here when I was nine."

"My turn," she says, not wasting any time.

"Truth or dare?" I counter.

"Truth."

I mull over the words and finally settle on, "Are you really as tough as you seem?"

She doesn't smile. "Yes. And no. Your turn."

"Truth," I say.

"Are you as cool, calm, and collected as you seem?"

I huff out a laugh. "Sometimes."

"And other times?"

The laugh slips from my lips. "I'm a fucking mess."

"My turn." I can't tell if the quick back and forth is

driven by her desire to reveal something about me or to be revealed herself. "Ask me another question."

"Why did you drink before they could say who your brother ... You know ...?"

Pen glances at the window seat where Chloe is asleep against the sill. She rolls, sensing our eyes, and Pen lures me onto the front porch. The breeze is warm, the night sky hidden behind gray clouds. I expect Pen to explain, but instead she's silent, proving once again that Chloe's secrets, unlike everyone else's, are safe with her.

Beneath the light whistle of the wind, crickets chirping, I say, "You're a good friend."

She ignores the comment, sitting on the lid of an old paint can. "It's your turn."

I sit down next to her. "I'm ready."

She narrows her eyes. "Okay, for all the marbles, this one's a two-parter. One truth and one dare. Truth," she breathes. "Do you want to kiss me?"

I don't look away. "Yes."

She doesn't look away either. "Dare." She leans in. "Do it."

My hands move first, thumbs grazing her cheeks, fingers in her hair. It's soft and she's warm and for a long time I just look at her, closing the space centimeters at a time while I take in the lashes that are stuck together by mascara, the birthmark buried under her left eyebrow, the small dimple on her chin. I stare, sorting every piece into things that feel good and things that hurt like hell, into things I never want to forget and things I'll do whatever it takes to make sure I never have to.

But before I have a chance to savor those first few breaths slipping between her lips, they're pressed against mine, falling and climbing their way back up. I taste her lipstick, her tongue, and it makes me dizzy. Her hands are on my knees, and then on my waist, on my shoulders, both of us gripping each other like we're clinging to the edge of a cliff. Afraid of falling off. Or hoping that if we do, we'll fall together.

Suddenly, Pen stops moving.

She stops breathing, my wild heartbeat the only sound.

I open my eyes and she's not staring back. She's staring at the street. At the car parked in front of Angel's house, cigarette smoke slithering out from the open window.

The engine purrs as the car pulls forward. Just in time for Angel to step outside. For J. P. to say hello to him too.

Angel pulls on Pen's arm. "Get inside. Now."

She straightens, shoulders heaving.

"Pen…"

"No." Her stare sharpens. She charges down the steps. "Stay away from us!"

Angel wrenches her back. "Are you out of your mind?"

My heart races.

"Stay away from the restaurant!" Pen shouts, trying to tear herself from Angel's grasp. "Fucking stay away!"

"The restaurant…" For the first time, J. P. smiles. He looks at Angel. "That's just what I stopped by to talk about. Your father's been a little harder to get ahold of these days, so I thought I'd try working things out with the new manager instead."

"Work what out?" Pen looks to Angel too. "What's he

talking about?" She seethes, but the faster her breaths, the more transparent she becomes. Beneath the anger, beneath the shock, her eyes glisten with fear.

"Nothing, Pen. I told you to go inside."

"Now I know where I recognize you from." This time, J. P. points a finger gun at me. "You're the kid that's always hanging around with that cop." He shifts the cigarette in his mouth. "Surprising, considering..." He ashes his cigarette onto the street. "You two must be close."

My heart is in my throat, suddenly made of thorns.

Because I was right.

He knows.

He knows.

How does he *know*?

Angel steps in front of me. "Maybe my father doesn't want to talk to you because you're a fucking asshole."

J. P. just laughs. "I see the apple doesn't fall far from the tree." Then he flicks his lit cigarette at Angel's feet. "I don't give a shit if he doesn't want to talk to me. You tell him that he doesn't have a choice." Then he lifts a hand, smile returning to his face. "I don't want to keep you from your party. Just let your father know I was looking for him. And that if I don't hear from him, maybe I'll stop by again. When it's a little less crowded." J. P. leans on the gas, letting the engine growl, and speeds off.

11

Pen

I MOVE SLOWLY, ONE limb at a time, everything stretching before I even attempt to open my eyes. I know as soon as I do I'll be spinning, and I have no idea how far I am from a bathroom.

When the world doesn't topple over, I get to my feet. I've been curled up in a sleeping bag on the floor of Angel's bedroom, Chloe next to me, one of his hoodies pulled over her head.

I tiptoe past her. A few steps into the hallway and my head is already pounding. But the alcohol-induced hangover isn't nearly as bad as the withdrawals I'm having from that kiss.

That kiss.

It was strange and scary, but also like sinking really slowly into something warm and good and safe. But I can barely concentrate on the memory of Xander's lips, the words we said. All I can think about is El Martillo. Watching us. A warning in his eyes.

The first time my father helped out a family who owed El Martillo money, J. P. just found someone else to extort. That's what he used to do. But that was before the whisper networks, the warnings to stay away from him, that he was a loan shark. A crook. But whispers were all it was. No one went to the cops. And even though people like Officer Solis want nothing more than to throw him in prison, they tread carefully too, understanding that El Martillo, like my father, is a thread woven so tightly into the fabric of our community, that one snip could unravel everything.

I find Angel in the kitchen and plop down at the table in front of him. "Since when did these games get so goddamn vicious?"

"Since everyone at work started hating each other." Angel sits down across from me. "Miguel and Sang tried to go at it the other night. I had to send Miguel home early."

"Over what?"

"Some bullshit. Apparently, preliminary prank wars took a wrong turn somewhere and Sang ended up losing an eyebrow."

I pinch the bridge of my nose, trying to halt the headache long enough to remember Sang's face. How could I have missed the fact that he was one eyebrow short last night?

"So, what did you do about it?" I ask.

Angel exhales, sits back. "Nothing yet." He fiddles with his spoon. "Every time I try to make changes or reprimand someone, it's a mess. I'm just not that guy. I'm not the disciplinarian."

"You're the guy who throws anti–Nacho's Tacos parties."

"Exactly." Angel looks away, realizing he's revealed too much.

"I haven't found anything else yet," I say, trying to coax him out of his pride. "Maybe since some time has passed..."

"No."

"No? That's it?"

He can't look at me. "It doesn't matter what you want, Pen. What matters is what Dad wants and he wants me to do it. *Me.*"

The word hits me in my gut. Because he's right. For some awful, unfair reason, our father has always wanted Angel to take over the restaurant. Even though he doesn't want it. Even though he doesn't love it like I love it. But our father knows that, and he still chose my brother over me. Maybe he always will.

Angel's voice softens. "I'm sorry, Pen."

"No, you're not."

"I am. It's messed up and I know that."

"So, do something about it." Tears prick the back of my throat. I swallow them, angry.

"Pen..." Angel starts to crack too. I'm eighteen years old and he still can't stand to see me cry. "Last night... you saw."

My knuckles blanch around the edge of my seat. "What does he want?"

"Dad won't say."

"But he wants something...."

Angel doesn't respond, and my pulse quickens.

"Angel...?"

He chucks his bowl of cereal in the sink, his back to me.

"Angel, please just tell—"

"Just stay away from the restaurant, Pen. Until this thing blows over, and then I'll talk to Dad. Like I promised. Just..." He faces me. "Trust me. Please."

"Will it...?" I still. "Blow over, I mean. Do you think—?"

He squeezes my shoulder, exhales. "It'll be fine."

Chloe stumbles into the doorway, rubbing the sleep out of her eyes. In Angel's oversize hoodie she looks like a toddler.

"Coffee," she croaks.

Angel shrugs. "Sorry, kiddo. Guess you'll have to get it on the way."

She grimaces but I can't tell if it's because Angel doesn't own a coffee maker or because he just called her *kiddo*. Probably both. Last night I drank when Java said Angel's name, even though I wasn't sure whose name he'd say next. Sometimes I'm sure Angel and Chloe have something going on behind my back, but other times he calls her kiddo and I'm sure they don't. If Java had said someone else's name from the restaurant, one of the other waitresses or maybe one of the girls behind the bar, it would have crushed Chloe just like it's crushing her now that Angel is more interested in a half-empty carton of orange juice than her.

"What time is it?" Chloe asks, redirecting his attention.

"Time for you to be serving the first plate at La Puerta Abierta."

La Puerta Abierta is the church across the street from

the restaurant where our father sends all of the restaurant's leftovers.

"Oh no. . . ." Chloe rushes to the bathroom and twists on the faucet.

"Who else did you schedule?" I ask. "They should already be setting up, right?"

Angel grips his scalp. "Oh shit. I keep forgetting to schedule someone in your place." He digs in his pocket for his cell phone. "Who got the least shit-faced last night? Do you remember?"

I shake my head. "Ninety percent of the people you'll try to call are probably passed out in their front yard right now."

"And I have to be at the restaurant in thirty minutes."

I follow him to the door, he and Chloe snatching their keys at the same time.

"I can help."

He ignores me and I try Chloe next.

"We rode together last night anyway. I can help you with the donations and then you can drop me back off at my apartment."

Angel jumps into his truck and calls to Chloe through the open window, "Do not let her inside that church," before speeding off.

I turn to her. "You know you can't serve that crowd alone."

She groans. "Fine. But only because I'm still hungover."

We reach the side door that leads into the church's dining hall, Chloe rapping on it with her foot. When it pushes open, Mrs. Rodriguez, one of the church volunteers, is already in her hairnet.

"Oh good, you're here." She holds the door open for us. "Since the restaurant was closed last night, your father already dropped off the food."

Last year when Nacho's closed because of Aarón's electrocution incident, my father and I stayed up until 2:00 AM cooking for the church so they wouldn't miss out on the donations.

I move the pots of refried beans and rice, setting them down on the burners that are already warm, and I wonder how long he stayed up last night making all this food. I wonder if he did it alone.

Mrs. Rodriguez hands me an apron. "Penelope, I thank God every day for your father's help." She lowers her voice. "Our membership has nearly doubled, the women's shelter is at capacity, and we've got three new families living in the rooms below the sanctuary."

"They're living at the church?"

"Do you remember Señor Ramos, who used to own the millinery shop? He took a loan from El Martillo. When he couldn't pay it back, ICE showed up at his house. Thank God he wasn't home. Your father brought them to the church in the middle of the night. They've been staying here ever since."

I remember the smell of El Martillo's cigarette, the gleam in his eye as sharp as the tip of a blade. I knew my father was getting in his way somehow.

"Did he bring the other families too?" I ask.

Mrs. Rodriguez nods. "The man is a saint."

The anger I've been carrying starts to dull. Jagged edges

smoothed down by sadness instead. It sits like a lump at the pit of my stomach.

The double doors leading into the dining hall finally open, and the crowd moves toward us.

One woman has a blue pin stuck to her jacket—a token of sobriety that the shelter gives out to tenants who've stuck to their ninety-day commitments. There are children with her—a boy in a shirt that's too small, and a girl who's holding one of her sandals, the clasp broken.

Chloe ties on an apron and comes to stand next to me. "Tacos set. What'd I miss?"

I nudge her in the direction of the growing line, people still pouring in from outside.

She faces away from Mrs. Rodriguez. "Do you think we have enough food?"

"We better."

Goldie is first. He's always first.

His eyes widen as the food hits his plate. "Don't be stingy, now."

"Oh, Francis, we've got to save enough for everyone," Mrs. Rodriguez teases.

He stiffens at the mention of his real name. Even though "Goldie" is just a reference to the way his gold crowns flash from his ice-cream truck when he drives down the street, he still prefers it. Chloe and I used to chase him down, his own trap music mixtape playing over the speaker instead of the normal "Do Your Ears Hang Low" or "Pop Goes the Weasel." When business was slow, my father would let him park in the Nacho's Tacos parking lot, catching people on their way in and out of the restaurant.

Mr. Martín is next. He's always next, and I assume he has some kind of deal with Goldie.

He tips his fedora at us, eyes wandering over to Mrs. Rodriguez. "Lookin' good today, Mrs. Rodriguez."

She blushes.

He's always trying to get her to go out on a date with him. She's been a widow for as long as I can remember. My mother's tried to set her up a few times, but no one's ever good enough.

"Penelope, when's your father gonna send over some more of that capirotada?" Mr. Martín lets out something between a sigh and a whistle. "Reminded me of the bread pudding my mother used to make when I was a kid."

I smile. I'd been the one to add capirotada to the menu during Lent a few years ago. I liked that it had a history, a sense of tradition you could taste. My father liked that it kept us from throwing out so many expired ingredients.

"Or better yet," Mr. Martín says, "I'll tell him myself."

I turn just as the door slams shut. My father is carrying in another box of food. He stops when he sees me, but not long enough for me to read his face. I hold my breath, waiting for him to throw me out, to fire me again in front of everyone. But he doesn't.

"Oh, thank goodness." Mrs. Rodriguez takes the food. "I was worried we were going to run out."

"And if that ever happens, you call me. No one leaves here hungry." My father pulls an envelope from his back pocket. "For the Ramos family."

She squeezes his hand before taking the money.

While I'm still holding my breath, I watch as he stops to mention something to Chloe about paychecks.

And then he leaves.

Without saying a word to me.

I stare down at the food, trying to blink away the sting. Wishing I was numb already. Smiling and making small talk as if I already am. But as soon as the crowd clears, the serving trays and utensils all packed up, I bolt for the back door.

Chloe follows me out, dropping the last of the dishes in her trunk. "What did I say before?"

"It's not going to be okay," I say. "You saw him. It's not."

This time she doesn't argue. She just wraps her arms around me.

Once we jump in her car and she starts the engine, it isn't long before I realize we're not heading in the direction of the restaurant.

"Don't we have to drop off these pots and pans?"

She stares straight ahead. "Look, I'm doing this because I'm your friend, and going to the restaurant is only going to make you upset."

I slump in my seat. "So, you're taking me home."

"So you can shower and get dressed for your interview at El Pequeño Toro."

"I don't have an interview at El Pequeño Toro."

She smiles.

12

Pen

EL PEQUEÑO TORO IS a cement block that specializes in making Mexican food miniature, and it is the final frontier in my search for employment.

The manager, Josie, leads me to a corner booth, old crumbs stuck between the seams of the plastic cushions. They're bright orange and shaped like sombreros.

"I've got to tell you, Pen, when your résumé turned up, I was surprised that you had such extensive experience in the restaurant business. Seven years, I think you said."

I nod, afraid of divulging too much about my previous place of employment and being forced to answer how exactly I got myself fired from my family's restaurant.

"So, Pen, what is it about El Pequeño Toro that inspired you to apply for a job here?"

Because once I passed the drug test, I knew I'd be a shoo-in. "Well..." I clear my throat, painting the smile on thick.

"I have a lot of experience cooking Mexican food, and it's something I really enjoy."

"And what would you say are some important leadership qualities you possess?"

"I managed the restaurant where I used to work. Well, unofficially." Josie's eyebrows quirk up. "I mean, it was more like they were grooming me for the position. I had a lot of responsibilities taking care of schedules and payroll, and managing the kitchen."

"Interesting. And where did you say you were previously employed?" She flips through my résumé again. "Oh, yes, Nacho's Tacos." She looks to me for confirmation and I nod again.

I wait for her to make the connection between the Ignacio Prado who owns Nacho's Tacos and the Penelope Prado whose résumé she is currently salivating over. But then she flips to my availability, jotting notes as she asks whether I'm free to work nights and weekends. I tell her I am, and suddenly she's grinning from ear to ear.

"Listen, Pen, I'm not supposed to say this until we've had HR run your background check, but..." She lowers her voice, eyes twinkling. "After the bad luck we've had recently with new hires turning out to be...unreliable, I don't think we can pass up an opportunity like this. You seem like a very responsible young woman, and I think it's safe to say we'd love to welcome you to the team."

She reaches her hand out, waiting for me to take it.

"Oh..." My stomach drops. "Thank you."

I shake her hand, trying to dredge up the relief I should be feeling instead. But there is none. Her hand in mine, it feels like I'm about to step foot into my worst nightmare, which it turns out is not being broke or homeless, but serving previously frozen, production line–quality Mexican food to people who wouldn't know real Latin cuisine if I stuffed it down their throats.

I feel like an imposter. But what's even more terrifying is the fact that Josie doesn't see me as one. She's looking at me as though I belong, as though I'm actually excited about this new opportunity. What was the word she used to ask why I applied for the job? Oh right—*inspired*. What *inspired* me to apply for the job?

What *inspired* me was self-preservation, but as I watch the other employees going through the motions, everyone with the same numb expression on their faces, I'm worried that whatever parts of me are worth preserving won't be strong enough to survive this place.

When I get back to my apartment I throw myself on the bed, which hasn't been made since I moved in. Music's been blaring all day—EDM this morning when Chloe dropped me off, and now a steady stream of heavy metal. I can't tell if two adjacent apartments are competing for Biggest Dick of the Year or if one of my new neighbors just has really eclectic taste...and also possibly a hearing problem.

Underneath the noise, I hear a faint knock. I expect it to be followed by the laughter of those smart-ass kids. But there's nothing. I creep to the door, peer out the peephole, and see the smiling face of an old woman.

I ease the door open. "I'm sorry. I thought you were these kids who keep coming by and knocking on the door."

"And I usually pride myself on being the first to greet the new tenants. I'm Mrs. Damas." She points across the hall. "That's me in 613."

I reach out a hand. "I'm Penelope Prado. It's nice to meet you."

"Here." I didn't even notice the large basket of baked goods she's holding. "Just to say welcome."

"Oh...thank you."

"Still settling in?" she asks.

"Trying to." I wedge myself in the gap between the door and the frame in an effort to hide the mess behind me.

"I thought I smelled something divine coming from your apartment a few nights ago. Were you baking?"

"It was a raspberry cake."

It strikes me how many days have passed since I baked something. Not just because of the time I lost, but because without Hugo and Lola and Mrs. Nguyen, there hasn't been anyone to share my food with. I guess I hadn't realized before how important that part is to me.

"It smelled delicious." She pulls a piece of paper from her pocket and slips on her reading glasses to examine it. "Actually, I was just in the middle of baking, and it seems I've run out of a few things." Her eyes crinkle as she hands me the list. "Would you happen to have any of these on hand?"

I scan the ingredients, glad that I recently *borrowed* a few things from the restaurant. "Let me take a look."

Before I can stop her, Mrs. Damas follows me inside. She doesn't mention the mess and neither do I. Instead, I search the pantry, lining up the ingredients on the kitchen counter for her to examine. She picks up a glass bottle of rosewater, then a bag of coconut palm sugar.

"You're an experienced baker."

I shrug. "I just like to experiment."

She picks up another bottle. "Dandelions. What do you use them for?"

"Sometimes I like to mix them into an oatmeal cookie batter. They're also great in sorbet." I go back to the pantry, shoving aside bags of flour and sugar before pulling out a bottle of lavender extract.

"Penelope..." Her eyes flash to mine. "Would you be willing to give me a hand? If you're not busy. I would love the help."

I'd planned to spend the day moping, but as soon as Mrs. Damas asks the question, I'm reminded that I have a choice. That even without my family, without money, without knowing what's coming next, maybe I can still be in control of something. I can still be myself.

"I'd like that."

I follow Mrs. Damas back to her apartment, the heat drawing me to the kitchen. There's a painting on every inch of wall space—landscapes mostly, except for the lone portrait of a man, brow covered by the same hat that sits atop her bookshelf.

Mrs. Damas pats my shoulder. "Here, tie this on."

I slip on a bright yellow apron while Mrs. Damas shuffles around, opening drawers and cabinets and handing me utensils and bottles of different ingredients. The kitchen table is covered in empty plastic containers lined with foil. It looks like Mrs. Damas is getting ready to feed an army.

"Planning a party?" I ask.

Mrs. Damas takes some of the ingredients from me and adds them to whatever she's mixing. "I spend every Sunday baking for the women at Casa Marianella."

Mrs. Rodriguez had said the shelter was at capacity. No wonder Mrs. Damas is making so much food.

Her fingers brush her lips, measuring the batter. "After my husband passed away, I didn't have anyone to bake for anymore." She pours the batter into two separate pans, and I help her load them into the oven.

"My father owns a restaurant, and we always take food to La Puerta Abierta. A lot of women from the shelter eat there during the week. I was actually just there this morning."

She pulls a bowl of dough from the fridge, peeling back the Saran Wrap. "Then you know how it feels." She motions with the rolling pin before handing it to me. "To feed someone who's hungry...it's a gift." She hands me a heart-shaped cookie cutter. "And to be able to help others the way I was once helped is a wonderful thing too."

"Did you stay at the shelter?" It's a personal question, one I have no right to ask, but I'm curious to know how she made it out.

"No."

The timer above the stove goes off. She pulls two pans from the fridge—a raspberry custard kuchen and a simple chocolate cake. She takes the cookies from me and loads them onto the last empty rack in the oven.

I'm afraid I may have overstepped my bounds when she finally says, "I came to this country when I was very young, just before the war reached France. Neighbors invited me to attend the local church, and it was the nuns who taught me English."

She places a cookbook on the counter, finger marking a page for the chocolate cake's caramel icing. She shows me the recipe and I start mixing, quiet as she continues.

"I was lucky. I had my family, friends, a community that we embraced and that embraced us back." She dries her hands on a towel before slapping a piece of dough against the countertop. "But things are different now. People have forgotten too much."

"The number of people the church serves has doubled." I pour the icing onto the cake. "A lot of people are really struggling."

Mrs. Damas nods, splitting the dough before winding it into a long braid. She tucks it into a bread pan and then into the fridge for proofing. "I wouldn't be able to sleep at night if I did nothing. As long as I can, I will."

It sounds like something my father would say, and just like this morning, I think of him without feeling angry.

For the next several hours, Mrs. Damas and I work in tandem—measuring, mixing, tasting, pounding, cutting. The warmth from the oven spreads until the numbness that followed me home from El Pequeño Toro disappears.

My hands are covered in batter when I finally register the buzz of my cell phone in my back pocket. I scrape off the raisins and dandelions (Mrs. Damas insisted that I make her my aforementioned dandelion oatmeal cookies). I catch it just before it goes to voice mail.

"Hello?"

"Pen?"

I freeze.

"Pen? It's Xander."

I ease out into the privacy of the hallway, fiddling with the doorknob, the strings of my apron, my body needing some kind of distraction from the things that are happening inside of it.

"Are you busy?" His voice is more hesitant after the long silence.

I clear my throat. "Actually, I'm helping a neighbor."

"Oh…"

I backtrack, attempting to be less blasé. "She's baking some things to take to the women's shelter by the restaurant. But I think we're almost done. Why? What are you doing?" *Stop talking now, Pen.*

"Well, I…just wanted to make sure you were okay."

I lean against the door, remembering Xander's face as El Martillo drove away. A new pang rises up in my chest as I realize the look I saw wasn't anger but fear.

"I'm fine," I say. "Really. What about you?"

"Well, that's the last time I'll ever go to one of Angel's parties." He lets out a nervous laugh, dodging the question.

I let him, laughing too. "Maybe it wasn't all bad before…"

He's so quiet on the other end of the line I think it's gone dead.

Then he says, "Actually, it was pretty great."

I smile, glad that he can't see it. "By the way, how exactly did you get my phone number?"

His smile is less invisible, a breathy laugh coming through. "Chloe… She slipped it to me before I left."

"Did you ask for it?"

He hesitates. "Not exactly. But I guess she wasn't really sleeping against the window. She saw the whole thing."

"Oh."

"Yeah."

"Xander?" A question forms on my tongue, my hand sweating against the phone.

"Yeah?"

Doing the scary thing right now feels a lot riskier than accepting the job at El Pequeño Toro. Which is exactly why I have to do it.

"Hello?"

"I'm here. Sorry…" *Stop being such a loser.* "Xander… are you… hungry?"

"Yes."

My cheeks flush and I feel like an idiot. "Do you want to maybe grab some food?"

"Tonight?"

"Pick me up around eight?"

"Eight. Okay, I can do that."

"Okay, eight."

"Okay… I'll see you then," he says.

"Yeah, see ya."

When I finally hear the line go dead, I slump down onto the floor, wishing I could sink straight into it. I fall back, the door yanked open behind me.

"It's true what they say, you know." Mrs. Damas hands me a small, foil-covered package, random bite-size pieces still warm. "The way to a man's heart is through his stomach."

13

Xander

WHEN I FINALLY DRAG myself out of bed, the alcohol having offered a brief respite from my normal nightmares, I find my abuelo and Mr. Daly on the front porch. Mr. Daly's showing off a beat-up mountain bike that he probably picked up at some estate sale this morning, and there are bags of takeout from the seafood place near the highway strewn across the card table in front of them.

Mr. Daly shoves a receipt in my hand. "Here, this is for keeping the old man from starving."

Abuelo kicks at his chair. "Who you calling an old man? You're the old man."

They're both in their late seventies.

"At least I can still drive," Mr. Daly says. "Look at that parking job." The car is halfway on the grass.

Abuelo waves a hand. "I didn't do that. The boy had it last night for work."

Mr. Daly examines me. "Work, huh?" Then he sniffs. "Doesn't smell like he's been working. Smells like he's been up to no good." He raises an eyebrow. "With a girl."

I take a step back. "You can tell all that just from the way I smell?"

"Did you have a date last night?" Abuelo asks.

"No. I told you, I was working."

He tosses his napkin. "I wasn't born yesterday. What's her name?"

I groan, feeling sixteen again. "I didn't have a date."

Mr. Daly leans forward. "Did you pick up a prostitute?"

"What?" I shake my head, hard. "No."

Mr. Daly turns to Abuelo. "You better clean that car out with some hydrogen peroxide and gasoline. The hookers around here ain't no good. And you." He faces me again. "You better have your member checked before he loses an eye."

"I didn't sleep with a prostitute!"

"And that's exactly what you tell the doctor."

My cell phone rings, saving me. I assume it's the restaurant, but I don't recognize the number.

"Hello?"

"Hello, this is Detective Lyle Freeman. I received a voice mail from someone named Xander Amaro, wanting to set up an appointment."

I head back inside, shielding the mouthpiece. "A voice mail?"

"Time stamp says 3:07 AM."

My face flushes, remembering. The phone in one hand, the business card the lawyer gave me in the other, dialing

Detective Freeman's number and stuttering through the details of my father's disappearance. It was the most I'd talked about my father in years, and to a complete stranger while I was just inebriated enough not to remember the next morning.

Detective Freeman clears his throat. "Look, kid, if you're serious about finding your dad, I can meet you Wednesday around four o'clock. There's a diner on the corner of Hill and Quaker. You know it?"

"Yes." I swallow, sweating.

It's just a voice on the other end of the phone, not even my father's voice, but it feels like he's listening. Like he's almost close enough to touch. There's a fire in my belly, but I can't tell what's fueling it—relief, fear, shame? I don't want to get my hopes up. I don't want to get hurt.

Detective Freeman clears his throat. "Hello?"

But I also don't want to give up. "I'll be there," I say.

He hangs up first, robbing me of the chance to change my mind. I don't know if I'm doing the right thing or if it's time for me to forget about the search. About my father.

The fire in my belly returns.

Do not give up.

You can't *give up.*

The restaurant parking lot is empty. I check the employee entrance, a single car parked next to the dumpster. I yank open the door to the kitchen, startled by the sound of my own footsteps. At this point in the afternoon, there should be music blasting from the dining room, Angel beating his tongs against the grill, plates sliding, a few breaking. But there's nothing.

I make my way across the kitchen, noticing through the pickup window that the dining room is empty too, chairs still stacked on tables.

Mr. Prado's muffled voice sounds behind his office door. He's alone, arguing with someone over the phone.

"I'm not opening those doors. I don't care how it looks. I'm not putting those kids in danger...." His voice sharpens. "You think I don't know that? I'm the one who hired them. I know how much they need the work." He exhales. "Look, I'll figure something out. Everyone will be taken care of. But I'm not using them as bait, and if you so much as suggest it again I'll..." He slams a hand against the wall. "It *is* a threat. I don't care if you're a cop. We're not goddamn pawns in J. P.'s game."

The door flies open, Mr. Prado towering over me before I can run or hide or wipe the stunned expression off my face and replace it with something that says *I heard absolutely nothing.*

He grips the phone. "I'm sorry, Xander. I forgot to call to tell you your shift was canceled."

"Oh." I take a step back. "That's okay."

"Seems we had a few more pests than we thought." He heads to the kitchen, nonchalant. "We gotta close up shop for another twenty-four hours."

"I'm scheduled to come in at one tomorrow. Should I—?"

"I'll call you." He disappears into the storage room.

I wonder if the other employees were relieved when Mr. Prado canceled their shifts today, too hungover to suspect anything was wrong. I wonder if Angel knows; if it has anything to do with El Martillo's surprise visit last night. But what could be so bad that Mr. Prado would have to close the restaurant?

My stomach drops.

What the hell is El Martillo planning?

The phone was to my ear before I realized who I'd dialed on the other end. In the ten seconds before she answered, I thought about hanging up at least a dozen times. I thought about telling her that the restaurant was closed again, about what I'd overheard her father saying on the phone. But the moment she answered, I could barely force out my own name. And then she asked me on a date. Pen Prado asked *me* on a date....

When I reach her apartment door, I stop, raking my sleeve across my brow. Music is blasting behind a door down the hall, the sound mimicking the panic inside me. I don't usually get nervous. Not when I was interviewing for the job at Nacho's, and not even when I was sitting in the lawyer's office, waiting for more bad news. That's all I've found over the past decade, so that's all I've ever expected, and it's those low expectations that let me function in a world full of land mines.

But Pen isn't a land mine. She's an atomic bomb, and even though she already kissed me, even though she's the one who asked me on this date, I still feel like every positive possibility that exists within this moment on the other side of her apartment door could self-destruct at any second.

I take a deep breath and knock, trying to listen for footsteps on the other side, as if anticipating the exact moment she opens it will somehow make seeing her less terrifying. I think I hear the clink of the chain falling free, a lock tumbling.

While I'm wiping the sweat from my forehead again, the door pulls open and Pen steps out of her apartment. She's wearing jeans this time, black ones with these shiny metal zippers on the pockets that jingle against her hips, and a bright red tank top that matches her lips.

"You look great," I say.

"Thanks." She smiles. "So do you." She looks down the hall, her eyes rolling as someone cranks the music to full blast. "All day," she growls.

I laugh but she doesn't, and suddenly I'm chasing after her.

She bangs her fists on the door. "Open up!"

A large man towers over us. I expect her to backpedal, but she holds her ground.

"I'm Pen." She sticks out her hand, formal, and for half a second, the guy actually looks intimidated. "I live down the hall," she says once he's firmly in her grip, "and I wasn't sure if you knew that I can hear every word to every song you've been playing for the past five hours."

His face doesn't change, and I can't tell if he's just stoned or if he genuinely doesn't give a shit. Probably both.

"I would appreciate it if you'd turn it down."

He tries to wrestle out of Pen's grasp. "It's a free country."

"I'm actually aware of that," Pen says. "Which means you are free to choose self-preservation and turn down your god-awful music. As long as one of you idiots can manage to find the volume knob. It's the little round thing about the size of your brain."

The big guy finally wrenches himself from Pen's hold, waving a hand at someone I can't see. The music shuts off and then the door slams in our faces.

I don't know whether I'm turned on or terrified. Maybe a little bit of both.

It isn't until I'm back down in the car that I realize the package of peanut butter cups Chloe instructed me to buy is still in my pocket. I pull it out slow before handing the squished package to Pen.

"I..." I grimace. "They melted."

She tears open the package, the smell of peanut butter filling the car. "Oh..." Then she laughs. "How did you know that my favorite thing in the world is eating melted peanut butter cups?"

I smile, relieved. "Lucky guess. Or...Chloe may have mentioned it."

"She likes playing matchmaker," Pen says.

I clear my throat. "Does she set you up a lot?"

"No," Pen huffs. "She tries, but the girl's got the worst taste in men. Hence her being in love with my brother."

"Oh..." I tap my fingers against the steering wheel. "So...you're not dating anyone?"

She dips her finger into the melted peanut butter. "Well, right now I'm going on a date with you." She licks the chocolate off, smiles. "By the way, would you like to know where we're going or would you rather it be a surprise?"

"I like surprises. Well, good ones."

I'm not used to seeing this playful side of Pen, and there's something fragile about it. Too fragile for me to bring up her father and the restaurant. But I can't stop thinking about the anger in his voice, and the fact that the employees might be in danger....

"Take a right on Carter Street and then a left at the second stoplight."

I put the car in drive, following her directions as clouds begin to cluster overhead. Windows cracked, it smells like rain.

"Now take another left up here. Pull into the parking lot in the back. I'm taking you through the secret entrance."

I put the car in park, the smell of rain swallowed by garlic and chili peppers and green onions. Pen leads me through the back entrance just as it starts to sprinkle, steam from the kitchen ushering us inside. Out of the fog, a girl with gold clips in her hair gives Pen a hug.

"Manee, this is Xander. Xander, Manee."

"Wait a second." Manee raises an eyebrow. "Is this a *date*?" She grabs a pair of menus. "You know what that means, Pen." She leads us away from the dining room and through a beaded archway.

"Oh, Manee, this really isn't necessary—" Pen drags her feet.

"Nuh-huh, you two get the sweetheart table."

She leads us to the most romantic corner of the restaurant and seats us in the embrace of an oversize seashell.

"So, the usual, Pen?" Manee bites the cap off her pen and starts scribbling.

"Actually, it's a special occasion," Pen says. "So I think

we'll start with some moo ping and shrimp dumplings. Then I'll take my usual, and..." She eyes me, lighthearted again. "How hot do you like it?"

I clear my throat. "You know me."

"He'll take the drunken noodles with chicken, and the jungle curry. Ped bab cone Thai ka."

Manee smirks.

Pen continues, "Then we'll finish with some chocolate roti and coconut ice cream."

"And some waters?" Manee suggests, pointing to me with her pen. "Looks like this one's already broken a sweat."

I wipe myself with a napkin. "It's just a little warm in here."

"And it's about to get a lot warmer. Ped bab cone Thai ka," Manee mumbles, laughing to herself as she saunters back through the beaded archway. "Yeah, right."

"What did that mean?" I ask Pen.

"It means we want everything to be *authentically spicy.* None of that Americanized bullshit."

"Oh..."

"Yeah..."

Pen taps her foot underneath the table. I scrape my hands on my jeans, waiting for the ease of the other night.

"So, uh..."

"Here you go, guys." Manee comes back with our drinks. "And your first round of food should be out in a few minutes."

"Thanks." I reach for my glass and almost knock it over.

"Are you feeling okay?" Pen asks after Manee's disappeared back through the wall of beads.

"Great," I say, praying that she can't see where the sweat is collecting just at the edge of my hairline.

I don't know why I'm so nervous. Actually, I do. It's because the last date I went on was sophomore year, and the last time I liked a girl this much was...never.

I take a big gulp of water, some spilling on my shirt. "Is there a bathroom around here?"

Pen points back through the main dining room. "That way."

I slip through the beaded archway, almost getting tangled in them, and spot the bathroom next to the kitchen. I jiggle the knob but it's occupied, so I give myself a pep talk in the hallway instead.

Stop acting like a fucking idiot.

Just be cool. Be cool.

I shake out my shirt, trying to get some cold air against my skin.

"I gave you a good deal, and look at all you've been able to build with it."

My spine snaps to attention. I know that voice.

I creep to the kitchen door, and through the steam, I see him. El Martillo. He stands over a man in a chef's coat, the man's fists clenched at his sides.

Just behind him is Manee. Her bright smile gone. But there's a resemblance between her and the chef. Same birthmark on their left cheek, same forehead lines. I spot the name embroidered on his chef's coat. Wattana. The same name on the menus Manee gave us.

"I'm sorry, Mr. Wattana, but the terms were clear. You fall behind on payments and I start taking this place apart, piece by piece." El Martillo's eyes flick to Manee, and my stomach clenches.

"I'm not giving you another cent." Manee's father stands his ground. "I don't care what the contract says. I owe you nothing, and if you don't leave right this second, I'm calling the—"

El Martillo grins. "Mr. Wattana, you have been here too long." He takes a few slow steps closer to Manee's father. "You think you've put down roots." He motions around the kitchen. "But these are weeds. And either I can dig them up, or you can keep paying for your plot whether the paperwork says to or not."

Then he glances over Mr. Wattana's shoulder, right at the kitchen door window. Right at me.

I duck, a door wrenched open behind me. An older man exits the bathroom and I throw myself inside, sweaty hands fumbling for my cell phone. I find Officer Solis's phone number.

The door pushes open again, but I can't make myself turn and look.

"Has Mr. Prado been teaching you how to be a hero?"

I freeze, the sweat on my brow turned cold.

El Martillo takes the phone out of my hand, darkens the screen. "You haven't been working for Nacho very long, so I'll give you the benefit of the doubt." He pulls a cigarette from his pocket and lights it. "That man is not invincible, and neither are you." He ashes his cigarette on my shoes. "And you can either trust me on that and keep your mouth shut. Or I can show you exactly what I mean."

I wish I was as brave as Pen. I wish that I could force

words to my lips, that I could scream. That I could hurt him.

But he's right.

I'm not invincible.

Not in this country. In this body. In this brown skin.

I'm afraid.

"I think we have an understanding." He grips my shoulder. "Now, go enjoy the rest of your date." He winks. "As they say, first impressions are everything."

My cell phone lands at my feet, the screen cracked. For a long time, I just stare at it like it's something dead.

"Xander?" There's a light knock and I tense. "Are you still in there?"

I ease the door open, but I can't meet Pen's eyes.

"Oh no, you don't look so good." She presses the back of her hand to my cheek. "You feel warm."

I can't speak. I can't move.

"Let's take a rain check, huh?" She plucks the car keys from my pocket. "I'll drive."

It's raining when we leave the restaurant, five to-go cartons balanced on my lap as Pen backs out of the parking lot. On the way to her apartment, we drive in silence, Pen probably attributing mine to the volcano inside me about to erupt. Instead, there's something else coming to the surface.

"Pen?"

This is our first date, and all that keeps racing through my mind is that I can't lie to Pen on our *first* date. I don't know how she'll feel about me being undocumented, if it'll make her wary, if it'll make her want to run. What if she thinks there's no future with me, no reason to even finish this date, let alone go on a second one?

But if El Martillo knows, he can't be the only one. I don't want Pen to find out from someone else and think I was lying to her all this time.

She glances over at me. "Yeah?"

I try to figure out how to bring it up without ruining the last few days and all the ones we haven't spent together yet. I just want that part—the *yet*—to still be intact after I've told her everything.

I let out a deep breath. "I have to..."

"Oh no." She swerves onto a side street, water splashing the windows.

"No, Pen, I don't—"

We skirt to a stop, my hands barely catching hold of the food before it goes flying.

I brace myself for another jolt before moving slowly to look at Pen. "I don't have to puke."

She puts the car in park, lets go of the wheel. "I'm so sorry. I thought you were feeling sick."

"No, I'm...I'm not sick."

She stiffens, searching my face. "Then what's wrong?"

"I..." *Just do it.* "I have to tell you something."

She sinks in her seat. "What is it?"

"Do you remember the other night when El Martillo showed up at your brother's party?"

She nods, quiet.

"Well, I think...somehow..." I want to stare at the rain, at the floorboard, anything but her face. "He knows that I'm undocumented."

Her hand is on mine, her touch even more terrifying. Because I don't know what's behind it—understanding or goodbye.

After a long silence, her grip on me tightens. "Nothing's going to happen to you." She looks up, waiting for me to look back. "My father won't let it."

It takes everything in me not to fold, melting right there in her lap. I swallow the tears instead, focusing on her touch, on the way she's closed the distance between us.

"I'm sorry I didn't tell you sooner."

She shakes her head. "It wouldn't have mattered. It *doesn't* matter."

"I don't want to be a liability at the restaurant. I don't want El Martillo to use me to—"

"Hey." She moves closer. "You're not the first undocumented person my father has hired, and you won't be the last. He'll protect you. I promise."

I exhale. "I'm sorry I ruined our date."

"What do you mean? This date's not over yet." She's smiling, the sight almost cracking me in two. "Open up those to-go bags."

I do as I'm told, Pen directing me on what to taste and when. She wasn't kidding about the heat. A few bites in and the skin under my eyes is already sweating.

I mull over what I want to say next, hoping that she doesn't feel like my status is something we have to awkwardly avoid. It's hard to talk about, but I'm so sick of secrets.

Sometimes it feels like my entire life is one big secret. I've always been hiding from someone—the federales and thieves who targeted me and other migrants heading for the border, ICE agents once I'd made it to the United States, then neighbors and teachers and police officers, pretty much anyone who I thought might have the power to report me as being undocumented. And now El Martillo.

I don't want to have to hide from Pen too.

"You know you can ask me anything," I say. "I'll tell you the truth. I promise."

She mulls over the words even longer than I did. "Can I ask you...Why do you go by Xander? It's just really... American."

"And I'm not?" I smile, trying to ease the tension. I'm relieved her first question is an easy one. "Officer Solis started calling me that. I used to hate it, but one year on the first day of school, I decided to try it out. Then I started to see how much more comfortable people were saying it, how much more comfortable they were around me."

"But do you feel like it's...you? Or do you feel like it's who others want you to be?"

This question's harder to answer. "I don't know. Sometimes it feels like a choice, and sometimes it doesn't. Sometimes it feels like the only weapon I have against being an outsider...and sometimes it feels like a weapon other people use against me."

"Alejandro." Pen tries out my given name.

"Hearing you say it reminds me of my mother." I grow quiet.

Pen reaches for me again. "Xander..."

"That's me," I say, "for now."

"I like it."

We finish the rest of our dinner, empty cartons lining the back seat. All of a sudden it feels like every physical sensation is magnified by a million. My stomach gurgles; Pen's puffed out like a balloon. I can't imagine moving, but the longer I sit still, the hotter it gets.

Pen looks over. "You're dripping."

"I think I'm going to explode."

Her lips scream red. "For real this time?"

"Oh God, it's so hot. Do we have any water?"

Pen searches the bags from the restaurant. "Shit."

I close my eyes, teeth gritted. "Oh God."

"You said that already."

Beneath our panting, mouths desperately trying to suck in air, rain still pounds against the hood of the car. I look from the window to Pen. Then we both reach for the doors, falling out into the downpour. We look straight up, mouths open as we try to find some relief.

Pen laughs, choking.

I hold out my hands, trying to funnel the drops into my mouth. "It's not working!"

Pen flings her arms around me. "Here, try this."

My lips throb as she crashes into them, and it's the opposite of relief. It's agony. But I can't let go. Even though it hurts. Even though it scares me. I don't let go. I won't.

14

Pen

MY FINGERTIPS SKIM THE door handle of El Pequeño Toro, and then I stop. I count the fear in needle pricks, every moment of discomfort that's led up to this one—putting on my uniform, catching my reflection in the bathroom mirror, pulling into the parking lot. This morning has already been full of impossible tests, but I'm here and I can't turn back.

The door pushes open, knocking into me. I shake the surprise from my face just in time, one of my new coworkers looking down at me with an amused smirk.

"You all right there?" he asks.

"Oh, I…" I straighten. "I'm great."

He lifts an eyebrow. "Look, Josie's not here yet, so if you need to go to the bathroom to cry or something, go right ahead."

"I don't cry," I snap, a little shocked at how big of an asshole this guy is.

"Right, just wait till your first shift's over." He clips on his name tag: DAVID.

Needle prick number four—David's assumption that I am weak and can be easily reduced to a soggy puddle of shame.

I step to him. "Is that some kind of threat?"

He winks, amused again. "Only if you want it to be." He crosses his arms. "Making little girls cry... it's sort of a specialty of mine. There's an art to it, really."

He's more pathetic than sinister, but it still ignites a pang at the pit of my stomach. Because I know that for the next several hours, the next days, weeks, David will be watching me. And I have to decide in this moment who I want him to see.

I cross my arms in response, feigning the same wicked amusement. "And my specialty's making little boys piss themselves, so I suggest that if you don't want to be the one in tears, you'll stay the hell out of my way."

He hangs his head back, laughing. Then, without warning, he grips both of my shoulders, grinning even wider. Before I can shove him away, he says, "I think I'm going to like you." Then he disappears to the back of the kitchen.

For a minute I just stand there, trying to calculate where I went wrong. I can still feel his grubby hands on my skin, his enthusiasm—or maybe it was admiration—making the hairs on my arms stand on end. It definitely wasn't terror. Why the hell wasn't he terrified? Why the hell did threatening him compel him to put his hands on me? Why the hell didn't I punch him in the fucking nose?

Because you're weak.

The voice passes through me like a chill and I try to shake it off.

As I come around the corner, I spot the shift manager, Claudia, in the back of the kitchen, freezer door propped open against her back as she lugs out boxes of food. David walks right past her, fingers racing across his cell phone. He hops up onto the counter next to me, legs swinging as he laughs at something on the screen.

I look from David to Claudia. "You're not gonna help her with that?"

He barely glances up. "Claudia doesn't like when people try to help her."

"So what does everyone else do? Just stand around until we open?"

He chews the dead skin from his thumbnail, spits it out. "Pretty much."

Regardless of whether or not Claudia might bite my head off for offering to help, I can't stand to share any more breathing space with David.

When I come up behind her, she stiffens.

"Do you want me to get some of these boxes?" I ask.

Without a word, she heaves one into my arms and I fall against the wall. She rolls her eyes before nodding to the empty counter where she wants me to drop it. I suck in a deep breath, but the weight shifts, almost toppling me over. I drop the box down on my fingers, trying to wince as quietly as possible as I pull them free.

Claudia glares. "I told Josie I didn't need another lightweight."

"Trust me," I shoot back, taking offense, "I'm no lightweight."

She rests her hands on her hips. "You used to work at another restaurant?"

I nod.

"Well, forget everything you learned there. You're in the bowels of the culinary world now, and whatever fancy shit you know, you won't be needing it here." She motions for me to come closer. "I'm only going to show you this once, so pay attention."

Claudia turns on the fryers as the grill sizzles on her right. She shows me the prepackaged foods, explaining how to read the labels before pulling the first batch of menu items to drop into the fryer.

"Only six in each basket or else they'll be cold in the center."

Because they're frozen, I remember, shuddering. There are a few foods that are better the next day, but Mexican isn't one of them. Especially if you're making dough or any kind of masa. I prod at one of the ice-cold empanadas and it feels like something dead. I imagine eating it probably feels the same.

Claudia leads me to a stack of cardboard cutouts, slaps one on the counter, and begins to fold.

"Ten per minute. Three empanadas in each box."

And here are their coffins. I wonder if they have one big enough for me. *Here lies Penelope Prado. Aspiring chef turned premade Hot Pocket peddler.*

Something dings. Claudia unloads the fried empanadas onto a metal tray and places them in a tall warming drawer.

She drops the next batch in the fryer. There's another ding. Fried burritos are done. They go in the warming drawer too.

Twelve dings later and we get our first drive-through customer. Claudia yanks a headset down over my ears, motioning for me to watch the screen above the cash register as she enters the order. Two breakfast empanadas, two fried burritos, four churros, two Diet Cokes—one with no ice—and three packets of hot sauce. The food is illustrated on the touch screen for easy navigation, but Claudia doesn't even look. She's got one hand reaching to fill the first drink when they ask her to add an extra burrito to their order.

She barely looks them in the eye, each transaction lasting just a few seconds. Not long enough to notice what they're wearing or whether they're in a good mood. Not long enough to see them leave satisfied, to find out what they hungered for in the first place. It's not like Nacho's, where we were people's priests and therapists and surrogate grandchildren. Neighbors. *Family.*

You don't have a family.

The voice is poison, coating the back of my throat until it's on fire. But I don't cry. Not here.

Three customers come and go, and then Claudia says, "Okay, let's see what you've got."

As if the universe is equally as amused by my misfortune as David, the next person who pulls up to the order speaker is about a hundred years old and under the impression that she's at a 1950s burger joint.

Claudia nudges me.

"Uh, hola, welcome to El Pequeño Toro, can I take your order?"

"Hello?" The speaker crackles. "Well, I'm not sure if this thing is working, but I need two cheeseburgers, no onion, add mayonnaise, two orders of fries, two chocolate shakes, one with whipped cream and one without—"

"Ma'am?"

She still can't hear me. I slide open the drive-through window and peer out. The old lady has the driver's side door open, half her body hanging out of the car. The person behind her honks; four others idle in line.

Claudia glances at the clock above the cash register. We only have eighty seconds between taking someone's order and then their money. I have thirty seconds to finish this one and get the old lady out of the way.

I lean out the window and wave, trying to usher her forward. She's still shouting into the speaker box, totally oblivious.

I can tell Claudia's waiting for me to ask her what I should do, or maybe to take over herself. I won't give her the satisfaction.

"I'll be right back," I say before marching out the side door.

I'm a few inches from the old lady before she finally notices.

She waves a hand at the speaker. "I think it's broken."

"I'm sorry about that, ma'am."

She looks up at me, shielding her eyes from the sun. "What was that?"

I lean closer, voice raised. "I said I'm sorry about that. If you'll just pull up to the window I can take your order there."

She blinks.

"Screw this." I walk in front of the car, motioning with my hands for her to roll forward.

She does, one inch at a time. Suddenly, the car jerks, her foot too heavy on the gas. I stumble back, the front of the car almost catching my leg as I jump onto the curb. I land on the concrete, ankle throbbing.

David's leaning out of the order window. "Hey, look at the vieja whisperer."

I push myself onto my feet before hobbling to the door. The instant I reenter the kitchen, I smell something burning.

Both fryers are dinging, the batch of empanadas and burritos dark and crumbling.

"You couldn't keep an eye on these?" I yell.

David ignores me, greeting the old woman and entertaining himself by calling her crude names that she cannot hear and therefore cannot be offended by. She just smiles.

I dump out the burnt food, drop some from the warming drawer into a sack—without bothering to wrap them—and practically toss them into the old woman's lap. David's already got her credit card.

The next customer shouts in my ear. The fryers ding. I search for Claudia and find her cleaning up a hot sauce disaster in the dining room while David just stands there, doing nothing.

"Tell me, are you completely useless?"

He leers. "It's called nepotism. Josie's my aunt and I'm her *favorite* nephew. Speaking of Josie, here she is now."

The bell above the door sounds, Josie stepping inside.

I expect another warm greeting, but instead she's fuming. "There's a line all the way to the turn-in. What's going on back here?"

I want to point a finger at David, but he's already pointing one at me. "Pen's first day." He lays on the charm. "Give her a break, Aunt Josie. I'll take care of this rush." He snatches the headphones off my head, snagging them on my ponytail.

"What's that smell?" Josie sniffs, smoke billowing up from the fryers. "Christ!" She waves a hand, trying to get Claudia's attention. "I need you on this."

Claudia rushes over, her pants covered in hot sauce. "I thought Pen was on the fryers."

"Actually, I was on the drive-through—"

She glares at me as she brushes past.

"Uh, excuse me. Could we get some service over here?" A family of four waits at the register, the mother with a hand on the counter like she's ready to hurdle over it.

Josie angles us out of earshot. "Do you think you can handle this?"

"Yes, I—"

"Here, put this on." She hands me a felt mustache, one side covered in double-sided tape.

I turn it over in my hand, horrified. "What's this?"

"The rest of your outfit."

I look from the mustache to Claudia, then to David. "But no one else is wearing one."

"David has allergies."

My nose wrinkles. "He's allergic to double-sided tape?"

Josie sighs, annoyed. "The adhesive," she finally says. "He has very sensitive skin."

I almost snort. "And Claudia?"

"She's allergic to people." Josie snatches the mustache back and slaps it over my lip. She spins me toward the register. "Now, the customers expect to be greeted with a little Latin flair."

My brow furrows again. "Latin flair?"

"An accent," she whispers. "The gringos love it. Gives them the full experience." She smiles, nudging me forward. "Bienvenidos. How to help you today?"

I'm pretty sure one can have an accent without speaking in broken English. Maybe when she said "Gives them the full experience," she didn't mean *my* experience. She meant theirs. The experiences they've cultivated at places like this where the food is as authentic as this mustache stuck to my face and where the Latinx people they meet are characters instead of human beings. I can see the expectancy in their eyes as they wait for me to slip into the caricature they know and love.

I use my own voice instead. "What can I get for you today?"

Josie's lips tighten into a thin line.

I ignore her, punching in their order. But the whole time I can't help but remind myself that this is not a place where I can just make my own rules. I'm not the boss. Josie is. And as degrading as it is to pander to such harmful stereotypes, I can't pretend like there's no risk involved in me refusing to follow her orders. I can't get fired. Not on my first day. Not when I've already spent my last check from the restaurant.

I slide the bag of food across the counter, my eyes down as I tilt my words. "Gracias. Please come a-gain."

I'm grinding my teeth as the next customer approaches. Before I can summon enough desperation to force out a greeting, he's pointing a finger in the direction of the bathrooms.

"Men's is clogged. Just thought you should know."

"Oh, don't worry." David slides over and I'm relieved that he's at least decent enough to keep me out of foreign territory. But then he says, "I'll cover the register for you," once again exuberant at the misfortune that keeps hurling itself in my direction. He takes my place before I can object. "What can I get you, sir?"

I follow Josie to the bathroom, counting the linoleum tiles as we approach the door marked MEN. She hands me a plunger before going in first, only one of us able to fit at a time. I can hear her jiggling the handle, something making her gag. She comes back out, sweating.

"Toilet's clogged. Do you think you can take care of it?"

I want to say no, to snap this plunger over my knee and run as far away from here as possible.

"I'll take care of it."

I hold my breath and then I venture inside. A latex bubble floats in the center of the bowl. I stand there, watching it twist, and I think about how my survival rule about *always* doing the scary thing was not created with condom-clogged toilets in mind. Maybe it's a metaphor. Maybe it's a sign. I look closer but then I start gagging the same way

Josie was. And I realize that it isn't the universe trying to test me or send me a message. It's a condom in a fucking toilet.

And this is your life now.

Suddenly, I'm sliding down the wall. I land on the floor with a thud, my back pressed to the hard surface as I try to keep everything inside me from collapsing too. My lungs are the first to go, the smell of the stagnant toilet water making them clench. The dam in my tear ducts goes next. The rush forces my lips apart and I cover my mouth, not letting myself make a sound. I barely sniff, shaking as I try to cry as silently as possible.

Because it hurts to feel it all over again—losing the restaurant, losing my father, losing the only purpose I had for anything.

And because this is where David said I'd end up. And then I challenged him to a duel. A duel I'm in very serious danger of losing if I can't stop the storm inside me.

But maybe I don't want to stop it.

Maybe this time I want to be swept up, torn apart.

I close my eyes, imagining the sounds of the restaurant, the smell of my food coming out on steaming plates, the tastes resting on people's tongues.

Gone. Gone. All of it gone.

Because you lied.

Because you're weak.

Because you're broken. Broken. Broken.

No.

I cover my ears, trying to muffle the sound. In the corner of my eye, I see the scars. The places where I used to put the pain. Memories like a warm whisper in my ear. But just because the voice is familiar doesn't mean that it tells the truth.

The truth.

What is the truth?

That I'm a failure and a fraud and more fragile than I thought?

Or that I'm fearless. That I'm strong.

I stare down at my arms, looking past the scars at the veins underneath. Purple and pulsing with life.

I am fearless. I am strong.

I steal my breath back, chanting the words over and over in my head. Until it's not such a fight to remember, to believe it's true.

I am fearless. I am strong.

The voice is hushed.

I rise to my feet, remembering the way my father gripped my hands. The way he begged me to fight. And then that's exactly what I do.

I catch my reflection in the bathroom mirror and lock eyes with the girl staring back. I scrape the tears from my cheeks.

I am fearless. I am strong.

Then I stand over the toilet, staring down into the bowl. At a fucking condom.

I take a deep breath, reaching for the plunger.

Because this *is* my life.

And I can do this.

15

Pen

AS SOON AS I get home I peel out of my shirt and grease-stained Dickies. Then I just lie on the floor in my underwear, absorbing the cold.

"Pen?" I hear Chloe's voice on the other side of the door. "Pen, I know you're in there. I've come to rescue you."

I crawl to the door and yank it open.

Chloe's eyes widen, her body pushing me inside. "Geez, you always answer the door like that these days?"

"It keeps the nosy neighbors away."

"You smell like a gas station."

"Close," I quip, wandering the apartment looking for a clean towel. "We cook our empanadas in motor oil." I make my way to the shower.

"Don't wallow in there." She sets the bag she's carrying

onto the counter. "You've got five minutes and then you're telling me all about your date!"

I need more than five. It takes almost half an hour to get the smell of churros out of my hair. When I reemerge, Chloe's sitting on my bed.

"Figured this was an emergency." She hands me a tub of cookie dough ice cream. She already carved out half of it and swapped me some of her cookies and cream.

I dig my spoon in, inhaling the first bite.

"Slow down. It's not going anywhere."

I swallow. "I had to dig a condom out of the toilet."

She chokes, horrified. Then she laughs, taking another bite of her ice cream. "Remember, it's only temporary while you look for something else."

I nod only because I don't want to think about it anymore and my ice cream is starting to melt.

She nudges me. "So, are you going to spill, or what?"

"What do you mean?"

She raises an eyebrow. "What's up with you and Xander?"

I jab my spoon in and out of my ice cream, not sure if it's a flutter or a pang in the pit of my stomach. Because thinking about Xander doesn't just make me feel hopeful, it makes me feel angry. That he lost his parents. That he lives in fear. That I can't do anything to change that.

"Pen..."

"He's been through a lot." I don't know how to let Chloe in without divulging Xander's secrets. But they aren't mine to share.

"So have you," Chloe reminds me.

I think back to my breakdown at work. But instead of being buried by that feeling, I clawed my way back out. Somehow. And yet, it doesn't feel like a fluke. It feels like a fork in the road. One I might actually be able to navigate, one brave step at a time.

"Is that why you gave him my phone number?" I ask.

Chloe smiles, her spoon pressed to her lips. "Maybe I just had a feeling."

"What kind of feeling?"

She waves a hand. "Okay, so maybe less of a feeling, and more of a vision. A vision of the two of you kissing on Angel's porch when you thought I was sleeping."

I stare into my ice cream. "I don't know what you're talking about."

"You're ridiculous." She chucks a pillow at me. "You're telling me Pen Prado is too cool to swoon?"

"Pen Prado is too cool to kiss and tell, that's all."

She smiles. "Well, luckily, everything I need to know is written all over your face. You like him. A lot."

My cheeks burn, and this time I'm sure. It's not a pang, but a flutter. "Okay, maybe I like him. A little."

"And?" She shimmies her shoulders, gleeful. "You're going to see him again, right?"

"I'm going to see him again."

She perks up. "When?"

"Tomorrow night."

Chloe smiles to herself—a little proud, a little relieved. Then she nudges me. "But…is he going to *see* you?"

I know what she means. Am I going to *show* him? The parts of me only she and Angel are allowed to see, the parts of me that even they're not. I feel myself reaching for another disguise, another excuse.

But even if I wanted to hide from him, the problem is that... "I think he already has."

16

Xander

"SO, ARE YOU GOING to tell me where we're going?" Pen leans forward, examining the road signs.

"It's a surprise."

"Obviously it's a surprise." Pen shrugs. "Or a kidnapping, depending on whether you're a glass-half-full kind of person."

"Are you?" I ask.

"I'm more of a 'who cares, let's just drink it' kind of person." Pen leans closer, raises an eyebrow. "Are we almost there?"

I take the next exit, a speed bump jostling Pen back into her seat.

"Almost."

"Okay, I'm going to close my eyes."

I pull down a residential street, Pen smiling at the sound of the tires grazing the curb. I open my door, the smell of garlic and rosemary filling my lungs. As Pen steps out, she breathes deep, smiling even wider.

"Now?" Pen says.

In the dark, the small house is all candlelit, lace-covered windows. I lead Pen to the front door before telling her she can look.

She opens her eyes, taking a few steps back to get a better view. "Is this someone's house?"

I give a slight nod. "The chef... does sleep here."

"Chef?"

"Signora Caterina. She makes the best pizzas in town." I pause before knocking. "Well, *we* make them. But she facilitates using a lot of hand gestures and Italian curse words."

Signora Caterina's son greets us at the door with a nod before silently taking my cash and counting the bills twice. We wind past ceramic figurines of Christ and the Virgin Mary as he leads us to the kitchen.

He hands us each an apron before wedging us between two other couples already seated at the kitchen table. The couple to our left is copiously taking notes—they must write for some local food magazine or maybe a blog—and the couple to our right is nervously sipping on some wine. Signora Caterina's son doesn't bother offering us any.

Pen nudges me. "So the hidden cameras are where, exactly?"

I glance at another Jesus statue by the back door.

"Ah, that's why there's so many."

I lower my voice. "Their family's a little eccentric, but food's about the experience, right?"

Signora Caterina waddles in hugging a giant bag of flour. She heaves it onto an empty chair without a word before sifting it onto the table. Once the surface is lightly covered, her son places a large mixing bowl in front of each of us. There are smaller bowls in the center of the table: yeast, more flour, sugar, salt, olive oil, and warm water.

Signora Caterina motions to the bowl in front of her. Then she releases a string of indecipherable instructions as she mixes the yeast and warm water. It's a pretty basic dough, and Pen seems to work off instinct, catching a few of the Italian words as Signora Caterina transitions from one step to the next.

"Impastate con le mani." Signora Caterina mixes the ingredients by hand.

"Sale."

Pen adds a pinch of salt to our mix.

"Versate l'acqua sempre un po' alla volta."

I add the water while Pen slowly works it in. The couple next to us, who are already on their second glass of wine, pours too much, the woman giggling until Signora Caterina swipes their bowl and chucks the contents in the trash. The woman's face turns as red as her glass as they start from scratch.

Next is the oil. Signora Caterina slides past Pen and me, nodding in approval.

Pen whispers, "Signora Caterina doesn't mess around, does she?"

"She takes her family's recipe pretty seriously."

I help Pen turn the bowl, the dough plopping down onto the table.

"She's terrifying. But I like her style."

"I thought you might."

Signora Caterina slaps her dough against the tabletop, tossing it down and ripping it up. I take Pen's place, doing the same. Flour flies, dusting our faces.

One of the food bloggers drops his dough a bit too delicately and Signora Caterina pushes against his shoulder.

"I think she's telling him to put his back into it."

Pen smirks. "Let me show him how it's done."

She takes the dough from me. For the next three minutes, Pen uses it like a hammer, smashing the heads of nails only she can see. When Signora Caterina signals for us to put the dough back in the bowl, Pen's out of breath.

"You okay?" I ask.

She exhales. "I needed that."

Out of the corner of my eye, I actually see Signora Caterina crack a smile.

Proofing bowls go in an empty cupboard while Signora Caterina's son brings out some finished dough.

"Pirlatura."

We press the dough into a sphere. One of the food bloggers tries to get fancy and tosses the dough in the air. Signora Caterina tosses flour at him in response. She motions to the table, her hands pumping the dough back and forth along the flat surface.

My stomach growls as the dry ingredients are replaced by various pizza toppings. There's roasted potato, dried salami, mortadella, mozzarella, mushrooms, eggplant. The food blogger who's been the source of Signora Caterina's ire all evening goes in for a piece of sausage and she slaps his hand away. She holds up a finger, and her son brings out a steaming pot of sauce.

Pen breathes against my ear. "I knew there'd be a secret ingredient."

"Excuse me," the female food blogger starts nervously, "I thought we'd be learning to make the sauce."

Signora Caterina may not understand much English, but she definitely understands when someone is trying to steal her sacred family recipe. "Vattènne!" She shakes a dirty rag at them. "Vattènne!" When that doesn't work she twists it into a whip, snapping it behind them as they race for the exit.

Pen looks at me. "Does that mean we get to eat their pizza?"

———

Behind Signora Caterina's house is a small creek, four round tables backed up to her chain-link fence. It's strung with Christmas lights, a statue of the Virgin Mary wrapped in them too. A small stereo sits on the sill of an open window, "Por Ti Volaré" humming from the speakers.

For a long time Pen just stares at me, a kind of wonder on the edge of her lips. She finally shakes her head. "This is without a doubt the weirdest restaurant I've ever been to."

"You're welcome?"

Her finger catches the condensation on her water glass. "Tell me, am I the first girl to meet Signora Caterina?"

I take a drink, my throat dry. "Yes."

"Why this place?" she asks, earnest.

"I don't know. You struck me as someone who likes to eat."

"I do."

"And this is one of the best places I know."

She sits back in her chair. "I've got to say, you were a natural in there. You're wasted playing second fiddle to Lucas."

"Oh yeah?" I raise an eyebrow. "You want to put in a good word for me with the boss?"

She laughs. "You know, I would, except I've sort of been banned from the premises. I'm probably the last person you want talking you up."

She's quiet and I immediately regret bringing up her father. But I'm not just reminded of Pen's tears the other night, I'm reminded of the phone call I overheard, of the danger the employees at Nacho's might be in. And of the fact that El Martillo knows my secret; that he can use it against me, against Mr. Prado whenever he wants. The only thing that gives me some relief is the fact that I don't have to keep it a secret from Pen. Maybe someday she'll trust me with her secrets too. That's what I really want to show her. That she's safe with me. That she can be herself with me.

Signora Caterina's son brings out our pizza, the pie hanging off the edge of the table.

"This smells amazing."

Three slices are gone before either one of us speaks again—Pen savoring every bite while I'm trying to figure out how to not screw this up.

As if sensing my worst fears, she says, "Do you remember how you said I could ask you anything and you'd tell me the truth?"

I swallow, mouth dry again. "What do you want to know?"

She faces the creek, thinking. Then she meets my eyes and says, "Everything."

I'm silent, a million thoughts racing through my head. Revealing my status was one thing. But that's not who I am. What if I start talking, really talking, and she doesn't like what she hears? What if I tell her the truth about my dad and this childhood hope I have that he still loves me, and she thinks I'm pathetic? What if I tell her how badly I want Nacho's to be my home too, how much I wish her family was my own, and she thinks I'm crazy? If I say the wrong thing, this could all be over—the way she's looking at me, whatever romanticized version of me is still living inside her head.

"I'm not afraid," she says.

"I didn't say you were." I crumple my napkin in my fist. "Seems like there isn't much you are afraid of."

She frowns. "Of course there is. That's not what I meant."

"I'm sorry." I watch the wind toss her hair. "I'm just..."

"Just what?"

"Terrified." I look down. "Of saying the wrong thing or saying too much."

"Of what I'll think of you?"

I nod, and my confession seems to disarm her.

She leans forward, trying to coax me out of my doubt. "Do you want to know why I asked you on a date?"

I want to say yes but I can't even open my mouth.

Her eyes soften. "Because it was scary."

I stare down at my hands. "I...scare you?"

She shakes her head. "Not you." She exhales, the tiniest tremor in her voice as she says, "I keep a running tally of the things that make me uncomfortable, constantly measuring how much something makes me feel anxious or afraid or...out of control." She twists a strand of hair between her fingers. "And the only way to make that feeling stop is to do something that scares me. I have to knock on a stranger's door and demand that they turn down their god-awful music." She lowers her voice. "Or I have to ask a cute guy out on a date."

"So it's like a game...."

"No." She looks down. "It's *not* a game. It's how I survive."

My voice softens, worried I've insulted her somehow. "You don't seem like you're just surviving."

She squirms in her seat, sitting on her hands. "I know how to play a role, especially at work. I know how to be a sister and a daughter and a boss. But now..." Her face grows still. "I don't know how to exist without Angel needing my help at the restaurant or without my little brother and sister needing me to make them breakfast. Lola used to fight me every day for some goddamned Froot Loops, and it used to feel like such a chore but now...I miss it." She chews on her lip. "I think I like taking care of people. I think I like the feeling of someone depending on me. Because when they do, it gives me a reason to be strong, to not give up."

It hits me that the source of Pen and her father's tension might be that they're the exact same person. Stubborn but loyal, guarded but always putting family first. If Pen's right about her father only keeping the restaurant open so he can take care of the neighborhood, she's the perfect successor.

"Why did you do it?" It's out before I can shove the words back down. I have no right to ask Pen why she lied to her parents, but her heartbreak is such a tangible thing that I have to know why it was self-inflicted.

"Because I was scared." She looks into my eyes. "I was afraid of living my mother's life. Being trapped. I know I want to be at the restaurant, that someday I want to open my own bakery—probably, pathetically, right next door. Or maybe even across the street. Somewhere within breathing distance of my father's food. *My* food." She shakes her head. "I should have known my father would never let me."

"Why not?"

She scratches the chill from her arms, eyes red. "I have no fucking idea, and that's the worst part of all of this. He won't talk to me, he won't explain. So I'm just left to wonder what the hell I did wrong. But I don't know. I don't know what's wrong with me."

She's on her feet, heading toward the creek. Lights twinkle across the water, churning with the moon's reflection. I follow her to the creek's edge, watching the waves stretch and knead it like dough.

I reach for her hand and she doesn't pull away. "There's nothing wrong with you, Pen."

She pinches her eyes shut.

I think back to that first day, Pen stomping around the kitchen, ordering people around, when just moments before I'd found her in the bathroom, teary-eyed, and wearing the same face she's wearing now. And I knew it was all an act, that the only reason she was so hard was because of her softness.

"Jesus." She lets out a tight laugh. "Why do I always have to cry when you're around?" She looks down at her feet. "Despite what you might think...or what you've seen with your own eyes, I actually don't like to cry. In fact, I hate it. Even if they're happy tears, even if they're just an ache in the back of my throat that no one can see. I don't like the way it feels."

"The way what feels?" I ask.

She stares into the dark, struggling for words. "The way it feels to *feel*." She hangs her head again. "I know that makes no sense. My parents, they used to call me their little statue because I never cried. Not even when I'd fall off my bike and scrape my knee. For as long as I can remember, the moment I felt something I didn't like, I would shut it off. It helped when I was working at the restaurant, because no one ever tried to pull any shit while I was around but..." She pauses, her cheek between her teeth. "The truth is, my parents were wrong about me being made of stone. Everyone is. I'm not cold because I don't feel anything. I'm this way...because I feel *everything*."

She inches away from me and toward the waterline. "In all the years I've been struggling with this, it's happened twice—the first time when my abuelita passed away, and the second time when I spent the first day alone in my apartment."

I suddenly realize that Pen isn't just talking about the

pain of losing the restaurant. She's talking about something deeper, something that's been following her around since she was a child.

"When I first came to the States, my abuelo enrolled me in this stuffy private school. It was terrifying. I couldn't understand anything anyone was saying, but for some reason I always felt like they were talking about me. About the kid with the funny accent and hand-me-down clothes and strange lunches that made the classroom smell." I let out a slow breath. "I refused to speak for almost an entire year, but I had to relieve the tension somehow."

Pen squeezes my hand. "What did you do?"

"Before my father left, he gave me his lucky rock. It was black with sharp edges. I used to squeeze it in my fist when no one was looking, trying to break the skin." I open my palm and show her the scar, deeper than the ones on her arms.

"I'm so sorry." Pen looks up at me, barely breathing.

"I'm sorry too."

We're both quiet for a long time, listening to the water trickle between the rocks.

"I take something," Pen finally says. "After my abuelita died, my parents took me to the doctor. It helps. But when things change, when bad things happen that are out of my control, it's hard...." She looks up, admonishing the moon or maybe God. "But maybe that's how it's supposed to happen."

"What?"

"Growing up," she says. "Maybe it's supposed to hurt this much."

I think of my father. Childhood hopes still burn between my ribs, but what if it's time to put them out? What if Pen's right? That growing up, that growing out of your old self, is supposed to hurt like hell.

"You're stronger than you think you are," I say, for both of us.

"I am strong." The resolve has returned to her voice. "Except when you're around." She looks away. "I like to keep people at arm's length. I like to be in control."

Our noses touch, my fingers brushing back her hair.

"You are in control," I promise. "Always."

Then I lean down, letting her close the space between us. This time when our lips touch, it's soft and tired and it feels like giving up. In the best way. Like giving up on a life of just surviving. Pen kisses me, and life isn't about just surviving anymore. It isn't about searching. It isn't about fighting. It isn't about being let down. It's about this. Needing someone who needs you back. Even if it's just in this one moment, Pen pressed against me, her hands fighting for an even stronger hold, a deeper kiss. I can feel that she needs it just as much as I do, and every cell in my body just wants to give it to her.

17

Pen

CITY LIGHTS HAVE SCARED off most of the stars. Two bright spots are all that's left to remind me that despite what Xander says, despite what I've been trying to convince myself and everyone else of my entire life—I'm not actually in control of anything.

I'm not in control of how Xander makes me feel, of the finiteness of this moment, of the fragility of my own fear. I stare up at those two bright spots, Xander's eyes closed as he unloads every burden onto our kiss, and I am not in control. And for the first time, it doesn't feel like the end of the world. It doesn't feel like an end at all.

Xander carries our leftover pizza back to the car, the sound of idling engines slowing our steps as we approach the street. Lights flash against the side of the house, red and blue racing across my skin. There's an ambulance up ahead, and four police cruisers.

Xander stops.

In the other direction is a dead end, the creek running south and cutting off the road.

We're at least ten blocks from Nacho's Tacos, the cruiser license plates unfamiliar. I don't know if these cops know my father, if they know our neighborhood, or if they believe it belongs to someone else.

"I'll drive," I say.

Xander sinks into the passenger seat, staring straight ahead.

As we approach the scene, lights swell against the windows. A cop lifts a hand, slowing me to a stop. I can hear Xander hold his breath.

I roll down the window, try to seem relaxed. Between my ribs, my heart pounds.

"We're unable to clear the street. Watch for my signal and then you'll need to maneuver onto the sidewalk."

There are two men facedown in the front yard adjacent to the ambulance, both in handcuffs. My stomach tightens as a child is carried out by one of the paramedics, her Tweety Bird nightgown ripped at the knee.

"What happened?" I say before I can stop myself.

The officer examines me more closely. "Do you live in this neighborhood?"

My face warms. *Why the hell did you open your mouth?*

When I don't answer, he says, "It's late. Do your parents know you're out here?"

I try to force out a sound, anything to get him to back away from the car. But suddenly I can't open my mouth.

Because he's not looking at me anymore. He's looking at Xander.

"I'm just on my way now." My knuckles blanch around the steering wheel. "I should get home before they start to worry."

He narrows his eyes, head tilted. "Put the car in park."

My stomach drops. "If I could just pass—"

"I said put the car in park."

My skin crawls, remembering the officer who slammed my father against the hood of our car. His voice was just as cool—the kind of unnerving placidness one wears when there's a gun strapped to their hip and a get-out-of-jail-free card stuck to their chest.

He yanks the passenger door open, Xander cowering under the glow of his flashlight.

I can't move. "Please, don't—"

"Step out of the car."

"No." It's barely more than a whisper, air desperately fighting its way to my lungs.

Xander's frozen too.

Gravel crunches, another uniform appearing behind the glow of the officer's flashlight. "Everything all right over here?"

The officer with the flashlight shines it from my face to Xander's. Sweat trickles down Xander's brow.

"Penelope?" the second officer asks.

My mouth quavers, "Yes?" as his face comes into view.

Officer Dunne. He and Officer Solis eat at the restaurant every Tuesday night.

He forces the other officer's hand down, the light no longer burning my eyes. "It's late and your father's probably worried. Go ahead on home."

"Not until I see some IDs." The first officer motions to Xander. "Come on, kid. What? You don't speak English?"

Officer Dunne puts his hands on his hips, looks from me to the passenger seat. "What kid?" Then he shuts the passenger door. "All I see is Ignacio Prado's daughter on her way home."

"What the hell is this, Dunne? Are you out of your—?"

"Put the car in drive, Pen."

I nod, still shaking.

Officer Dunne motions to the sidewalk on the other side of the ambulance, helping me navigate around the cruisers. Before the first officer can get Xander's license plate, I tighten my grip on the steering wheel and speed out of the neighborhood. When we reach the access road, flashing neon signs replacing the emergency lights, Xander's still frozen.

"Xander...?"

He doesn't answer and I feel sick. Then I hear his breath hitch, his body quaking against the seat. I pull up to an empty gas station, parking away from the streetlights. Xander's hairline is speckled with sweat, and all I can think about is what *he* must have been thinking about. Getting sent back. Losing everything.

I reach for him. "Xander, I'm so sorry."

He doesn't speak. He doesn't move.

"I'm sorry. I shouldn't have said anything. I shouldn't have—"

Without a word, he wraps his arms around me. He's still shaking, and it rattles me too, my hands pressed to his back. His own are clenched. After a long moment, he lets go, and I reach for his hands next, trying to coax his fingers into loosening from their fists. He opens his right hand and I see the scar where it runs from palm to index finger. My fingertips trace the skin, trying to read the memories buried underneath.

My eyes drift down to my own forearms, to the faint scars I thought were hidden until the night of Angel's party when Miguel Medrano asked me how I got them and I actually told the truth. For a long time they were a private reminder of the places I've been, of the pain I thought I could control. Xander follows my eyes, staring just as closely, and I realize that the scars are a reminder for him too.

He pinches his eyes shut. "No matter how long I've been here, there's still a part of me that doesn't feel like I belong. Because I know there's some people who just don't want me here." He stares at the flickering streetlight. "I should be used to people not wanting me around....At least when my mother left me at the bus station, I could watch her go. But my father just disappeared."

"Did he come to the States?"

Xander nods. "I know he was here for a little while, that he talked about going to California."

"Do you think...?" I hesitate, not sure how close Xander's grief is to the surface or if after more than a decade of waiting for his father to come back, he still feels hope.

"That he might not want to be found?" Xander exhales. "I think about it all the time. Sometimes I choose to believe that he hates me, and for a while, I stop looking." A faint smile tugs at his lips. "But then I remember how he used to sit me on his knee, his teeth clicking like I was a jockey in a horse race. I'd wrap my small hands around his thumbs while he shook me until I laughed."

My chest aches with a million of the same memories— my father teaching me to whistle while the two of us cracked pecans on the back porch, my thirteenth birthday when I woke up to find two tickets to the local theater's production of *A Midsummer Night's Dream* under my pillow, my first day at the restaurant when he paraded me around, introducing me to every customer, his face full of pride as he told them I was his daughter.

Xander's voice wavers. "He loved me once. I know it. That's why I can't give up."

In that moment, Xander's resolve is a reminder for me too. That I love my father, that he loves me back, even if it feels like we're strangers sometimes.

My father loves me. That's why I can't give up.

Xander holds out a business card with the name and number of a local detective. "I don't know how much the fee is yet. Probably a lot of money; probably money I shouldn't be spending on someone who may not even want to see me. But...if he doesn't want to be my father, I need to hear him say it. I need to see it in his eyes like I did the day my mother left." He flicks the card, thinking. "Do I sound crazy?"

"No, not at all." I lean toward him. "You sound brave."

A weak smile breaks through as he says, "You make me feel like I could be."

The lone streetlight barely grazing the hood of the car finally goes out, the darkness making it easier to pretend. That Xander's safe. That I'm strong. But he needs me to be, and I decide in that moment that maybe I don't have to pretend anymore. Maybe I never really was. Maybe I can be strong for both of us, not because it's how I survive, but because it's who I am.

18

Pen

"I NEED YOU ON drive-through. I'm taking my break." David holds the headset over my bandana, letting it snap against my ears.

"You just took a break thirty minutes ago."

He shrugs. "And now I need another one."

The next order is already coming through the earpiece. I can barely make out each item over what sounds like a car full of teenage boys laughing and shouting in the background. I punch in what's clear, but they roll to the window before I can read it back to them. I slide open the plastic screen, and in the driver's seat is Miguel Medrano.

Stay calm, Pen. He's just another asshole customer— emphasis on the asshole.

Miguel's jaw drops as he takes in my getup, including the felt mustache stuck to my upper lip.

"Penelope Prado." He whistles between his teeth. "How the mighty have fallen."

My pulse ticks up as I register the hushed voices of the other passengers. *Penelope got fired, remember? Her dad must really hate her. She looks pathetic. I heard she's homeless now. I wonder if that mustache is real.*

Miguel frowns. "¿Por qué la trompa?"

I bristle, trying not to pounce.

"We miss you at the restaurant, Pen. But I guess when you get an opportunity like this..." He gestures to my uniform. "...you just can't pass it up."

I lunge for him, dragging him through the window by his shirt.

"Holy shit!" Behind me, David's frozen in horror (or again, maybe amusement—it's hard to tell), his cell phone slipping from his grasp.

Miguel writhes like a fish. "You crazy bitch! Let go of me!"

I twist his collar until he's choking, the other losers in his truck scrambling for his feet as they try to pull him back inside.

Claudia rushes over. "What's going on back here?" When she sees Miguel halfway through the order window, me with a death grip on his shirt, she stops. "Pen, let go of him."

"Listen to your *boss*, Pen," Miguel croaks out.

I want to make him squeal again, but he's right. Claudia is my boss and if I want to keep my job—which, let's face it, is legitimately on the line right now—then I have to do what she says. So I grit my teeth...and then I let go, his friends pulling him back into the front seat of his truck. They call me a puta before speeding off.

"You're going home," Claudia says.

I expect an obnoxious quip from David, but he doesn't make a sound.

I don't either. I just grab my stuff from the back and storm out.

"So, wait a minute. Are you fired or are you not fired?"

Chloe sits at Mrs. Damas's kitchen table, testing out a few of the new items we've made for the women at Casa Marianella.

"I'm...not exactly sure yet."

Mrs. Damas folds some lemon zest into the icing she's making. "Well, it sounds to me like this Miguel Medrano is one rotten egg."

"Oh, he is," Chloe says. "He even burned off another employee's eyebrow."

I cross my arms, fuming again. "He should have been fired so many times. I tried to do it myself once, but my father wouldn't let me." I get back to stirring my chocolate ganache. "It doesn't make any sense. He's worthless. And a brat. And I hate him."

"Have you ever stopped to consider that your father's seen something in him you haven't?"

"Trust me, he doesn't possess a single redeeming quality."

"Unless he does." Mrs. Damas smiles. "Unless you just haven't looked closely enough."

"Maybe that's your problem with David too," Chloe teases. "You just haven't gotten to know him well enough."

I jab my spoon at her. "Listen, I come here to bake. Not to become a better person."

Mrs. Damas passes behind me before drizzling the icing over her lemon-buttermilk pound cake. "You can't do one without the other."

Chloe's nose wrinkles. "Really? Because Pen's been baking for years and she still—"

I shoot her a look. "And I still what?"

She reaches for another biscochito, raising it in surrender. "You still make the best butter cookies I've ever had."

"That's right." I untie my apron. "I think that's everything, Mrs. Damas. Same time next week?"

She nods. "Yes, yes. Thanks so much for your help today."

I yank Chloe away from the sweets, crumbs spilling from her lap as we head for the door.

"You girls have fun."

Back in my apartment, Chloe immediately flings herself on my bed. "Okay, I need to hear about this second date, which by the way was less than twenty-four hours after your first date."

"So...?"

"So, you haven't gotten sick of him yet."

I slump down beside her. "*We've* spent almost every day together the past seven years and I haven't gotten sick of *you*."

She looks up at me, batting her lashes. "That's because you love me."

I shrug. "Sometimes."

She digs a finger in my side and I swat at her, laughing.

"So," she asks, "do you think you're falling in love with him?"

I roll my eyes. "We've only gone on two dates."

The truth is, I don't know how to explain to her that something has happened to my insides at the cellular level, and now he's all I can fucking think about.

She senses it anyway. "I think you're falling in love with him."

"Has he said anything?" I pull the blanket over my shoulders. "At the restaurant. Has he said anything to you about me?"

She's quiet, whatever joy was just bubbling beneath the surface gone out in a flash.

"Chloe?"

She scrapes a hand down her face. "He told me not to tell you."

My chest squeezes. "Xander?"

"No." She pinches her lip between her teeth. "Angel. He told me not to tell you...that I haven't been at the restaurant." She finally faces me. "No one has."

"What do you mean no one's been at the restaurant?"

"I mean, Nacho's never reopened. After the pest control people left, your father called and canceled everyone's shifts. And then the next day he called and canceled them again."

"The restaurant's closed....But why?"

Chloe stares at her feet. "Do you remember when El Martillo showed up at your brother's party?"

I nod.

"Well, apparently he showed up at the Johnson catering too. He and your dad exchanged some words."

"But that was weeks ago...." I shake my head. "I don't understand."

"I don't know all of the details. I've been doing my best to just stay out of the way. Your dad and Angel have had more than a few blowups in his office. I didn't want to get caught eavesdropping, and Angel won't tell me much. But I think El Martillo made a few veiled threats, and your dad's worried he'll make good on them."

"Veiled threats? About the restaurant?"

She shrugs. "Maybe."

Suddenly, I'm turning down the street to my parents' house. I don't knock, my old key sliding into the lock as footsteps rush to the door. My mother is holding a baseball bat, the panic on her face quickly replaced by relief and then anger as she pulls me inside.

"Pen, it's almost ten o'clock."

"Where's Dad?"

She sets down the bat, brushes her hair out of her face. "He's not here."

"Where is he?"

She straightens, matching my tone. "He's working."

"No, he's not."

Her shoulders slump. She knows that I know.

She turns her back on me and heads to the kitchen. A fresh pot of coffee bubbles, my mother taking it off the heat before pouring herself a cup. Then she pours one for me too, setting it down across from her. I don't sit.

"I want you to tell me what's going on," I say.

"The police are going to take care of it."

"You know that's not true. If Dad trusted them to take care of it, the restaurant would be open right now and El Martillo would be in jail. But he's not. And the longer this goes on, the more it seems like...like we're protecting him. Letting him off the hook."

"You think we've suddenly lost sight of the difference between right and wrong? It's complicated, Pen. Too complicated to explain to you right now."

"Because you don't think I'll understand or because you're ashamed?" The second the words come out, I instantly want to shove them back down.

My mother's voice is stern. "Your father has given up everything to protect his family, to protect this neighborhood. For that, we will never be ashamed."

My stomach drops. "What do you mean, *given up everything*?"

She looks away.

"Mom..." It feels like the ground beneath me gives way. "The restaurant," I force out. "It's still ours, isn't it?"

My mother reaches for my hand. "Pen..."

I know what she wants to say, but I don't want to hear it.

"Pen, I'm sorry."

When I get back to my apartment there's no music blaring. No muffled voices coming from a television somewhere.

At first, I'm relieved. I might actually get some sleep. But suddenly the quiet slows my steps, my heart racing the second my front door comes into view.

It's ajar, the gap just wide enough for me to make out the mess. I stop, waiting for footsteps, voices, any sign that they might still be inside my apartment. But the quiet spreads, luring me closer.

The mattress is upside down, blankets on the floor. The trunk at the foot of my bed has been emptied too, clothes scattered. I don't dare tread closer, skin pricking as if their eyes are still on me. I back into Mrs. Damas's door, my hand falling limp as I attempt to knock.

I'm shaking so much by the time she answers that I can't even get the words out. She looks over my shoulder to my apartment and then she drags me inside.

"Are you all right?" She hands me a glass of water.

I just hold it, unable to drink, to speak.

"I'm calling the police." Mrs. Damas presses the phone to her ear. It rings once. "Yes. I want to report a robbery...."

At the same time, I open my contacts and start scrolling. My finger hovers over Xander's name, but then I hear the sirens. I slide down to my father's phone number and hit CALL.

———

Ten minutes later, Officer Solis stops him and Angel in the doorway, explaining what happened. "They're searching the neighborhood and taking witness statements. A tenant said she noticed someone in a hoodie using the access stairs. Didn't look like one of the residents."

My father never takes his eyes off me, his expression

darkening as he reconciles the details relayed by Officer Solis and the empty look on my face. Angel's fuming.

"We need her to walk the apartment and tell us if anything is missing."

My father comes over to me slowly. He takes both of my hands. "Are you okay?"

I croak out, "Yes."

"We need to go inside the apartment so we can tell the police if anything is missing. Can you do that?"

I nod.

I follow my father past police officers and curious neighbors. Angel hangs back, Officer Solis trying to calm him down. I catch his eye and I can't shake the fear before he sees, the dread draining the color from my face and igniting him all over again.

"You find him. You find him before I do."

"Angel, we're doing everything we—"

"It's not enough. It never has been. But I won't let—"

Officer Solis drags Angel down the hall, Angel's voice still raised.

My lips barely part. "They think...it was *him*."

My father doesn't respond, steering me over the threshold instead. The first thing I see is the bookshelf Xander put together. Everything glass is broken, the shelves snapped as if someone drove their foot into them one by one, my childhood memories scattered like fallen leaves.

I immediately reach for the pieces, trying to scoop things up, to put them back together.

"Uh, miss..." An officer approaches. "We're still in

the process of photographing everything. So if you could please—?"

"I'm sorry."

I let my father lead me from one broken thing to the next while I list everything that's missing for the officer—some jewelry, my laptop. But they didn't take as much as I thought. Maybe that wasn't the point. Maybe the point... the reason why they...why *he* did this...was to make me feel *this*. To remind me...and my father that we can break. That he knows how to do it. That it's *easy* when you're the one with all the power...And we're the ones with everything to lose.

We make our way around to the kitchen. The pantry's been ransacked, food scattered all over the floor. The fridge door is open, more food spilling out. I move to the center of the room, tracing every crack and tear and sharp edge. Until each breath I suck down is just as sharp. Until I can't breathe at all.

My father pulls me to his chest. "You're safe, Pen. You're okay. I'm here." He grips me harder. "I'm here."

19

Xander

I ARRIVE TOO EARLY at the diner and have to order a stack of pancakes to avoid looking suspicious. I take a few bites, the last one scraping all the way down. I chug my orange juice, but the sugar only makes me more jittery.

"Xander Amaro?" A man sits down across from me. "Detective Freeman." He reaches out a hand.

"Nice to meet you." We shake.

He doesn't look like a private investigator—no fedora or long trench coat. Instead, he's wearing denim shorts and white sneakers, a pair of sporty sunglasses with purple frames resting in his spiked silver hair.

"I think I was able to get most of the information I need from your voice mail. I can start working on your case as soon as this week. But before we move any further, we'll need to talk about price."

I think back to the lawyer's assurance that Detective

Freeman is not only thorough but honest. Unfortunately, she didn't say he was cheap.

"I charge by the hour, and depending on how complex the case, I could clock in anywhere from five to twenty hours a week."

"What's the rate?"

"One hundred dollars. But I request that new clients pay an up-front retainer—five hours' worth of work—and then I check in with you to discuss how much more time I might need."

"So that's five hundred dollars?"

He nods. "Look, Xander, people don't recommend me to their clients because I'm the cheapest guy on the block. They recommend me because I'm not in the business of screwing people over. I can't tell you how many people have come to me after having already shelled out thousands of dollars to another PI who just up and disappeared." His brow furrows, sincere. "If you're committed to this, then so am I. I can promise you that."

<hr />

Back in the car, I scratch Detective Freeman's price onto the back of his business card, trying to calculate how many more hours I'll need to work before I can pay the retainer. But then I remember that Nacho's is closed and will be for the indeterminable future. Maybe I should try to find another job. Or maybe I can offer to help Mr. Daly clean out his garage...and his house...and his backyard.

When I pull into the driveway, my abuelo and Mr. Daly

are marveling at an old record player in the back of Mr. Daly's truck.

"Give us a hand, will you?" Mr. Daly grunts, trying to shove the console to the end of the truck bed.

I help him carry it into the living room. The place is packed, so we just drop it as close to an outlet as possible, Mr. Daly excited to get it plugged in to see if it works.

"You didn't think about testing it before you bought it?" I ask.

"These things are indestructible." He waves to a collection of cardboard boxes on the other side of the room. "Crack open the third one to the left and hand me one of those records."

I clear a few of the other boxes out of the way and realize that they're sitting on top of a five-foot console that looks almost identical to the one we just carried inside.

I take a step back. "Uh...did you know this was here?"

Mr. Daly wipes his brow, exasperated. "Of course I knew it was there. Now I've got a matching set."

Just as Mr. Daly drops the needle on *Songs in the Key of Life*, my phone buzzes. It's Angel.

I step out onto the porch, hoping he's calling to tell me the restaurant is open, which would mean I could pay Detective Freeman as soon as next week.

"Hello?"

"Where are you?" I can hear traffic in the background.

"At home. Why? Is the—?"

"I'm picking you up in five."

He's pulling into my driveway in three, waving at me to

hop in. Lucas slides to the back seat. He's stone-faced, and it makes me uneasy.

"What's going on?"

I didn't have time to pull on my Nacho's shirt before I ran out to the sound of Angel's honk. He stops me before I can yank it over my head.

"You won't be needing that."

"Where are we going?" I ask.

Lucas faces me. "We're going to find out where that son of a bitch J. P. is hiding."

I look from Lucas to Angel. They look like they've been up all night, and there's something destructive beneath the dark shadows under their eyes. It's laser-focused, and I wonder how much they've really thought this plan through. Maybe they don't even have one.

"What happened?" I ask.

Angel practically growls. "He broke into Pen's apartment last night."

My heart stops, ears ringing. "Is she—?"

"She's fine," Angel says. "She wasn't there. But he ransacked the place."

She wasn't there.

She *wasn't* there.

But she could have been.

There's a dent in Angel's glove compartment before Lucas can pin my shoulders to the back of my seat, my breaths coming hard and fast as Angel peels out onto the street. He runs a stop sign, and that's when I spot the gun against his hip. The sight of it sobers me for a second, and I realize we're not on our way to turn El Martillo in or even to beat the shit out of him. We're on our way to kill him.

When we finally pull up to the house, low-hanging tree branches knocking against the roof of the truck, I'm not in my body anymore and I don't know how to force myself back inside.

Angel is pure adrenaline, Lucas trying to get him to stay low, as we approach the house. We slide along the exterior, and beneath the carport I can see El Martillo talking on his cell phone as he makes his way to the driver's side door. There are other voices, at least two.

I press myself to the wall, turning my head so I can whisper in Angel's ear and tell him we should go back to the truck to call Officer Solis. But before I can open my mouth, Angel steps beneath the carport, the revolver pointed straight at El Martillo.

Hammers click, one after the other, three guns aimed back at Angel.

"Oh, hell no." Lucas takes a step, but I push him back.

"Call Officer Solis."

And then I give El Martillo's henchmen another target. When I reach Angel he's shaking, and all I want is to take the gun from him. It's El Martillo who signals for the others to lower their guns instead.

"I think I know what this is about." El Martillo snaps a finger. "I heard the restaurant's been closed for a few days. Pest problem. That's a shame. Nacho's has the best tacos in town."

"I think the pest problem is you." Spittle rests in the corner of Angel's lips. I can tell he wants to scream.

El Martillo laughs, taking a step closer. "And you've—

what? Come to exterminate me?" He winks. "And let me guess. You're some kind of sidekick?" He's an arm's length away now.

"You went after my fucking sister. That's why we're here."

"Ah." El Martillo rubs at his chin. "It's a family matter. See, that's the problem; the real reason the restaurant is closed. Because your father thinks he's running a charity, not a business. To him, everyone's family." He shakes his head. "But that's too many mouths to feed. Cuts into my profit margins."

Angel narrows his eyes. "What do you mean *your* profit margins?"

El Martillo puts his hands on his hips, amused again. "Hell, kid. I thought you were the manager." He wags a finger. "Maybe I *should* pay your sister a visit. Seems like she's the real brains of the family." He grins, looking right at me. "And the beauty to match."

I swing but he hits me first, landing a punch to the right side of my face. My mouth fills with blood. Before I can choke on it, he grabs me by the shirt collar.

"You want me to make you disappear, boy? You think I haven't done it before?"

I spit at him, blood sticking to his face.

He grits his teeth before giving one of the gunmen a signal.

The bullet cracks like lightning, the pain so deep I can't even feel it. The wind dusts my face, sweat trickling down. I try to sense the wound, but when I open my eyes there isn't one, the gunman facedown instead.

Four police officers spread out, guns drawn. El Martillo lets go of me, hands raised. Officer Solis snatches me off the ground before dragging me to his cruiser while Angel and Lucas are pushed into the car up ahead.

"Are you okay?" Officer Solis asks once the doors are shut.

I don't know how to answer. I check myself for wounds one more time.

"Xander?"

"I'm okay."

We follow the other patrol car, El Martillo and the others being cuffed behind us.

"What the hell was that?" He watches me in the rearview mirror. "Xander, what the hell were you thinking?"

"Angel." I swallow more blood. "J. P. went after Pen. He ransacked her apartment."

"I was there last night, but no one's found anything to peg it on J. P. Do you have some kind of proof?" He's desperate to find something tangible that will connect J. P. to a crime—any crime. He exhales. "They'll sweep the house. Maybe we'll get lucky."

I try to watch the road, the lines zipping past at the rate of my pulse. But I keep catching my reflection in the window.

"I'll press charges for the assault," I finally say.

Officer Solis glances back, probably not sure if he heard me right.

"How much time do you think he'll do for that?"

"Xander…" There's no enthusiasm in his voice, not even relief.

He pulls over, letting the other cruisers pass us. He

looks back over the seat, examining my wounds, searching for the fear that used to keep me quiet. But I don't want to stay silent. I can't if it means Pen could be in danger.

"Please." I'm choking again, tears welling up at the base of my throat. "Please let me do this." I picture Pen, her fingertips tracing my scars. If I testify against El Martillo I can protect her. I meet Officer Solis's eyes, willing him to see the strength underneath all of this brokenness. "I *have* to do this."

20

Pen

"LET HER SLEEP."

"But it's almost dinnertime. I want Pen to—"

"Shh. Come on. Let's close the door."

Clammy fingertips brush my face.

"Lola, no . . ."

I roll, my first instinct to swat at whatever's tickling my skin. But then I blink and see Lola. My mother's got her by the arm, trying to drag her into the hallway.

I smile. "Did somebody say something about dinner?"

I yank her onto the mattress, tickling her as she squeals.

"Pen, I have to pee!"

I kiss her on the cheek, sitting up. "Okay, go pee. I'll meet you in the kitchen."

Lola skips down the hall.

"And wash your hands," my mother calls after her.

She lingers in the doorway and in the stillness, the

memory of why I'm here hits me in the gut. I remember my apartment door, cracked, my slow footsteps revealing the mess on the other side. I remember the sirens and that sinking feeling that something awful had happened, was happening.

We didn't leave the police station until almost 2:00 AM. I glance at the clock—it's ten till six. I've been asleep for hours but I still feel like I'm in a fog. I know it's all over my face, and I look away before my mother can see. But then she crumbles next to me, wrapping her arms around my neck.

She waits for me to lean on her, and I want to, but it's too dangerous. The helplessness isn't just in my head this time. It's not just a feeling I can't control. It's a place. A trap. And if I fall into that trap, it won't just derail me again. It will destroy me.

"I'm so sorry, Pen." She squeezes harder, probably trying to picture what it looked like. Or trying not to.

I do the same, attempting to lure my mind away from the thought: *What if?*

What if I'd been home?

My stomach turns and I almost show her how much it hurts. How much it scares me. Because I know the answer. If I had been home...they would have broken me the same way they broke everything else.

I strip out of my mother's embrace and head for the bathroom. Lola's standing on the footstool, washing her hands as she sings the ABC's. She's only on the letter *M* and I try to hold myself up, to keep the bile down, but I can't. I fall onto my knees and heave into the toilet.

Lola stumbles off the stool, my mother leading her out by the hand. "What's wrong with—?"

"Let me get you something," my mother calls back, her voice just as weak as I am.

But as I stare into the mess, heaving again, I don't let myself cry. Not with Lola watching, not in my parents' house, where my mental illness is supposed to be invisible. Instead, I breathe deep, replaying the night over and over in my head—every possible scenario until the shock has worn off. Until the urge to scream is stuffed down so deep that the rest of me goes numb too.

I don't feel the warm towel against my forehead or the small droplets of water as they race down my cheek. It isn't until I see Hugo pressing it to my face that I realize I'm not throwing up anymore.

"Thanks, Bubba."

He's stoic, and I know he knows that I'm not sick but that something else, something worse, is trying to come to the surface. But he doesn't ask if I'm okay or what happened. He probably already knows the answers to that too. Or maybe he's remembering why I don't live here anymore and realizes that I probably wouldn't answer truthfully anyway.

And beneath the numbness, it's that thought that cuts me open. That he might be angry. That he might not trust me anymore.

"I'm sorry, Hugo."

His tiny fist tightens around the washcloth. "If you never would have lied, this never would have happened."

He drops the rag on the floor and brushes past my

mother as she carries in a glass of water and something to help with the nausea. She hesitates, having caught the last of what Hugo said.

I look up at her. "He hates me."

"He loves you." She sets down the glass. "Why do you think he's so angry, why he's so scared about what happened last night?"

"He shouldn't even know about what happened last night."

Her lip trembles. She looks away. "You used to not think I was such a horrible mother."

I know she wants me to say that she's not. She needs to hear that our relationship isn't entirely ruined. But even though I'm not as angry as I was before, I still can't make myself say it. I still can't forgive her.

"Take this." She drops the pills into my open hand. "And then get dressed. There's someone here to see you."

When I step out onto the front porch, Xander is sitting on the steps. He stands, looking me up and down—long enough for me to notice the bruise on his right cheek—before burying his face in my neck. For a long time he just holds me, and I can feel his heart racing, his hands slowly curling into fists against my back.

"I'm okay," I say, because he needs to hear it. I lean back, far enough to see his eyes. "What happened to you?"

He swallows, staring at my hairline. "Angel told me what happened."

My heart starts racing too. "And what did you do?"

"We found J. P."

I let go of him, trying to reconcile the fear with the fact

that he's standing right in front of me. "What did he do to you?" I search for the same brokenness I found in my apartment; an ache, a tremor, an ounce of regret. Xander and Angel could have gotten themselves killed. Because of me.

Xander's mouth twists. "Just a scratch."

I shake my head, angry. "Funny."

"I'm sorry." His voice is firm. "I'm sorry for what he did to you. I'm sorry I wasn't there to—" He squeezes his eyes shut. "I'm so sorry, Pen."

"It wasn't your fault." I take his hands. "He's hurt so many people. The 'why' doesn't matter." Anger starts to push past the fear, but instead of snuffing it out, I let it rise. I let him see. "What matters now is what we're going to do about it."

Xander looks down. "If I go to the police and press charges, maybe they'll actually be able to put him away."

"You would do that?"

He nods, jaw clenched. "I would do anything for you."

He makes it sound so easy. Like there is only right and wrong. Black and white. But what about all the gray? All that Xander would risk by putting himself under that microscope?

"I can't let you do that. It's not worth it."

It's not worth losing you, I want to say. Nothing is. Because I need him. Especially now.

He wants to argue, but I press my lips to his before he can say a word. While my mother and Lola and Hugo watch from the window. While Angel pulls into the driveway.

Xander grips me in handfuls, breathing deep and reminding me that I'm real. That he is too. That in this moment, in each other's arms, we're safe.

Angel gags, joining us on the porch. "I've already lived through one traumatic experience today, now you're gonna put me through another one?"

I punch him in the arm. "You idiot, what the hell were you thinking?"

His brow furrows. "Hey, Xander gets a kiss and I get assaulted?"

I hit him again, eyes welling up. "Don't ever do anything like that again."

He squeezes me, resting his chin on the top of my head. "I didn't just do it for you. I did it for Dad. For all of us."

I look up. "Where is Dad?"

"Back at the station."

"Good."

Angel crosses his arms. "Oh no. What are you thinking?"

I cross my arms in response. "I'm thinking that Nacho's Tacos is officially reopening tonight."

"Come on, Pen. That's crazy. Dad'll flip."

I shake my head. "No. You and Xander got to play hero. You got to do something about what happened. Now it's my turn." I glance back at the window, Lola and Hugo sitting at the kitchen table. "I can't just go back in there and wait for something to be done."

And I can't let this feeling fester. It's not the discomfort I'm constantly trying to chase away with a sharp bite and bold decisions. Or even the fear I've been using as fuel. It's a darker, colder thing.

"And this has nothing to do with you wanting to go back to the restaurant?" Angel asks.

"It has everything to do with it." I picture the torn booths, the folklórico dancers, and old ticket stubs. Then I imagine the emptiness where there should be flames and food and family. A skeleton as hollow as the ones painted on the walls. "Dad may have fired me, but it's still my home. I'm not letting El Martillo take it away from me or the people who live in our neighborhood. They need to see the lights on and to know that he can't do this anymore. That we won't let him."

"She's right." My mother stands in the doorway, looking from me to Angel. "I'm tired.... Your father will never admit it, but I know he is too." There's a sense of defiance in her eyes and I almost don't recognize her. "But we can't give J. P. another cent, another second."

Angel asks the question we've all been wondering. "What kind of deal did they have?"

My mother looks down. "Your father made too many deals with the devil. That was the problem. When people would come to him for money, claiming that J. P. was threatening to reveal their status to the police unless they paid him, your father would hire them to do odd jobs around the restaurant."

"That's no secret," I say. "Everyone knows Dad would hire almost anyone who asked."

"What they didn't know," my mother says, "is that... your father knew what they were going through because he was tied up in J. P.'s web the same way they were."

My heart is in my throat, trying to punch its way out. "What do you mean?"

"We were kids. Your father had tried getting the

money from a bank, but every single one of them turned him down. J. P. gave him some money to open the restaurant. He was one of the first, making J. P. seem like a legitimate businessman to all of the other people in the neighborhood."

"That's the real reason Dad's always helping people?" Angel asks. "Because he feels guilty?"

"Dad's not responsible for what El Martillo does," I say. "He never could have known that he'd turn out to be such a monster."

"But he did turn into a monster," my mother says, "and in our own small way, we've been feeding that beast, letting it grow bigger and bigger. Every year he wanted more money, and your father tried to push back, but there was always so much at stake." She looks at Xander, face pained.

"What do the police know?" Angel asks.

"Everything. But it wasn't enough, especially with all of J. P.'s connections. They tried to convince your father to keep the restaurant open. To wait and see if J. P. would make good on his threats."

My stomach drops. "Of course he would."

Angel clenches his fists. "You mean they wanted to use us as bait?"

"Your father refused."

"But then J. P. did make good on his promise." Xander reaches for me. "By going after Pen."

"And now they're holding him at the station." I find my mother's eyes. "But he won't be there for long. In the meantime, we have to open the restaurant. We have to take back control."

Opening the restaurant was too much of a risk for my father. But what about what's at risk if we don't? If we don't do the scary thing, if we don't even try. We'll be stuck in that fear forever, and I know what it's like to be stuck. It's the predecessor to disappearing altogether, which is even scarier than whatever El Martillo might be planning. Maybe tonight, when people are actually safe enough to be seen, is our only chance.

"You take care of calling in the employees," my mother finally says, "and I'll take care of everyone else."

21

Pen

BY THE TIME WE get to Nacho's, the parking lot is already full. Every employee is dressed and ready to sling some tacos, to start a fight. They huddle together, talking about what happened to my apartment the other night, trading theories about what else El Martillo's been doing behind the scenes.

We reach the front door and Angel pulls out the keys.

He tries to hand them to me. "Do you want—?"

I fold his fingers over them. "No, you should do it."

He slides in the key and turns the lock. Our footsteps echo in the dark, a single line of sunlight brushing the faded prayer card stopping me in my tracks. I press my hand to it, hoping for magic, like the day I finally told my parents the truth.

Behind me, Angel grazes it too before reaching for the

lights. Then Xander. Then Lucas. Everyone taking a bit of luck on their way inside.

The stagnant air smells like cleaning supplies. Not like my father's food. Not like home.

Soon, questions begin to swirl among the employees. *Where's Nacho? Have you seen Mr. Prado? What are we all doing here?*

The murmurs reach a lull, and I realize that everyone's looking in my direction. At first, I think it's because they want an answer to their questions or for me to galvanize them with some kind of speech. But then I realize it's because they haven't seen me at the restaurant in so long.

People I trained, people I helped hire, people I used to give shit to on a daily basis—they all stare at me and I can't help but wonder what they see. A failure? A total bitch? That might be who I wanted them to see—someone cold and in charge. But is that who they remember?

Before I can analyze each expression, Chloe breaks through the crowd and then she's hugging me. I can feel her tears down my neck, and suddenly there's someone else pressed to us both.

Andrea wraps her arms around me. "I never thought I'd miss you yelling at me."

Then so does Mari. "Or you doing my eyeliner before every shift." Her wings are crooked and they smudge even more against my shirt.

Solana finds a way in, Java and Struggles coming up behind her. Between strands of hair I can see Sang and Lucas. Chelo inches closer, patting someone on the back.

"Oh, come on." Angel uses his height to sandwich her between him and Miguel Medrano. "You know you love us."

She growls.

"Don't fight it," Angel whispers.

Everyone laughs and then Chelo smiles.

Lucas pulls Xander in and I immediately find his eyes. And I know he's feeling what I'm feeling. Accepted. *Loved.*

His eyes well up, and it gives mine permission to do the same. Then, one by one, everyone is letting go of something. Their fear of losing the only home they've ever known. Their fear of never finding somewhere to belong in the first place. We hold on to one another until the permanence of it sinks in. Until our close proximity has us laughing instead of in tears.

"I'm glad you're okay," Chloe whispers.

"I love you." It's the first time I've said it, but she knows. That she's not just my best friend but my sister.

The windows rattle, a heavy bass bumping from one of the cars outside. Through the window, I see Goldie's ice-cream truck parking across the street, his mixtape blaring. There are others farther down the street selling helados and shaved ice, people already venturing out of their houses to get in line.

"Hell yeah." Lucas high-fives Sang. "Block party!"

I spot my mother standing with Mrs. Rodriguez from La Puerta Abierta, both of them directing people who are setting up tables and chairs.

Behind me the restaurant speakers crackle, the beginning of "Suavemente" making the hairs on my arms stand on end. Xander's at the stereo, finger on the volume dial as he cranks it up.

Angel howls, out of his mind. "You heard the man. Let's get to work!"

Lucas races between people, chanting the lyrics as waitstaff removes chairs from tables. Everyone takes their places, and then Chloe opens the doors for customers.

Every Nacho's Tacos regular finds a seat, tables scraping across the floor as people push them together. We appease them with cheap liquor and chips and salsa while we thaw meat and prep ingredients. We work double-time, sending out dishes family style instead of taking orders. People aren't here for the food, anyway.

Xander and I carry out plates to people in the parking lot. They've set up coolers and card tables, some families sprawled out on quilts.

Mr. Martín's sitting in a lawn chair with a few other churchgoers. "I haven't seen this many people out in years." He removes his hat, holding it against his chest. But he isn't marveling at the turnout. He's staring at Mrs. Rodriguez across the street.

I nudge him. "You two aren't getting any younger, you know."

Mr. Martín laughs, blushing. "You really think I got a shot?"

"I think you'll never know until you try."

"Wish me luck?" He gives us a wink before making his way across the street.

We continue winding through the crowd, getting caught in the stream of a bubble machine, kids with water guns giggling so much they can barely aim. Their mothers fan themselves, bare feet stretched out in the grass. A soccer ball rolls against Xander's foot and he kicks it back to the group of kids playing near Goldie's ice-cream truck.

When we near the end of the street I stop, taking it all in. From the corner of Monte Vista Boulevard, the view in every direction is of people sitting on porches, playing music, smoking cigars. Beneath the staccato drums of bachata and the rhythmic beat of cumbia, beneath the voices of Selena Quintanilla and Vicente Fernández and Juan Luis Guerra, you can hear the crack of Coke cans, the slap of children's bare feet as they race up and down the sidewalk, the swish of women's skirts as they sway to the music, the high trill of el grito as that music possesses men's souls.

And as the sun begins to set, no one goes back inside. No one hides because no one worries about being found. Tonight, El Martillo is a bad memory, Nacho's Tacos is the safe haven it's always been, and our neighborhood is the little piece of the American dream that so many of these people risked everything for.

As I take Xander's hand, I wonder if he feels it too. The smile on his face is hesitant, and I wonder if he's trying not to think about El Martillo the same way I am.

"How do we make this last?" I ask.

He looks down at me. "I don't know." Then he exhales. "Maybe...it's as simple as doing what we want. Doing it in spite of being afraid."

"What do you want to do?" I ask.

The smile he's been fighting finally anchors. "I want to eat a slice of your famous coconut cake. Maybe two."

I find his lips, clapping erupting behind us.

"Yeah, Xander," Lucas hollers, "I see you."

Solana yells, "Get it, Pen."

Xander's lips break into a smile but I hold on, not caring that we have an audience, despite their whistles and cheers.

Java fans himself before pretending to faint. He lands on Aarón Medrano, who actually cracks a smile for once.

Xander's laugh finally breaks our kiss. "Are you ready to be back in that kitchen again?"

I face the entrance I've walked through a thousand times, remembering what it felt like to walk out of it the day my father fired me. My entire world was shattered, the things that used to define me suddenly disintegrating.

That feeling of being lost tries to nudge its way in again.

You don't belong here.

You never did.

And that's the fear that's holding me back. That without my father here to tell me to go inside—that this is where I belong—reclaiming my place here means nothing.

I take a deep breath, shoving the voice down. Because maybe I don't need him to tell me that I belong. Maybe I can walk into that kitchen because *I* know it.

"I'm ready," I say, leading the way.

Back in the kitchen I take my familiar position between the grills and the plating station. I stare down at the scuff marks worn into the concrete, my shoes fitting perfectly within the outline. As I combine the heavy cream and coconut milk for my signature cake, I feel myself slipping into a skin I haven't been allowed to wear. But I don't need my father's permission.

Suddenly, the energy shifts like all the air's been sucked out. The flames on Angel's grill get a little hotter. Or maybe the flames are inside me, sensing who's in the doorway before I dredge up enough courage to turn and look. Everyone else already is, their necks craned as they watch him enter. Waiting for him to train his sights on his first target.

My father's stare beats down on the back of my neck, and I wait for him to make a scene. Even the restaurant patrons are leaning back in their chairs and watching us through the serving window.

Angel gives me a quick nod; a look of solidarity. *I've got you.*

I should know by now that he always has. I hold on to it, waiting....

I told you that you didn't belong here.

Now he's going to prove it.

My father takes a step closer and I brace for another fight.

But instead, he ties on an apron and joins Angel at the grill. He's between us, Angel charring a flank steak on one side, me stirring my cake batter on the other.

My heart pounds as I pour it into a pan, some spilling over the sides. I force down a deep breath, voices finally starting to sift in again as people call out orders and ask for supplies. Then I start on the filling, my eyes straight ahead as I try to guess what my father is thinking.

He dips a finger into the bowl in front of me, presses it to his lips.

I'm frozen.

"Needs more lemon."

My face flushes and he wraps an arm around me, pulling my forehead against his stubble. The shock of his touch almost knocks the air from my lungs. Suddenly, tears are streaming down my face, but I don't try to stop them.

And for once, it feels good. To be this transparent. To be forgiven.

In the midst of the reignited chatter, dozens of new tickets coming through, I notice Officer Solis make his way inside the restaurant. My father goes out to the dining room, greeting him with a handshake. When they head to my father's office, I follow, squeezing inside just before they shut the door.

The space is much too cramped for the three of us. Suddenly, the looks on their faces make it feel even smaller.

"What's going on?" I ask.

My father grips his chin. "It's about the robbery."

My stomach drops. "Is . . . *he* going to jail?"

Officer Solis searches my eyes, as if he's not sure how to say, "He didn't do it."

I find the wall, knees buckling just as my father leads me to a chair. He's kneeling, speaking in my ear. But I don't hear a sound. I don't feel him next to me. All I can feel are my hands, gripping my knees, shaking. Because it doesn't make sense. I could *feel* him there in the middle of all that chaos.

I could *feel* him. It was *him*.

I look up at Officer Solis. "Who...?"

"Someone in the building." He sighs, kneading his chin. "Couple of stoners a few doors down from you."

I remember the music, the smoke. I remember gripping the guy's hand. I thought I was putting on a show for Xander, for myself. I thought I was taking control, but all I did was invite the chaos in closer.

My father asks what I can't. "What does that mean for J. P.?"

Officer Solis grimaces. "We had to let him go."

I snap up. "What about what he did to Xander?"

Officer Solis just shakes his head. "It was on his property. Lawyers claimed self-defense." He sighs. "I'm sorry, Pen."

What he means to say is he's sorry that it wouldn't matter what El Martillo said. That it doesn't matter what El Martillo does. His money, his power, screams *I'm innocent*, and in this world, that is enough.

22

Xander

I SIT CROSS-LEGGED, REORGANIZING the shoebox that contains my father's entire existence and trying to decide what Detective Freeman might find useful. I stack the photographs, topping them with a Post-it of old phone numbers. I fold in the letters from the consulate, dates highlighted where they correspond with a timeline I drew on a sheet of notebook paper. I clip two postcards to it—the last times my father reached out to my abuelo before disappearing on him too. Both arrived before I did, one from Florida, another from New Mexico.

I barely hear the creak of the staircase before Abuelo reaches the landing. He stops, leaning a hand against the wall to catch his breath. I slide the box under my bed, jump to my feet.

"Abuelo, what are you doing up here? You know you shouldn't—"

He pushes past me, stepping into my room. I don't remember the last time he made it all the way up the stairs; he doesn't seem to either, his eyes flitting across the walls, just as bare as when I first arrived. They finally settle on the bed, and then he slumps down onto the mattress, coughing into his handkerchief.

I hand him the glass of water on my nightstand, but he pushes it away.

"Abuelo, are you okay?"

He stares, still red-faced, and then, without a word, he holds out Detective Freeman's business card.

My fingers twitch, wanting to reach for my pocket. It must have fallen out when I was helping Mr. Daly move that old record player.

I stare at the floor. "I was going to tell you."

He pinches his eyes shut. He knows I'm lying.

"Do you know how long I've lived in this house?"

I sit next to him on the bed, too afraid of looking him in the eye.

"Almost twenty years. I've been in this house on this street in this town for almost twenty years." He turns to look at me. "Your father knows how long I've lived in this house."

I know my father knows where I am. I know that he could have come for me if he wanted to. But he didn't. Abuelo wants me to remember that. That he didn't just abandon me that day he left me in Puebla. But that he's made that choice every single day he hasn't called or written or come to see me. It was *his* choice.

"What do you think you're going to find?" Abuelo asks.

The truth is, I don't know who or what I'll find. All I

know is the pathetic hope that sputters between my ribs. And I can't speak it aloud, I can't show him that after all these years, after everything I've been through, all of the pain and mistakes that should have made me into a man, I'm still a child. My father's child.

It's all I can say. "He's my father...."

Abuelo takes my hand, squeezes. "You're right." He lets go. "*He* is." He stands, testing his footing.

"Abuelo, let me—"

He pushes my hand away. "No, mijo...."

I trail him down the stairs, and I'm sick. Because I knew looking for my father would make my abuelo upset. I knew it would make him think I was weak.

But I didn't know that it would break his heart.

I didn't know that watching it happen would break mine too.

All because of this hole inside me.

One my abuelo has been trying to fill since he took me in. But I wouldn't let him. I couldn't. Because I was still hoping...Because I was delusional. That's what Abuelo thinks. Maybe that's what I am.

Maybe that was okay when I didn't think I had anything to lose, but what if I do?

Abuelo doesn't let me help him the rest of the way down the stairs, even when he has to stop to catch his breath. He doesn't let me pour him some more water when the coughing starts up again. He doesn't touch the lunch I make him. He doesn't say a word as I tell him goodbye and head to the car.

I sit in the driver's seat, clutching the steering wheel, trying not to list the things I've already lost—my mother, my father, my home. And yet, the list of what's at risk still seems longer—if I find my father and make my abuelo hate me, if I don't....

I finally back out of the driveway, still not sure what I'm supposed to do. But I need to trade the sight of him for a brokenness I can actually fix.

When I pull up to Pen's apartment complex, she's sitting in her car, clutching the steering wheel the same way I was. For a while I just watch the way her brow furrows as she stares up at the window of her apartment.

No one tells you that when you become the victim of a crime, you're the one responsible for cleaning up the mess. But at least Pen isn't trying to do this alone.

I tap on her window and she cracks the door.

"Hey." I back up, letting her out.

"Hey."

This time we both look up. In the daylight it doesn't look so menacing, but then Pen inhales, breath hitching.

I reach for her. "Are you okay?"

"I...don't know." She shakes free from whatever had her gripped. "Just ready to get it over with, I guess."

"It's only been a couple of days. Are you sure—?"

She nods. "I need to do this."

They're the same words I said to Officer Solis. If anyone understands Pen's need to combat the helplessness she feels, it's me. Maybe that's why I'm here instead of Angel or even Pen's father. Or maybe she didn't tell them she was coming.

When we reach the elevator, I finally ask, "Do your parents know you're here?"

She sighs, tucking a loose strand of hair back into her

ponytail. "It was...vaguely discussed. Officer Solis called to let us know it was clear for me to come and clean up." The doors ding open. "They don't know that I'm actually coming back for good."

I stop. "What do you mean you're coming back?"

"It wasn't him." She shrugs, strangely indifferent. "It was a couple of stoners angry that I busted their balls."

"That doesn't mean they weren't dangerous."

"I know." We reach the door. "But according to Officer Solis, they did cry like babies while being cuffed."

I want to indulge in her attempt at humor, but I can't. I don't want Pen staying in this apartment alone no matter who ransacked it. Because even if El Martillo's involvement wasn't real, my fear sure as hell was. She wavers and I can see that hers is still intact too.

"Pen..."

She stares at the door handle, at her warped reflection within the brass. Before I can pull her away, before I can lead her downstairs and back to our cars, she clenches her jaw and twists it open. Then she steps inside, doing the thing that scares her, checking off another invisible adversary in her quest to being unbreakable.

But when her hand grazes the wall, light buzzing on above the kitchen sink, the floor is mostly bare, shadows disappearing behind neatly stacked packing boxes instead of debris.

Pen takes a step toward the center of the room, her body tensed and waiting for another ambush.

There's a light knock, the door still cracked. An old woman peeks inside, spotting Pen.

"Mrs. Damas?"

The old woman smiles. "I didn't realize you'd be back so soon. I was hoping..."

"Did you do this?"

She takes Pen's hand. "We saved what we could. Anything broken is still in those boxes to the left. I didn't want to risk throwing out something important. I just...wanted it to look more like home when you finally came back."

Pen doesn't speak. She stares at the boxes, letting Mrs. Damas pull her into a hug.

"Thank you," Pen finally says.

"You're welcome, dear." Mrs. Damas leads her to the pantry, unbroken herb bottles and canisters full of baking ingredients stacked neatly on the shelves. "The property manager hired someone to clean up the mess in the kitchen. He was worried about pests." She opens the fridge next. It's stocked full of food. "I told everyone to wait, that all of this would go to waste before you'd be back, but they couldn't help themselves."

"The other tenants?" Pen marvels at the fresh ingredients.

"Your neighbors, Pen." Mrs. Damas's eyes crinkle. "It breaks my heart that you haven't had the best experience with some of the people on this floor, but we're more of a family than you know."

For a long time Pen is quiet, looking from the shelves to the boxes to her freshly made bed. Then she stares at the walls, maybe trying to see the people on the other side, to reconcile them with the careful hands that have rescued her from having to relive that night all over again.

"Will they know…?" Pen meets Mrs. Damas's eyes. "That I'm grateful. I really am."

Mrs. Damas pats Pen's hand again. "When you're ready, you can tell them." She heads for the door, squeezing my arm. "Now, I'll leave you two to reorganize things." She winks at Pen. "Let me know if you get hungry."

When the door falls closed, Pen's still staring at the boxes.

"You don't have to go through them if you're not ready," I remind her.

She leans against the counter. "What if there's no such thing?"

"What do you mean?"

She looks down. "What if there's no such thing as being ready? What if the only difference between being ready and not being ready is a decision?" She looks up, gaze pinned to the boxes like they're just another adversary. "A decision I make."

"Is that why you're making yourself stay here tonight?"

Pen said her constant need to do the *scary thing* isn't a game, but she's still keeping score. And if coming here today, cleaning up her apartment and then forcing herself to sleep in what was just twenty-four hours earlier a designated crime scene is worth enough points to risk her unraveling, then that must mean she's not playing alone. To Pen, her adversary is real, and even though there might not be a clear way to win, in Pen's mind there's a dangerous way to lose, and it's a possibility every second she's not doing something to make herself feel powerful.

"I thought I wanted to be home." Pen huffs. "Even my

mom said something about me coming back to live with them. But I already know what'll happen if I do. We'll all fall back into the same routine, and it will feel good for a while. Safe. Familiar. But then six months will go by, or maybe another year, and it'll be time to rip the Band-Aid off again."

"What Band-Aid?"

"The Band-Aid that is my adolescence." Pen gestures around the room. "That's what this whole thing was supposed to be about. Not just a punishment, but a chance to become an adult. Because I made adult decisions like not going to school and then lying about it." She scratches at a chip in the countertop. "And even though I regret hurting them, I don't want to stop being able to make those decisions."

"Because you're ready...or because it scares you?"

Pen meets my eyes. "Both."

She finally makes her way over to the boxes, kneeling in front of the broken things first. She starts sifting through the box and we work in tandem, Pen taking things out slowly, cradling them in the palm of her hand before handing them to me to toss into a trash bag or work into the living sculpture on her rumpled bed.

Most of these things I've touched before, the bookshelf of Pen's childhood memories I assembled now in pieces. But she doesn't linger too long on what's been broken. Instead, she empties one box after another until all that's left to do is put it back together.

By the time we finally finish, the sun is starting to set, the curtainless windows letting in the last beats of light. They're pressed to the floor, ethereal thumbprints in bursts of blue and pink.

Pen collapses on her bed, watching the light shrink. There's nowhere for me to sit but right next to her, and suddenly her proximity is a small flame.

A few hours ago, we were standing in a concrete box, desperately trying to rewind Pen's memories of that night until we were standing in her bedroom again. Now we are. We're sitting in Pen's apartment on her bed, and it's the most awkward I've felt around her since the night we first met.

My fingers stretch, wanting to reach for her. She watches them too, but I don't know if she's willing them to stay still or if she wants me to come closer.

She moves first, fingers lacing with mine. "Thank you for coming with me."

I squeeze, letting my index finger rest against the underside of her wrist. "Anytime."

She draws tiny circles against my skin until I'm buzzing. I tighten my grip on her and she sighs.

She sits up and I hold my breath.

Her cheeks flush and then she says, "I'm...starving."

My cheeks burn too. I smile. "I definitely worked up an appetite."

She lets go of me and makes her way to the fridge. "Should we see what's edible in here?" She leans down, examining the shelves. After a moment she starts mumbling to herself. "Two and then...There might be...Got that, good...A little...Oh yes, perfect."

She plops the ingredients down on the counter and shuffles over to the pantry to continue her monologue. Then she ties on an apron before dumping some dry ingredients into a bowl without measuring.

"What's that?" I ask, making my way over.

She lifts a finger. "This is a secret recipe, which means no questions."

She adds some eggs to the bowl before leading my hand to the spoon. I stir, something tart and sweet creeping into my lungs. Pen zests an orange and chops some dark chocolate and almonds. Then she mixes up something else warm and gooey in another bowl. She dips her finger in, pulls it out slow, tasting it.

She takes back the batter I'm stirring, some sugar still on her lips, and then she adds the orange and chocolate chunks. She reaches for a cupcake tin on the bottom shelf, filling each one halfway before sprinkling brown sugar over the tops. They go in the oven and then she scrapes some fallen batter off the bowl, licking it from her finger before finishing the icing.

"Open."

She leads the spatula to my tongue, her skin smelling like citrus, and then I don't think. I take the spatula out of her hand and drop it back into the bowl, taking her finger in my mouth instead. It's sweet like a warm cup of coffee. The dark chocolate hits me next, making my cheeks ache, and then the tartness of the orange peel. She tastes like morning.

Pen watches my mouth, barely breathing, and then the bowl topples to the floor. I'm pinned between Pen and the counter. Our mouths are open, foreheads pressed hard against each other. Her eyes urge me on, but my own are full of questions—where to put my hands and my mouth.

She presses her lips to mine and it doesn't feel like it did the first time, fervent and afraid, this temporary cosmic bang muffled by alcohol. This time we're right in the middle of it, of the flames and the heat and the power. It feels deliberate and important, and I wonder if she can hear the *tick tick tick* inside me, her closeness winding me like a clock.

I grip her in handfuls, my bones aching like they're reaching for her too. Her tongue forces its way into my mouth, and somehow we make it to the bed. She tugs at the apron strings until they're tangled around her knee. She laughs, leading my fingertips to the bare skin beneath her shirt. She finally gets the apron undone, the button on her jeans unfastened next.

The timer buzzes above the oven, loud and shrill.

Pen braces herself against my arms. She pulls back, both of us panting and slightly dazed. I wait for her to ignite again, but that fierce look in her eyes that made my knees shake has disappeared. She rushes to the oven, steam rises from the cupcake tin as she pulls it out.

I retrace my steps, every touch, trying to figure out where it went wrong. But then Pen carries one of the cupcakes over to me.

I take a bite, mouth watering.

"Do you like it?" she asks.

The flavors spark on my tastebuds, each bite revealing a new layer that takes me by surprise. I take another one and then it hits me. Long after I've swallowed, the taste grazing the tip of my tongue. Heat.

"Well?" she presses.

"Where's the spice coming from?"

Pen's mouth twists, the tiniest bit wicked. "Secret ingredient. Ghost pepper flakes."

"It's unbelievable. I'm serious, it's the best thing I've ever eaten."

She glances at the floor, the mess that we made. "Even without the icing?"

"Even if it was dipped in toilet water first and served in a dirty diaper."

She laughs. "So, it's good, then." Her eyes brighten. "You think I'm good."

"No." I brush some brown sugar from her cheek. "I think you're amazing."

After dessert, Pen lets me commandeer the kitchen and make us dinner. I use the leftover chocolate to make mole poblano, Pen placing a half-broken candle between our plates as we use one of the empty boxes as a dining table again. The candle sits tilted in the gap between the cardboard flaps.

"I'm not sure that's safe."

"It's good ambience." Pen takes the first bite, lips puckered as she closes her eyes. "This is... What is this?"

"Mole poblano. My mom used to make it when I was a kid."

She shakes her head, fighting with whether to laugh or hold the flavors in her mouth. She takes another bite, nodding as if she's confirming it wasn't some kind of fluke. "I know what *this* is," she finally says. "But I meant you. What *are* you? I didn't know you could cook like this."

I fiddle with my fork. "Well, I do work in a restaurant."

She rolls her eyes. "No way you learned how to cook like this by plating six hours a day." She takes another bite, savoring it. "Is this why you wanted the job?"

"This, as in, did I want to cook?" I shrug. "Well, yeah. I like cooking."

She points her fork at me. "Mm-mm, you love it. I can taste it."

I look down again, not letting the smile make it past my lips. "Well, coming from you, that's a pretty big compliment."

She sits up, her chin on her knee. "Come on, I'm not some kind of prodigy. I just..."

"What?" I narrow my eyes at her. "Like to cook?"

She hugs her knee closer. "I love it."

"I can taste it." I hesitate before saying, "I could taste it before we even met."

Her brow furrows. "What do you mean?"

"I've eaten at Nacho's plenty of times, but that night we helped you move in and you cooked dinner for everyone, I finally realized what it was that kept me coming back, what keeps the entire neighborhood entranced and arguing over whether Nacho's enchiladas are better than their abuela's or if his famous coconut cake can cure a broken heart."

"Nacho's has been around a long time. People like a little magic, and the myths are good for business."

"But the magic is you." I lean closer. "People don't like the food because of the myths. They love it because of you." I reach for the loose strand of hair that keeps escaping her ponytail. "So do I."

She crawls over, hands against my shoulders, and when she looks into my eyes, I realize she's measuring the sincerity in them.

I don't hold back. "I think I'm in love with you, Pen."

She closes the space between us, her lips resting against mine. Careful this time. We hold each other, breathing together until my back is pressed to the floor, until exhaustion has Pen tucked into the crook of my arm, her head against my chest.

She looks up at me. "I love you for saying that." She kisses me on the cheek. "I love you."

I brush the flyaways from her face. "Do you believe me?"

"Yes."

"About the restaurant..."

She hesitates, drawing circles on my skin again. But then she says, "Yes."

Eventually, we make it back the bed, too stuffed and tired to take off our clothes. We don't need to. We've shown each other more of ourselves than we've revealed to anyone else, and for me that's enough. To know that I can let her see me, that she's willing to let me do the same, it's enough.

⸻

When I wake up, Pen is curled against my arm. Her eyes ease open and that's when I register the door grinding against the chain, the sound what had actually woken me.

"Penelope!"

Ignacio Prado stands on the other side, trying to ram his way through.

Pen snaps up, her voice a whisper. "Shit."

I slide to the floor wedging myself as far underneath the bed as possible. Pen jumps to her feet, wrenching the door open before her father can bust it down.

He charges inside. "Why aren't you at home?"

I watch her feet as she backpedals, still drowsy.

"Pen, I said why aren't you at home?"

She stops. "I...am home."

"You know what I mean. Why aren't you at home with your mother and Lola and Hugo?"

I can't see her face, but I can see her hands clenched around the hem of her shirt.

She lets go, exhales. "This is where I live, Dad."

"Are you trying to prove a point?"

"No, I'm—"

"Were you trying to hurt your mother? Because that's what happened when she woke up and you were gone."

He won't admit that he's just as hurt, but I know Pen must hear it in his voice.

"I wasn't trying to hurt anyone." Her hands are fists again. "I was *never* trying to hurt anyone. Why can't you just believe me?"

The bed creaks, mattress sinking as her father sits. He's quiet, and I wonder if he's realized what a mistake it was to fire Pen; if he's blaming himself for the distance, still unsure how to build a bridge safe enough for either of them to cross. But someone has to take that first step.

Pen slumps down next to her father. They sit in silence for a long time, Pen's toes a light pitter-patter against the floor.

"I'm sorry." She exhales. "I don't know what else to say, how else to show that...I'm so sorry."

"Is that why you're here?" her father asks. "Because you think you're still being punished?"

"I'm here because it was the right decision. You and Mom made the right decision."

I strain to hear them reach for each other, but then I realize that the other night at the restaurant was the first time I ever saw them embrace. When he first walked into the kitchen, every single employee held their breath, waiting for him to throw her out again. But he didn't.

"Angel said you had another job somewhere else."

"El Pequeño Toro."

He's thinking, quiet again for too long. Then he says, "Keep it."

She jumps to her feet. "But...what about—?"

"Pen..."

"The other night...What was that about if not—?"

"Penelope, we are not discussing this right now."

"But you...You made me think..."

She can't even get the words out. I wonder if she's thinking about the conversation we had last night, about how she's the heart of that place, the magic of her food doing just as much for the neighborhood as her father's good deeds. She deserves to fight for her place there, but he won't even let her do that.

Her father stands. "When it comes to the restaurant, I still need more time."

"How much time? What does that even mean?"

"It means it's my decision."

She turns her back on him, her voice unsteady. "You know what it means to me. You know how much this hurts."

But he doesn't. How could he? Pen's depression is

practically invisible, her ability to disguise the worst of it a necessity of living in her father's house. He's made her stone, and even now he can barely see the cracks. Or maybe he doesn't want to.

"And as long as you feel that strongly about it, you're not stepping foot back in that kitchen."

"Because I love it?" Pen snaps. "Or because you hate it?"

"Trust me, Pen." His voice is low and full of regret. "After almost twenty years...After what I've been through, you would too."

"Is that what you think you're protecting me from? Your life?" Her voice shakes. "What about *my* life?"

He reaches the door. "Go live it."

When it falls closed and I hear the latch fasten, I pull myself out from under the bed.

Pen stares at the floor. "That's it, isn't it? If the other night didn't change his mind...nothing will."

I pull her against my chest, trying to quell what I can feel are sobs. But she won't let them reach the surface.

"He's wrong," I say. "One day he'll see it."

"And what if he doesn't?"

"He'll regret it."

Her voice comes out cold, numb. "We both will."

My cell phone screams from the kitchen counter. I let it ring to voice mail. A few seconds later they call again.

Pen wipes her eyes. "It's probably work."

I flip through Angel's text messages. "I'm sorry."

"Lunch rush," she murmurs. "It's okay."

"I'm telling him I can't come in."

She halts my typing. "Don't. I'll be fine."

"But I'd rather stay here with you."

"And I'd rather not have both of us get fired from my father's restaurant." A faint smile cuts into her cheeks. It quickly disappears as she says, "Besides, I have to go to work in a couple of hours, anyway."

I examine her more closely, afraid of leaving her alone. "Is this you doing the scary thing?"

She looks down, tugging on the hem of my shirt. "I've been doing the scary thing." She meets my eyes again. "And I can keep doing it."

"But not alone. Not anymore."

She presses her forehead to mine. "Thank you." And then she pushes me out the door.

"Can I see you later?"

I won't be able to leave without knowing when I'll see her again. As if leaving without making plans will open the world up to all kinds of disasters, my entire life unraveling unless it's tethered to some moment with her in the future.

"I get off late tonight," she says. "But tomorrow I'm free around seven."

"Tomorrow, then," I say.

"Tomorrow."

She kisses me and I hang onto it for too long.

"You're gonna be late," she reminds me in a whisper.

I press my face to her neck.

"I'll see you tomorrow."

23

Pen

THE CITRUS PEEL I'M grating revives the memory of Xander's lips, the heat starting in my taste buds before traveling, inch by inch.

And then he said, *I love you.*

I wasn't sure if I was ready—for what I was feeling and what I wasn't. I was afraid of the fact that I wasn't afraid of him. Not even a little bit.

But what if I was wrong? What if I was just grasping for something permanent because everything else in my life felt like such a mess? What if my body and my heart and that voice in the back of my mind were just lying to me? What if that was all they'd ever done?

I've lied to the people I love before, I've lied to myself, but every word I say around Xander doesn't feel like one. The words he says don't feel like lies either.

. . . the magic is you.

You.

I stare down into my pancake mix, trying to sense something supernatural. Lemon zest, blueberries, vanilla extract, cinnamon. Ingredients placed in my pantry by strangers, random and not rescuing anyone. I don't feel like magic, and if there were something special about my food, my father wouldn't still be keeping me from the restaurant. Whatever spell I've cast over Xander hasn't worked on him. Because there isn't one.

Or maybe that's just another lie. One I'm telling myself, one my father believes out of fear that I'll turn out just like him. That I'll be happy about it.

I thought when we were working side by side the other night that he finally understood how my food makes me feel. But now I know that none of that matters. Not enough to change his mind.

But I can't change mine either, and even though I'm not sure if Xander's right, if there's magic in what I make, I know there's magic in the way it makes me feel. That's how I'm going to survive this, by creating each day from scratch. Starting with this one.

I pour the first pancake into the center of the pan, the sizzle a welcome sound. The last time I made pancakes was also the last normal morning before my lie ripped everything apart at the seams. I'd been so anxious, spoon furiously beating the side of the bowl while Hugo looked on, both of us completely oblivious to the fact that everything was about to change.

After I down an entire stack, I peer through the peephole, checking that the hallway's empty before easing out the door. I graze each key on my chain, my hand shaking as I slip the right one into the lock. It sticks and I take a deep breath, sliding it in straight. Footsteps rush past me and I tense.

The two kids I dragged down this very hallway for obnoxiously knocking on my door are sword fighting with foil-covered cardboard. They stop when they see me, swords falling at their sides. I expect them to run and hide but instead they stare, the younger one taking a tentative step closer.

He points to a piece of foil pinned to his chest. "This is my hall monitor badge. My mom made it for me."

I lean closer, HALL written in marker and spelled with one *l*. "I like it."

He looks down, cheeks red. "Thanks."

"We'll watch your apartment while you're gone," the older one says. "If you want..."

There's a hard knot in the back of my throat. "Wait here."

I head back inside my apartment, pulling some leftover cupcakes from the fridge. The two boys are waiting a few inches from the door when I step back out.

"For your services." I hand them the cupcakes, and they immediately peel back the foil. "You two shouldn't be working for free."

As I head toward the elevator, their cheeks are already stuffed. The doors ding open and they run off, swords raised. They're arguing over who gets the last cupcake, the doors closing just as the loser is beheaded, the winner swallowing his spoils.

When I arrive at El Pequeño Toro, not a single trace of sugar left on my tongue, I'm immediately afflicted by the same permanent scowl that every other employee has mastered in an attempt to scare away customers.

At first, it's just a twitch, a weight tugging at my mouth. Then I finally let it sink there. Honestly, it doesn't matter whether I smile or frown or bare my teeth. The little felt mustache, which has now become a mandatory part of my uniform when I'm running the drive-through, will hide any emotions, or lack thereof, that I choose to express.

The emotion I'm feeling at the end of my shift is a mix between impatience and indifference until Josie comes over to inform me that David had a family emergency and she needs me to cover his shift too.

For the next four hours I push buttons and count change and shove bags into people's hands without so much as blinking. Just as I'm on the verge of collapse, Claudia clocks in behind me.

I don't dare attempt small talk, but over my shoulder I can sense her staring.

She comes up beside me, refilling the condiments by the drive-through window. "I thought your shift ended a couple of hours ago."

"I'm covering for David. He had a 'family' emergency."

She refills the napkins, finding other things to organize or clean up in my work area. I don't know why she's hovering and I don't really care to ask.

"I didn't think you'd come in today," she says.

"I'm on the schedule." I push food into a sedan, closing the window before they can ask for more hot sauce.

Claudia stops, the disdain that's usually on her face replaced by something softer, something that makes both of us uncomfortable. "I heard about what happened," she finally says.

The memory flashes across my face, just for a second. I pass another order through the window before quickly keying in the next one.

"Pen, are you okay?"

"I'm fine." It's what I'm supposed to say, and just like everything else, if I pretend hard enough, maybe eventually it'll be true.

But today, the first day after returning to my apartment, a felt mustache stuck to the sweat above my lip, my skin and hair covered in grease, it's not. And Claudia knows it.

"You shouldn't be here."

I want to tell her that it's either here or alone in my apartment again. Alone with the doubt, with that little loud voice that feeds on it. But I don't trust her. I almost tell her that too.

"My parents used to own the gas station on Real Street. They needed money to help send my sister to college, and El Martillo offered them a deal that was too good to pass up." She leans against the counter, the admission making her shrink. "When they couldn't pay it back, he took everything. The gas station. Our house. The six of us had to move into a two-bedroom apartment."

"I'm so—"

She lifts a hand, probably not trusting me either. But then, why is she telling me this?

"I put up with this shithole so I can help them pay bills, but every time I'm working a shift from hell I can't help but picture his face. And I'm reminded that this place and every cancer-serving dump like it is a weapon too. A trap set to keep us from venturing outside our neighborhood, to keep us from thinking for even a second that we can."

"Is that what you want?" I ask.

"Don't you?"

The escape I yearn for isn't outside our neighborhood. It isn't even beyond Monte Vista Boulevard. It's in my own head, El Pequeño Toro just a manifestation of the fears I wrestle with every single day. But this place, those fears—they don't define me. They shouldn't define Claudia either.

"You could do it, you know. . . ."

Claudia's eyes soften but she doesn't entertain the thought. "Not anytime soon." She shakes her head. "Go home, Pen. I'll make sure you stay clocked in until the end of your shift." Then she takes my headset, gentler than the last time she told me to leave.

After an entire day of scowling, the smile feels foreign on my lips. I head back to the lockers, removing my mustache before scraping off a layer of grease with a few paper towels.

I find a pen in Josie's cubby, scribble the number to Nacho's on the back of Claudia's hand. "My father's restaurant. You should ask for an interview."

She stares down at the ink. "Are they hiring?"

"Always."

"Then . . . why don't you go back?" she asks, not condescending, just curious.

I head for the door. "I will."

It's the opposite of what I was feeling this morning—uncertain, defeated—but the words come out before my fears can stop them. Maybe today *is* a day for pretending, for unfiltered hope and second chances. Even if it's not my father giving me one, maybe I can give one to myself.

———

The radio is a soft buzz in the background when Mrs. Damas opens the door.

"I smelled you baking." I raise a basket of ingredients. "I thought you could use some help."

"One day you better start charging me for your services," Mrs. Damas says on the way to the kitchen.

"If only..."

There are cupcakes cooling on the counter, a Bundt cake halfway piped with cream cheese frosting, and some chocolate melting on the stovetop. It smells like heaven.

"I'm serious," Mrs. Damas says. "While it's admirable that you prefer to use your skills helping little old ladies bake for charity, I think you're missing out on a lucrative business opportunity."

I tie on an apron. "I'm not exactly in a position to open my own bakery. I make eight dollars an hour. To save up for something like that would take..." I pause, attempting the calculations for half a second before I realize I'd need to work "about a million hours."

Mrs. Damas tsks. "What ever happened to taking risks?"

"I do take risks. Every day that I walk into the black hole that is El Pequeño Toro."

"Then don't."

Mrs. Damas pops out each cupcake while I smear icing over the tops.

"Don't what?"

"Don't walk into that black hole ever again."

My brow furrows, the spoon slipping from my fingers. People from my neighborhood don't take risks. We have dreams, sure. But the numerous threats involved in their pursuit keeps us from pining for things beyond our reach. We don't shoot for the stars or even the moon. Instead, we pray for roots. Something to tie us down, to ensure that the places and the people we love are never taken away from us.

As much as I hate working at El Pequeño Toro, the thought of quitting my job molds a pit in my stomach. "I can't just quit. I have to pay rent."

She turns to me, serious. "What is your dream, Pen? The thing that keeps you up at night."

I place the cupcakes in a Tupperware container.

"I know it's on the tip of your tongue."

It is, the thought warming my cheeks the longer I refuse to speak it aloud.

"What's the harm in telling the truth?"

The harm is in the hope. But what's worse is feeling it and trying to pretend like you don't.

"I want to bake," I finally say. "I want to own my own bakery right in the center of the neighborhood. I want to feed the people I care about. I want to help them the way my father does."

"Have you ever told him that?"

I shake my head.

"Why not?"

"He'd tell me not to do it."

"And would you listen?"

I flick my ponytail over my shoulder. "I don't know. I listened to my parents when they told me to go to school. But that didn't last long. I guess I'm just as stubborn as they are. But what do I really know about owning my own bakery? What do I know about anything at all?"

"Make me something."

I take a step back. "Now?"

She nods. "Make me something you'd sell at your bakery."

"And what?" I grimace. "You'll tell me if it's good enough to actually do it?"

"I already know it'll be good enough. We're doing this to convince you."

I stare at the ingredients for a long time, pulling things forward, changing my mind and swapping them out. I think back to the "test" I was given at Maureen's bakery, Tiers of Joy. She wanted French, complex. Something to show my skill. But that's not why I bake.

As I mentally scroll through the desserts on Nacho's Tacos' menu, nothing is a puzzle, and when I think about what I'd serve in my own bakery, there's only one thing that matters—how does it make me feel? That's why I bake—to feel in one bite all of the things I temper when I'm trying to stay in control; to remember who I am when it feels like that control is slipping from my grasp.

I reach for the coconut flakes and condensed milk—just

two ingredients—deciding that if I'm going to make Mrs. Damas something from my dream menu, it's going to be just as simple as my reason for cooking in the first place.

I mix the coconut and condensed milk in a bowl, and then I spread it out over the bottom of a baking sheet. I pop it in the oven, leaving the light on so I can see when the edges have started to brown.

We're boxing up the last of the baked goods for the women at Casa Marianella when the timer sounds for my cocada. I pull it out, letting it cool.

"It looks lovely." Mrs. Damas leans closer, breathing in the roasted coconut. "And your signature flavor."

I inhale too, using a butter knife to cut the bark into jagged pieces. She cracks one in half, examining where the flakes have settled within the condensed milk. Then she takes a bite, holding it in her mouth until it ignites a smile.

"It's delicious."

I rest a piece on my tongue, sugar dissolving like tiny sparks, the coconut rising like sweet smoke to the back of my throat. I don't realize my eyes are closed until Mrs. Damas speaks again.

"That feeling, Pen, is passion." She takes my hand. "And the thing about passion is that it's born the second you are. You love baking not just because it's in your blood, but because it's in your soul."

I think back to the doubts I was wrestling with this morning. I can believe Mrs. Damas when she tells me that cooking is in my blood. I can even believe Xander when he tells me there's magic in the things I make. But I don't know if I can believe that it all means something. That it matters.

"It might be my passion. . . ." I face Mrs. Damas. "But is that enough?"

She smiles, surprised, saddened. "Of course it's enough. You are *more* than enough."

I think about how good it felt to walk out of El Pequeño Toro earlier, how it wasn't just Claudia who gave me permission to leave, but myself. Maybe because I wanted a second chance. Because I deserve one. But it's not enough to want something, I actually have to let myself do something about it. That means not wasting any more time being stuck in this self-doubt that is a leech and a liar and the most dangerous kind of amnesia. That means facing my fears head-on, not because doing the scary thing is how I survive, but because, this time, the scary thing is the right thing.

Mrs. Damas and Xander are right. I don't belong at El Pequeño Toro. Maybe I don't belong in my father's restaurant anymore. But my food is fucking magic and I won't stop making it.

24

Xander

CHLOE'S ROLLING SILVERWARE AT the hostess stand when I walk inside the restaurant. "I'd wipe that smile off before Angel sees."

My face is hot. "What smile?"

"The one Pen's kisses have permanently plastered to your face."

"I don't know what you're talking about."

Someone chuckles.

I turn and see Lucas.

"Oh no, the boss is not gonna like this." I'm not amused, and he pats me on the back. "Don't worry, your secret's safe with me."

I look to Chloe next.

She raises her hands. "My lips are sealed."

"But seriously, though." Lucas leads me back to the kitchen, hand covering his mouth. "If anyone else around here finds out, you're toast. There's nothing these losers love more than some good chisme. And you sleeping with the boss's daughter—"

"NO."

Andrea and Mari slide around the corner, Mari with her hand over her mouth while Andrea's hands are pressed to her cheeks in shock. They look like two of those wise monkeys from that Japanese proverb.

Chelo steps around the corner next, eyes bulging. "Who's sleeping with Pen?"

Andrea shakes her head, hands still cupping her cheeks. "Xander—"

"I'm not sleeping with Pen," I snap.

My voice ricochets, and every utensil stops moving at once—the Medrano brothers pause midchop, soapsuds dripping down Struggles's forearms as he clutches a plate, fish and chicken starting to burn as the starters stop and stare. Everyone except Angel. He's got his headphones in, tongs drumming against his grill, totally oblivious.

Lucas presses a finger to his lips, motioning for everyone to keep quiet, before dragging that same finger across his throat. Without a word, everyone gets back to work. The fact that they're not using it to humiliate me, or worse, get me fired, must mean my initiation phase is finally over. I'm relieved.

"We still on in five?" Miguel waves over at Lucas.

Lucas nods. "You get the stuff."

Miguel heads back to the storage room.

"What stuff?" I ask.

Lucas rubs his hands together. "We found the perfect

way to celebrate the reopening of Nacho's. Speaking of which…" He snatches one of the finished tickets off the spike before maneuvering over to where Solana is checking her cell phone.

He brushes past her—"sorry"—pressing the sticky side on the back of her shirt. His face scrunches as he tries to stuff down a laugh.

I eye him. "What are you doing?"

Solana heads back out to the dining room, passing Andrea on her way to the bar. I didn't notice before that Andrea has three tickets stuck to the back of her shirt. Java pops up from behind the bar and he has six.

"Just a good old-fashioned game of pin the ticket on the waiter." Lucas crosses his arms, beaming with pride. "It's all part of the opening ceremonies."

"Opening ceremonies for what?"

Miguel lugs out two giant jugs of pickled jalapeño juice.

Lucas wiggles his eyebrows. "Prank Wars." He waves Angel over.

"All right, here's the deal," Angel says. "Winner gets to clock out early and still gets a cut of the tip share from the rest of the night."

"Rules," Lucas adds. "You have to finish the entire jug and keep it down for at least ten minutes."

"Did someone say something about clocking out early?" Andrea suddenly reappears.

Mari's right behind her.

"Come on, you two can't possibly clean out this entire jug." Miguel motions to their stomachs. "Where the hell are you gonna put it?"

Andrea glares at him. "Watch us."

"Well, I guess now we're working in teams." Lucas looks around the room. "Who wants to step up and be Miguel's partner?"

Everyone turns to look at Aarón, expecting him to volunteer. When he notices us looking, he puts his headphones in and gets back to chopping.

Struggles comes around the corner. "I'll play. Chokehold and Super Shocker have a match tonight. I never get to catch the livestream."

Miguel scans the room, completely ignoring Struggles.

"Come on, man," Struggles pleads. "I won't let you down."

"Fine." Miguel spins the top off the first jug. "But you better not fucking puke on me."

Andrea and Mari lean over their jug while Miguel and Struggles crouch over theirs like animals.

I gag at the sound of those first few gulps, covering my nose. "Whose sick idea was this? It's not even a prank."

Lucas lowers his voice. "It *is* a prank if the contestants have no idea that they weren't even on the schedule today."

I pause. "So...they're competing to go home early on a day they weren't actually supposed to work?" I shake my head, still not seeing the genius in all this. "Are they getting paid?"

"Everyone but Miguel." Lucas snorts. "Prank's on him, dude. Chloe's idea. Apparently, he harassed Pen at work and now Chloe won't rest until she's imagined a million ways to torture him."

I remember Pen mentioned something about dragging

him through the order window. I look on with a new sense of appreciation. Ironically, Miguel is the one struggling the most, his face already green and half of each sip finding its way onto the floor.

"Hell no." Angel kicks a rag over the mess. "You spill and you forfeit."

I look over at Andrea and Mari, still chugging, both stone-faced.

Lucas shakes his head, awestruck. "Holy hell..."

Miguel shoves Struggles. "Fucking keep drinking, man."

Struggles pushes him back. "Dude, you do it!"

Angel holds his nose. "I can't watch any more of this."

Miguel starts gagging and I have to look away too. The girls near the finish line, Struggles huffing and puffing as he tries to keep up. That's when Miguel topples over, clutching his stomach. The girls finish off their jug, and I can practically hear the pickled jalapeño juice sloshing around inside them. Struggles falls back, defeated, and then he hurls all over himself.

Andrea leans over him, holding her nose. "Your shift ends in half an hour, dumbass."

Mari shakes her head. "And it'll probably take you that long to clean this up."

The girls high-five, and then they wobble like two pregnant women toward the exit.

Before Struggles can lift himself out of the mess, Mr. Prado walks in, almost stepping in it. He spots Angel, motions with a finger for him to follow him into his office. The door closes.

We all hold our breath, partly because of the smell but

mostly because we're trying to hear what kind of punishment is in store. A few minutes later, Angel steps out again with a stack of paychecks. But instead of handing them out, he hands them to me.

"I need you to take care of passing these out tonight. Do you think you can handle that?"

"Me?"

He leans closer, shielding his voice. "My dad is fucking pissed, and I'm going home. He asked me to pick someone else to take care of it."

Angel ducks out the back door, no one saying a word. While Struggles and Miguel finish cleaning up their mess, I make the rounds, passing out paychecks. I don't open mine until my shift is over and I'm sitting in my car.

I rip open the envelope and find a check for $564. Enough for Detective Freeman's fee, to possibly find my father; enough to make my abuelo hate me in the process.

When I pull into the driveway, Abuelo is sitting on the porch playing cards with Mr. Daly.

"How's the job treating you, Xander?" Mr. Daly chews on a cigar.

"It's good, thanks."

A few days ago I would have pulled up a chair and played a few hands with them. But right now I can't manage more than a few words.

Mr. Daly notices the tension, looking from me to my abuelo in this exaggerated *what the hell is wrong with you two* kind of way. Neither of us speaks and Mr. Daly huffs, slamming his cards down.

"Straight flush."

He knows not to try to force my abuelo to talk. The last thing he needs is to end up on his bad side too. Then he'd have no one to play cards with.

The sun inches lower, glinting off something big and white in Mr. Daly's backyard.

"What is that?" I ask.

Abuelo groans. "More junk."

Mr. Daly jabs a finger. "That there is not junk." He heaves himself out of his seat, smiling from ear to ear. "Follow me."

We pass through the side gate, the truck coming into view. It's tall and wide, like a box truck only bigger.

"You starting a moving business?"

"Hey, that's a good idea," he says. "But, actually, I was thinking of sprucing it up, maybe using it for traveling."

I follow him around the other side, spotting the faded logo of a barbecue restaurant.

Mr. Daly taps the metal exterior. "Used to be a food truck." He laughs. "Food must not have been very good."

"How much do you want for it?"

"Do what now?"

I stand straighter, feigning confidence even though I have no idea what the hell I'm doing. All I know is that I'm making a choice, and maybe it's out of fear—fear of finding my father and being disappointed, fear of Pen feeling powerless—but something in my gut is telling me to make it. "How much do you want for it?"

"Now what are you gonna do with a big thing like this?"

I hold my ground. "How much?"

He crosses his arms. "Well...let's see, I paid four

hundred for it, add on a two-hundred-dollar finder's fee and then another..." When he starts mumbling to himself I roll my eyes. "That comes out to...about a thousand bucks."

"But you paid four hundred. Do you really expect to turn this thing into an RV? When was the last time you got out of Austin?"

"I'm retired now. Maybe it's time to see the world. Live a little."

"You've been retired for seven years."

Mr. Daly huffs. "Well, what do you want with this piece of junk anyway?"

"I thought you said it wasn't a piece of junk." Abuelo's leaning against the gate, arms crossed.

I sigh, doing my own calculations. "Six hundred."

"Six?" Mr. Daly snorts.

"Will you sell it to me for six hundred?" I ask. "Or not?"

He takes his hat off, knocks it against his knee. "Eight hundred."

"Six-fifty."

"Come on, kid, this is business."

"Business..." Abuelo shakes his head. "You're a crook. And Xander's not a customer. He's family."

Mr. Daly rests his hands on his hips, eyes squinting in the sunlight. "Hell, why'd you have to bring up family? Huh, old man?"

"Because it's all you've got," Abuelo says.

Mr. Daly looks at me. "Six-fifty and you've got yourself a deal."

"Five," Abuelo calls out.

"Five?" Mr. Daly's fuming again.

"Five. Xander gets the truck and you made a hundred bucks today."

I reach out a hand to shake on it.

"Christ. Fine, kid, you got it."

"And you'll let him keep it back here while he works on it," Abuelo adds.

"What?"

"We don't have room."

"Fine. But I don't want you clankin' around at all hours of the night."

"I'll work on it in the mornings before my shift," I say. "I'll be quiet, no mess. You'll hardly know I'm back here."

Mr. Daly wipes his brow again. "It's been a long time since I was so expertly conned out of my own money."

Abuelo narrows his eyes. "What'd you just say?"

"I said you two should team up. You'd be millionaires."

For the first time all day Abuelo manages to crack a smile in my direction, and not for the first time, it's a reminder that family is so much more than a memory, so much more than blood. It's caring about another human being even when you can't stand the sight of them, caring about what they care about even when it seems pointless or even dangerous, caring enough to forgive them when those dangers end up hurting you both.

25

Pen

I DELIVERED MY TWO weeks' notice via email. On my last day, Josie cried, I finally told David what an asshat he really is, and Claudia surprised me by saying she'd finally called Nacho's. Her interview is this afternoon.

I shoot her an encouraging text message: **Play up your previous manager experience. Trust me, you've got this in the bag.**

She responds a few minutes later: **What about my shining personality?**

I text back: **Very funny. Actually, I think you'll find that you and my father have a lot in common. He'll like having another ringleader in that kitchen.**

I can see she's typing then stops, starts typing again, stops. I'm afraid I've scared her off when she says: **What have I gotten myself into?**

Then I tell her the same thing I told Xander the night

of Angel's party: **What you've gotten yourself into is the most faithful and fucked-up family you will ever meet.**

All I get back is a smiley face.

I thought about calling my father to put in a good word for her, but I asked Angel to do it instead. It won't matter. He'll hire her on the spot like he does everyone else.

Chloe plops down on the floor. Her eyes widen. "Are these all for me?"

"Yes." I transfer the best of each batch to a serving tray before pushing it in her direction. "Now, I want you to very *slowly* and very *objectively* taste each one. I need to know which ones are worth putting on the menu."

"Menu." Chloe holds a bite of a miniature sopapilla in her cheek. (At least I came away from El Pequeño Toro with one good business idea—miniature is much more portable). "Sounds so official."

"Well, that's what I'm going for." I reach for my checklist, bite the cap off my pen. "So, what do you think?"

"Delicious." Chloe reaches for the pan de polvo.

I hand her a glass of water. "Can you at least cleanse your palate first?"

"Sorry." She takes a sip. "I think I'm stress eating."

"Stress eating? Why?"

She swallows, reaches for the pan dulce next.

"Chloe…"

She takes another bite and I snatch the bread out of her hand.

"What's going on?" My heartbeat ticks up. "Is it the restaurant? Did something else—?"

"No." She shakes her head. "Nothing like that. The restaurant's fine. Everything's fine."

"Then what's the matter?"

She shrinks, bracing for some kind of blowback. Then she says, "Angel asked me out on a date. Tomorrow night." She leans back, still waiting for me to overreact.

I stuff a wedding cookie in my mouth instead.

"I knew this would happen." She finishes her pan dulce. "Now you're stress eating too."

"I'm not stressed."

"But you're angry."

"I'm not angry."

"Then you're—"

"I'm fine." I exhale, staring down at the powdered sugar on my jeans. Over the past five years, Chloe's heard every reason why I think she and Angel aren't a good match—that he's a flake, that he's incapable of thinking about anyone other than himself, that he thinks everything is a joke and needs to grow the hell up—and she still wants to be with him. Which means that I have to be a good friend and let her. I meet Chloe's eyes, knowing she'll need to see a genuine smile if I'm ever going to sell this. I muster up the best one I've got and then I say, "If this is what you want...then I'm fine."

Her arms latch around my neck. "Thank you."

"Okay, okay." I wrench out of her hold. "Let's not make this a big deal. Besides, I have a few orders I need you to help me deliver. We're on a time crunch."

Chloe stuffs the last of the polvorones into her mouth before taking one of the small boxes of pastries. I grab the other two. One order of marranitos, one order of apple pie empanadas, and one order of my famous coconut cake. I fold each lid before smoothing out a PEN'S PASTELES sticker over the top flaps. Chloe designed it on her laptop in my signature red.

At the door, I take a deep breath, let it go, and then I take the three steps across the hall to Mrs. Damas's apartment.

Chloe shrugs. "Well, this is convenient."

The door opens, Mrs. Damas out of her apron for once. "Pen, so glad you're here. We've been looking forward to this all afternoon." She leads me and Chloe inside, introducing us to the three old ladies sitting on her couch. "This is Pen, the girl I was telling you about. She's starting her own baking business and is letting us have the first taste of some of her signature desserts."

"Where would you like these?" I ask, lifting the boxes.

"Oh, right here." She motions to the coffee table.

Chloe and I exchange a look before slowly folding back the lid on each box. The women lean forward, inhaling, big smiles on their faces. But the first bite... that's what's most important.

I rest my chin in my hands, trying to hide my expression and the fact that I'm dissecting their every move. One of the women takes a bite of one of the marranitos. She sighs. The other bites down on one of the empanadas and she goes completely still, eyes closed. But while I'm watching them, Mrs. Damas is watching me.

"You see what happens when you follow your passion, Pen?" She smiles. "You feed people's souls. You feed yours too."

26

Xander

SUNLIGHT GLINTS OFF THE fresh coat of paint, burning my eyes. No longer black and white, the truck looks like a giant piece of candy. I picture Pen's face in the order window, the smell of coconut wafting from the opening, the scent corralling people on the street.

When I first started fixing it up, I thought I was only doing it for her—and if I'm being honest, selfishly, for me too. But somewhere along the way I started imagining it rolling by, tracing the veins of our neighborhood, the magic of Pen's food pumping new life into the people who live here.

I don't know if that's what Lucas or Struggles or Officer Solis see when they look at Pen's truck. But just the simple promise of her food has been enough to keep them going under this blazing Texas sun. Unfortunately, all they're getting today is mine.

I come around with burritos and bottles of water, Lucas taking two of each before dousing his entire face. He winks at me conspiratorially before twisting the rag he's holding and popping Struggles right on the ass.

Struggles howls. "Ouch, dude! That fucking hurt!"

Lucas laughs. "Sorry, but you missed a spot." He squats in front of the truck, rubbing his thighs. "You're not getting low enough. Wax on, wax off." He motions with his hands. "Haven't you ever seen *The Karate Kid*?"

Struggles crouches, his scrawny legs shaking.

Lucas nods. "Lower…"

Struggles forces himself into a deeper squat as he waxes the front bumper. When he isn't looking, Lucas comes up behind him, towel twisted in his fist again. He swings it slow, aiming just between Struggles's legs. Then he rears back, popping Struggles right in the junk.

Struggles screams, writhing in the grass. "You motherfucker!"

"What are you two idiots up to now?" Officer Solis steps down from the truck. "You're ruining Xander's big romantic gesture."

"He's out of his mind." Lucas crosses his arms. "I'd never spend this much time and money on a girl."

"Which is why you'll be single the rest of your life." Officer Solis hands me the keys. "Plumbing's done. I tested the flow and pressure. Everything looks good." He peels Pen's premade label from the exterior.

Chloe snuck it to me so we could copy the logo onto the truck. We all step back, admiring how much it looks like her design. The couple that painted the sidewalk outside the restaurant worked on it all day yesterday. Wouldn't charge me a cent when I said it was for Pen.

The same thing happened every time I needed new parts. When the generator turned out to be a dud, the car repair shop down the street found a used one for me in a few days. When some of the electrical was shoddy, Angel called up the handyman who fixed the power at the restaurant after Aarón Medrano electrocuted himself. When the compressor went out, Mr. Daly hunted down a new minifridge, nicer than the one we had before. And not a single person asked for money.

They couldn't see the vision in my head, the hopes and dreams I have for the neighborhood. But it didn't matter because they all had visions of their own. The Prados have given them that—permission to dream again—and not just because of the bravery they showed reopening the restaurant, but because of the bravery they show every morning that they open those doors, welcoming people in no matter where they come from or where they think they belong. At Nacho's, everyone belongs.

Officer Solis steps back to admire the fruits of our labor. "It's more than a gesture, Xander...." He nods. "More permanent."

I know he's hoping the word will stoke something in me, an admission that I finally feel like I'm home. That Pen is the place I was looking for all along. But after two weeks spent renovating this truck, Angel letting me hijack employees' shifts to scrub down old kitchen equipment and repair every inch of the inside, Pen's "fucked-up family" spending just as much time on her dream as I have, I've realized that in so many ways they've become my family too. That's the permanence I've been looking for. That's *my* dream.

I examine the truck again and think about all those hands that have helped put it back together; all of the people who've helped keep it a secret. My brain starts adding up the hours and the sweat before focusing on just the sheer size of the thing. My stomach knots, afraid that's all Pen will be able to see too.

I turn to Officer Solis. "Do you think it's too much?"

He laughs. "It's definitely too much." Then he grips my shoulder. "But she'll love it. She'll love *you* for doing it." He nods back to the truck. "So, when's the big reveal?"

"I'm supposed to see Pen before work."

"Well, it looks like a million bucks."

I shake Officer Solis's hand. "Thanks..." I tighten my grip. "For everything."

He pulls me into a hug, musses my hair. "Don't mention it."

"Shit, what time is it?" Lucas glances at his phone before heaving Struggles onto his feet. "We're gonna be late."

I toss them two more burritos on their way out. "Thanks for your help."

Lucas jabs a finger. "You tell Pen I want free pastelitos for life!"

I laugh. "I'll see what I can do."

"And don't forget," Lucas adds, "championship's tonight. You never know who might be up for top prize."

"You mean I better watch my back."

"Hey." He shrugs. "I gotta go out with a bang."

Prank Wars has been going on for the past three weeks straight. As a result, Lucas now has a tattoo of a dachshund in a hot-dog bun on his left ass cheek, Sang is down to zero eyebrows, Andrea has a broken wrist, and Java is missing a tooth.

I've come out unscathed only because I'm used to having eyes in the back of my head. I check every doorway before walking through it, I'm never the last to leave a room, and I keep a haphazard routine so that no one can anticipate where in the restaurant I'm going to be or how I'll get there. It's a lot of work, but it's also the most fun I've had...ever.

My phone buzzes. Pen's just a few minutes away. I walk the yard again, picking up scraps, trying to scrape the dirt from my hands. I'm at the edge of the street when she pulls up to the curb, the wind catching her hair as she steps out of the car.

I take her hands before she senses where to look, the truck slightly visible above the fence.

"What's going on?" she asks.

"Just...close your eyes."

My heart races as I lead her through the side gate.

"Where are we going?" she whispers.

I face her in front of the truck, both of us angled within its shadow.

"Okay." I take a deep breath. "Open your eyes."

She blinks, expressionless for a full thirty seconds, and I think I'm about to be sick. But then she approaches the truck, her hand brushing the logo. She's still silent as she rounds the front, her hands leading the way as they grab hold of the headlights and the grill, the driver's side mirror.

I open the door, Pen climbing in first. She plops down in the passenger seat, eyes roaming the dash. I show her the features up front, still waiting for her to say it's too much. But she doesn't. She doesn't say anything at all.

"Can I show you the rest?" I ask.

She follows me back to her workspace, where I point out the two sinks, the various storage compartments for all of her supplies, and the new fridge. I'm leaning into the cool air, showing her how far back it goes, when I realize that she's no longer looking. Instead, she's gripping the countertop, staring out of the order window.

The tears are invisible at first. But then I notice her blanched knuckles and short, tight breaths. I come around to face her, searching her eyes.

"You believe I can do this...."

I can't tell if it's a question, but I answer it anyway. "Of course I do."

She reaches for me with the same fervency that she did the night I showed her my scars up close. Only now it's her fears on display. Even though she has nothing to be afraid of.

"Thank you for doing this." She holds me closer, voice small. "But you didn't just do it for me, did you?"

I ease back, afraid of asking what she means.

"All the money you spent..." She shakes her head. "I don't even want to know how much. That was the money you were supposed to use to find your dad, wasn't it?"

My mind races, searching for anything I can say or do that might prove she's wrong, that no part of this was self-ish or cowardly.

I don't look at her as I say, "Maybe I found something better."

"Or maybe that's what you told yourself to justify throwing all of your money at my dream instead of your own." She takes a step back. "I just need to know...."

"What?"

"That you don't regret it. That you won't."

I reach for her hands. "I won't."

"Not the truck," she says, pulling away again. "Your father."

I've been pushing away thoughts of my father for weeks, reaching for a wrench or a screwdriver every time they started to creep up again. It's also helped that Angel has been giving me more responsibility at the restaurant. Exhausting myself is the surest way to forget. But never for long, the questions I've been haunted by since he left more unbearable now than ever. And Pen knows it. She can see it all over my face.

"I won't," I say again, even though it isn't really an answer to anything. I still don't know what I should do next, especially now that I'm not doing it alone.

Or maybe that's just an excuse too. Maybe I won't let myself start looking again until I've exhausted every single one. Or until I stop making them.

"I'm sorry," Pen finally says. "I shouldn't have said any-thing. After you did all this..." She presses her forehead to my chin. "It's amazing. It's the most amazing thing anyone has ever done for me."

I'm still not sure if she believes that last part, but I don't want to spoil this moment, especially if it means being transparent in the process. I want this to be about Pen.

I reach into my pocket, pulling out the keys. She perks up at the sound.

"There are some conditions."

Her mouth quirks up. "Conditions..."

"Even though I'd like to take credit for this entire thing, there are actually a lot of people who helped make this happen, and therefore a lot of people expecting free food for the rest of their lives."

She rolls her eyes. "Haven't even opened up shop and you're already cutting into my profits."

"I'd argue, but we both know Lucas can *eat*."

Her eyes widen. "Lucas helped?"

"Everyone at the restaurant pitched in. Officer Solis too. When the people in the neighborhood heard it was for you, they wanted to give whatever they could."

Her eyes well up again. "I can't believe so many of you kept this a secret."

"It wasn't easy."

Her face darkens. "None of this has been."

I know she'd rather be at her father's restaurant, the truck not a substitute for standing in that kitchen and not a solution for all of the broken things about their relationship. Maybe it's nothing more than a distraction for both of us.

"Things are going to get better," I say, trying to turn this grand gesture into an escape for her too.

"I know I should believe you." She stares out the order window again. "But I can't shake this feeling."

"Are you worried about El Martillo?"

She sighs, rubbing her temples. "I know you trust Officer Solis, but if the system worked, they would have locked him up a long time ago."

"And if we back down now, nothing will change. But if we stand up to him, if we keep living our lives, if your father keeps opening those doors, and if you keep making your food, maybe *something* will. Or maybe everything will."

Her eyes glisten. "I want to believe you," she says again.

"You don't have to believe me. You just have to believe in yourself." The moment's slipping away from us and I rush to bring it back. "Now, what do you say we break in this new kitchen and you bake me your famous coconut cake?"

Pen smiles, eyes flitting from me to the oven. "I think I'm feeling more of a sopapilla cheesecake vibe. Or maybe some fried ice cream, or margarita cupcakes."

I press my lips to her forehead. "Make it all and then sell everything and become a millionaire."

She laughs. "Ah, so that's what this is really about."

"It's about you."

Pen pulls me in close. "No. It's about us."

27

Pen

I STARE INTO THE side mirror, my reflection spliced with the logo on the side of the truck. The paint still smells fresh, lemon cleaner wafting from the dashboard as the air conditioner blows my hair back against the seat.

I feel like the captain of a small ship—instinct driving me against the current. But I've been swimming upstream my entire life and I know how to navigate treacherous waters. One breath, one stroke at a time out into that dark and scary thing.

But even if I get lost, I still have those stars. The ones I spotted over Xander's shoulder as he kissed me behind Signora Caterina's house. The ones I see in his eyes every time he tells me my food is magic. He wants me to summon it here, to feed the neighborhood bits of bravery and hope. To grow it inside them like tiny seeds.

I don't know if the truck is just a glorified mascot, if

my food will give people enough strength to turn their backs on El Martillo for good. But if my father's restaurant is people's safe haven, how wide of a safety net can I cast on wheels?

"So, I guess this means you can start making deliveries outside of a three-foot radius?" Chloe approaches the truck, rests her arms against the passenger side window.

"You kept this a secret. For weeks."

"Hey, at least it was a good one this time." She comes around to the driver's side. "Get out."

I raise an eyebrow. "Excuse me?"

She wrenches the door open, shooing me to the back. "You've got food to prep. Just tell me where you want to park. Remember, time is money."

I head to my workstation, thinking about all of the time and money Xander spent over the past few weeks. On me. Not just because he believes in my food, but because he's still struggling to believe in himself. To believe that he deserves to be loved. That's what he's so afraid of finding. Not his father. But proof that he was worth leaving in the first place.

As long as he avoids confronting his father face-to-face, he'll always wonder. Until that wondering hardens into something real, the doubts and fears turned to truths. That's what he was willing to risk every day that he spent money on this truck instead of paying Detective Freeman. Peace. He deserves it more than anything, and as I scratch items and prices onto the chalkboard in front of me, I decide that, with my food, with what little magic I may possess, I'm going to give it to him.

"Head toward La Puerta Abierta," I call to Chloe in the front seat.

"Scratch that." She looks back. "We're not going anywhere."

"Why not?"

She opens the driver's side door again, leaning out. "Because everyone's coming here."

I look out the window to see people moving up the street, barefoot or on bikes.

I quickly crack open cans and jars, Chloe pulling things from the bags I got at the supermarket. As soon as Xander left for work, I went on a supply run, keeping it simple like when Mrs. Damas first asked me to cook her something from my dream menu. But this isn't a practice run. That dream menu is posted on the outside of this truck and in less than five minutes, people will be ordering from it and expecting to feel what they do at Nacho's.

Make that less than one minute.

"Tell them the cocada's up first. It won't take long to harden."

"Okay, form a line, please." Chloe tries to wrangle the crowd like she does on a busy night at Nacho's. "Kitchen's just getting warmed up."

"I want cupcakes."

I hear hands against the side of the truck, the crunch of tiny shoes on gravel as kids jump to see over the order window.

"I want cookies!"

"Good morning, girls." Mr. Cantu is first in line. He tips his hat. "Nice day for a grand opening."

I come over to the window, smiling and shaking my head. "You painted this thing, top to bottom, didn't you?"

"Anything for the Prados." He blushes. "How do you like the logo?"

"I love it." I beam, reaching for his hand. "Thank you. So much."

Chloe raises an eyebrow. "And in exchange, you're hoping for the friends and family discount, am I right?"

He pulls out his wallet, handing Chloe some cash. "No discount necessary as long as you promise to put Pen's alfajores on the menu."

Chloe hands him a coffee filter full of cocada.

He rests an arm against the order counter. "And one other thing."

I crack an egg into a bowl. "What's that?"

Mr. Cantu lowers his voice. "I've heard some talk. About El Martillo."

I lower my voice too. "What about him?"

"That he's still around. That he's not happy."

"Well," I say, trying to sound tough, "we're not very happy with him either."

"He wants the restaurant, Pen."

My heart drops.

"He's always wanted the restaurant. And not just so he can knock it down and replace it with some expensive apartments or a Chick-fil-A. He wants it because it shelters. Because it saves. Because as long as your father's around, El Martillo's no longer a last resort." He leans closer, eyes earnest and full of faith. "But he's not getting it. We won't let him." He stands a little straighter. "When that SOB finally shows his face again, you don't dare let him run you out of this neighborhood. ¿Entiendes?"

My hands sweat; a confrontation with the neighborhood bogeyman seems like not just a possibility but an inevitability.

"You won't be standing alone." Mr. Cantu gestures to the growing line. "Remember that."

As I look out, I see the faces of so many people who only know me because I'm Nacho Prado's daughter; people who know my mother because she's taken care of someone they love. But even though my name isn't on the sign outside my father's restaurant, the smell of my food wafting from the open order window of the truck is still a siren song. A call to arms.

I turn to Chloe. "Let's rally these troops."

She takes a few more orders while I finish the topping for my dulce de leche panqueques. I whip the cream, watching the tiny ripples shift like sand as I try to summon the things I want folded into every bite. Hope. Courage.

While cakes sizzle on the flattop, I switch to biscochito, working defiance into the dough. I pound optimism into the pan dulce and coax compassion into the cajetas. Then, as we fill orders, people congregating with my food in hand, I watch those things rest on their lips before catching on their tongues and sliding down, down to their bellies, hitting their hearts along the way.

The sight hits mine too, as I realize that the magic isn't in the food itself. It isn't in the flavors or the technique or even the way it makes people feel. It's in the way it brings people together.

They continue to come in waves, working me into a rhythm. By late afternoon, I'm finally starting to get my timing down.

"I want two of everything."

I turn at the sound of his voice, my father standing in the shade of the truck. I don't know how long he's been watching me work, and I worry about what he sees. His worst nightmare. Another mistake.

But then I remember how Xander said Angel was letting him steal employees for a few hours during their shift to help him work on the truck. There's no way they were able to pull that off without my father knowing about it. How long *did* he know about it? What does it mean that he didn't try to stop it?

Chloe nods. "You got it."

We both start plating and wrapping things up.

Chloe rings up the total, and I shake my head.

"How many handouts have you given away today?" My father places a fifty-dollar bill on the counter. "Lesson number one: 'Free' is no way to run a business."

I want to remind him that free meals are a staple at Nacho's Tacos and that he's been running his "business" like that for years. But then again, Nacho's isn't really a business at all. What if that's not what I'm trying to build either?

"What's lesson number two?" Chloe asks.

My father tears open the foil on his pancakes before folding one into his mouth. He closes his eyes. "Lesson number two..." He opens them again. "Take care of people."

I come down the steps. "Doesn't that contradict lesson number one?"

He shrugs. "Sometimes."

He turns to go and I grip the doorway, fighting the urge to follow him, fighting the fear that's holding me back. I jump down onto the sidewalk and reach him just before he gets in his truck.

"You knew about this."

It isn't a question, and he doesn't respond.

"You paid employees to help Xander work on the truck. Why?"

He loads the food into the passenger seat. I expect him to ignore me again, but then he rests his arm against the open window, pausing to look back at the food truck one more time. "Because it's yours."

Up ahead I can barely see the street sign for Monte Vista Boulevard, Nacho's just on the other side. My eyes burn and I pretend to shield them from the sun.

"And the restaurant's not...."

He shakes his head, sighing, sick of having this same conversation. Except it's never a conversation. It's always me begging for a piece of him and him telling me no. No. It's always no.

"You want those walls? You can have them." He faces the end of the street too. "You want that kitchen? It's yours. But not the debt, Pen. Not the people who are hungry. Not the late-night phone calls that someone's son or daughter was picked up by the police, that they're being deported." He looks me in the eye. "You can't have the pain, Pen. The worry. I won't let you."

It isn't a question, and he doesn't wait for me to respond. Instead, he gets in his truck and drives back in the direction of the restaurant.

When the sun sets against the interior of the truck, my menu scratched out and the line finally gone, Chloe and I are sitting on the floor, back-to-back like after my move when we were both so exhausted we could barely hold ourselves up. And I can't stop thinking about what my father said. That I could have the parts of the restaurant everyone sees—the building and the menu and even the customers. But not the troubles they bring with them.

And I couldn't tell him...that the reason I love the restaurant is because it's a life raft. I love that whether people come in hungry or broken or hopeless, they always leave full. Not because they always have money or something else to give in exchange, but because he can't let them leave empty-handed. Because he cares. But for my father, caring is a curse. A curse he refuses to pass down to me.

Instead, he wants me to have something of my own.

Because he believes in me.

Because he loves me.

Chloe takes my hand, and I realize my eyes are wet. When her face comes into view, so does everything else— the truck, the mess, not just on the floor but on our faces too—and as I brush the flour from my cheeks, it hits me that I get to wake up tomorrow and do it all over again.

"What are you smiling about?" Chloe groans. "We're filthy."

"We are."

She nudges me. "But it's better than that stupid felt mustache?"

I exhale, settling into the filth. "So much better." I lean my head back, spotting the moon as it appears through the order window. *Because it's mine.*

Chloe reaches for the shoebox we used as a cash register. She drops it in my lap, bills flying. "How's that for validation?"

I scoop them up. "Pretty freaking sweet."

"Look at you making a pun."

"Maybe I'm in a good mood."

"Because all your dreams are coming true?"

I count out the money for Detective Freeman's fee. "Yes." *And now it's Xander's turn.*

―――――

I don't expect Detective Freeman to still be in his downtown office when Chloe and I pull up. The money's in an envelope, Xander's name and contact information on the front, ready to be stuck under the door. But when I spot him through the window, reading glasses on as he pores over a stack of papers, something tells me to go inside.

"This won't take long," I say.

Chloe's staring down at her phone. Her big date with Angel's tonight.

"How many times have you texted him?" I ask.

"Four." She blows a strand of hair out of her face. "That doesn't seem desperate, does it?"

"No. He should have answered after the first one."

"It's getting late. What if he's bailing?"

I don't know what to say. Bailing is absolutely something he would do.

"Maybe they're slammed at the restaurant. He'll probably call you by the time we get back to the food truck."

I'm not sure if Chloe believes me; maybe all of the awful things I've said about Angel's relationship potential over the years are finally sinking in. I should be relieved, but I can't take the heartbreak on her face.

"He'll call, Chloe. He wouldn't have asked you out if he wasn't interested."

Her cheeks warm, a smile cutting into them. "Yeah... I'm a catch."

"Amen."

Chloe follows me to the door. I let out a deep breath, knock twice.

Detective Freeman pushes it open. "Can I help you?"

"Uh, yes. My name is Penelope Prado. I'm a friend of Xander's."

He scratches his chin, thinking. "Xander...Xander Amaro?"

I nod.

"I haven't heard from him in several weeks. Is everything all right?"

"He's fine. He...actually doesn't know I'm here." I hold out the envelope. "I wanted to pay his fee for your services."

He doesn't take it, backing up instead. "Would you two like to come inside for a minute?"

We follow Detective Freeman into his office. He leans against his desk, looking from the envelope to my face as I try to appear as earnest as possible. I'm surprised he isn't jumping at the cash, but maybe that's actually a good sign.

"You said Xander doesn't know you're here?"

I shake my head.

"Look, I've got to be honest with you. The voice mail Xander left me was pretty loaded. It's obviously a very sensitive situation. When he didn't call to arrange paying for my retainer, I assumed he just wasn't ready." He pauses. "And when people aren't ready, it's not a good idea to force them, which is why I haven't called him about getting the process started. That's a decision he has to make."

"What if he never will?"

"Then that's his choice."

"I know he wants to find his father," I say. "He's just afraid."

"Which might mean that he's not ready."

"So, what if he doesn't hire you?" I straighten. "What if *I* do?"

"You want to hire me to find Victor Amaro...."

I nod, handing over the money. Xander might be too afraid to face his father, but what if I could convince his father to come to him? How much doubt could be extinguished by him showing up on Xander's doorstep? And if he decides not to come, just as afraid, Xander never has to know.

Detective Freeman finally takes the envelope before rummaging through a filing cabinet and pulling out a manila folder. He hands it to me.

"What's this?" I ask.

"What you paid for." He clears his throat. "He lives in New Mexico. With his wife and two daughters."

I picture each one, a puzzle piece locking in place, jagged edges revealing a hole where Xander should be. Unless they have enough of the picture without him. Unless they prefer it that way. My stomach knots as I'm struck by just an ounce of the fear Xander must have wrestled with when he called Detective Freeman the first time. He let it stop him. What would happen if I do the same?

I clutch the folder to my chest. "Thank you."

"Just be careful."

"Did he seem dangerous?"

Detective Freeman shakes his head. "I meant with Xander. I've done this work long enough to know that people aren't always prepared for what they find. Sometimes things work out, but sometimes they wish they hadn't gone looking in the first place."

28

Xander

LUCAS SLIPS ON THE third rung of the ladder, body shaking as he tries to hold in his laughter. We collapse on the roof of the restaurant, Lucas almost spilling the bucket of caramel.

Struggles tries to reach his finger in, Lucas swatting it away.

"You have one job, Struggles. Don't fuck it up."

"Feathers. I know. I'm on it."

"This prank is my pièce de résistance."

"What does that mean?" Struggles asks.

"It means it's gonna win me top prize this year. *If* you wait for my signal and follow the plan."

We drop to our bellies just as the back door of the restaurant swings open.

Down below, Angel's staring at his bright cell phone screen, probably pulling up Chloe's number. They've been giving each other googly eyes across the restaurant ever since he finally asked her out.

Lucas winks at me. Then he yells, "Big date tonight?"

Angel looks up just as Lucas tips the bucket of caramel over his head.

Angel stumbles against the dumpster, phone flying. "What the fuck!"

"Now!" Lucas yells.

Struggles shakes out the feathers, snorting as Angel coughs and tries to scrape the mess from his eyes.

He grasps at the dumpster, trying to find his footing. "I'm gonna fucking kill you!"

I stay low, hoping he doesn't see me. I didn't know who exactly Lucas was planning on pranking. All I knew was that being in on the joke was better than walking on eggshells inside the restaurant. I'm the only person who still hasn't been pranked yet, and if I'm lucky I may actually get through the next couple of hours without a scratch. Or covered in feathers. Or some other even more disgusting substance.

Angel's arms are outstretched as he feels for the door. Just as he finds the handle, the door flies open, knocking him back onto the gravel, covering him in rocks and grass.

"Goddamn you, Lucas—"

His threat's cut off by the rumbling of voices. Down below, Miguel charges after Sang, Chelo and Java trying to break them apart. Andrea and Mari run out after them, Solana and Gabby not far behind. As everyone circles around Miguel and Sang, Aarón appears on the stoop, as apathetic as ever.

Angel's still trying to scrub the gunk from his face. "What the hell's going on here?"

Everyone freezes, looking him up and down.

Sang points. "What the hell happened to you?"

Andrea shakes her head, examining the damage. "I thought you had a date with Chloe tonight."

"I did." Angel deflates. "And now I'm gonna be late!"

Lucas snorts, everyone looking up.

Java claps. "Nice one, dude."

Angel snarls. "It's not gonna be so nice when I beat his ass."

"How about we make that an official rule change?" Miguel lunges at Sang, Chelo yanking him back. "Prank victims may retaliate using physical force."

Sang rolls his eyes. "Victim? I lost two eyebrows because of you!"

Miguel fumes. "Yeah, and you…"

"And I what?" Sang smiles. "You know, admitting you have a problem is the first step."

"I don't have a problem. You put something in my fucking drink."

"Or maybe you just have a sensitive stomach. Did you eat ghost peppers again? We all remember what happened the last time…."

Angel breaks through the crowd. "Enough! The two of you have been going at it since last year's Prank Wars. It's time to end this shit." He steps back, everyone silent.

Sang and Miguel exchange a glance.

Angel waves a hand. "Go on."

Miguel's brow furrows. "Go on?"

"Fucking fight!"

Chelo releases Miguel, his fists raised. Sang squares up in response.

A car rolls past.

Crickets chirp.

Andrea sneezes.

"Someone throw a punch already!"

They throw themselves at each other, bodies tangling for half a second as their fists barely make contact. Miguel lands on his side, panting. Sang's on his back, cut up from the fall.

Chelo laughs. "You guys are pathetic."

Java shakes his head. "I came outside for this?"

The back door swings open again. Mr. Prado steps out.

He puts the pieces together in less than a second—Sang and Miguel on the ground, Angel covered in caramel and feathers, Lucas's and Struggles's feet hanging off the roof of the restaurant—and immediately realizes that we're all up to no good.

But he doesn't yell or snatch Angel up by the scruff. He just crosses his arms, everyone racing for the door like water backed up in a bent hose.

On my way back to my plating station, he stops me. "Xander, can you step into my office for a minute?"

My heart races as I follow him inside. It shoots into my throat the second he motions for me to close the door.

"Yes, s-sir?" I stammer.

"I've noticed Angel's been giving you more responsibility. Mostly things he doesn't feel like doing himself. But you've done a good job, Xander."

I let out a deep breath. "Thank you, sir."

"Do you think you can handle closing tonight?"

I straighten. "Uh, yes, sir. I can handle it."

"Good."

He looks down for a long time, and I think it's my cue to go. But when I reach for the door, he clears his throat.

"I stopped by the truck today. Pen's grand opening." He meets my eyes. "It looked good."

I knew paying the restaurant employees to work on the truck wasn't Angel's idea. It had to have been Mr. Prado's. But he never said a word; he never came by to see the progress. He let me be the one to give the truck to Pen even though he was the one who'd made it happen. Not just the labor, but every bit of luck along the way. People were only generous with their time and money because at some point in their lives, Nacho had done the same for them. It was his reputation that made Pen's dream a reality.

"It couldn't have happened without your help," I say.

He looks away again, still uninterested in the credit. "It was your idea." He stands. "A pretty grand gesture."

He sounds like Officer Solis, and suddenly I'm sweating again. Because now I know exactly where this conversation is going.

"You're a good kid, Xander. So I'm not going to give you some big intimidating speech."

My heartbeat ticks up as I wait for the *but*...

"All I'm going to say is that Pen is more precious to me than you could ever know...."

"I understand, sir."

"Do you?"

I nod, mouth dry. "Yes."

"Good....And depending on how well things go tonight, I think it might make sense to make a permanent change to your position. Angel could use an assistant manager. Especially one who's reliable."

"Thank you," I say, this time not just for hiring me but for giving me what I've been looking for all along. A place to belong.

He grips my shoulder like he can see it in my eyes. "You've earned it, Xander."

He opens the door, the sizzle of the grills forcing the lump in my throat back down.

Once Mr. Prado's out of sight, Lucas calls over the kitchen, "Okay, guys, we've got thirty minutes to get these customers out of here, and then it's time for the closing ceremonies."

I take over Angel's station, cooking the last few to-go orders before cleaning the grill. I still have a few more things to knock off my checklist when everyone starts gathering in the dining room.

Lucas waves me over. "You, my friend, get the honor of being my assistant." He taps a fake microphone he's fashioned out of foil. "Hello? Is this thing on?"

Java chucks a dirty washrag at him. "Get on with it...."

He clears his throat. "Okay, good. Welcome, everyone, to the eighth annual Nacho's Tacos Prank Wars Official Closing Ceremonies."

Chelo boos.

Lucas raises his hands. "I haven't even given out any awards yet."

"Exactly!" Sang snaps. "Now hurry up with all those bullshit awards you made up so we can find out who wins the crown!"

"Okay, okay." Lucas hands me a small foil taco. "First up, the award for best blast from the past (literally). Drumroll, please..."

The crowd obliges.

"Sang Nguyen for the sweet surprise he slipped into Miguel's drink this morning."

Sang lifts the bottle of laxative Miguel accused him of using to poison his drink. Miguel lunges for him again, Chelo yanking him back like a dog on a leash.

"Come on, you had your chance."

Sang takes his taco award before moonwalking back to his seat.

Lucas snorts, eyes watering as he tries to get out the next one. "The award for most..." He can't catch his breath. "For most..."

Andrea chucks her shoe. "Spit it out already!"

"The award for most creative use of shit goes to Miguel Medrano for his Dump in the Trunk, which has been roasting in Sang's car for the last four hours."

Sang stands, ashen, before bolting for the door. Miguel and a few others run out after him, Miguel ready to savor his revenge. We can see their silhouettes through the window, Sang rearing back, swinging, and missing Miguel completely.

Java rolls his eyes. "This is getting embarrassing."

Lucas runs through five more awards: most dangerous, best use of rancid meat, most disgusting visuals, worst side effects: smell, worst side effects: taste.

"And now, the moment everyone has been waiting for…" Lucas pumps his fist, riling everyone up as hoots and hollers mix with the deafening drumroll. "The eighth annual Nacho's Tacos Prank Wars top prize goes to…" Lucas falls to his knees, holding the taco above his head. "ME! For turning Angel into a giant cock."

Java jumps to his feet. "This shit's rigged!"

Andrea rolls her eyes. "How lame."

Lucas launches right into his victory dance, no one bothering to stay and celebrate with him. One by one they disappear out the front door, Java hitting the lights on his way out.

Lucas kneels in the dark, unperturbed. Beaming. He kisses his prize. "This is the best night of my life."

"Congratulations." I try to muster up some excitement, but I still have a few items on my closing checklist.

He doesn't move, just keeps staring at the ceiling.

"I'm gonna finish up."

I grab an empty crate on my way to the supply closet. I lean into the door, back first, the crate falling out of my grasp the second I see who's on the other side.

J. P. grips a can of gasoline, the smell making my eyes water. Everything is soaked.

He reaches a hand into his pocket and pulls out a matchbook.

"What are—? Why are you—?" Something else is speaking for me. The fear, maybe. I wish it would tell my body to lunge for him. But as he lights the first match, all I can do is listen.

"I remember when they started building this place."

His eyes flit across the walls. "I ate lunch here the day it opened. Best damn tacos in town."

The match burns down to the tips of his fingers. He blows it out. "This sort of thing…" He flicks the matchstick at me. "It's not exactly my style. I'd rather talk things out. Negotiate like real businessmen. But that's not what Nacho is." He shakes his head. "I knew that when I gave him the money for this place. I knew it when he couldn't pay it back."

"Mr. Prado takes care of the people in this neighborhood. He doesn't prey on them like—"

"You think he cares about you?" J. P. drops another lit match, his other hand swooping in to catch it before it can hit the ground. "See, that's Ignacio Prado's poison. He makes people think the world cares about them. And it's that trust, that belief that makes them stay even when it's dangerous. Even when they don't belong. He gives them hope, and there's nothing more destructive than that."

I think about my own hopes, how some days they're the only thing that keeps me going and on others they're the binds that tie me down. A trap I keep setting for myself over and over again. But hope is not the reason I'm stuck in this supply closet, seconds from being set on fire. Hope isn't the reason J. P. wants to destroy everything Mr. Prado has built.

The reason … is hate.

I see it coming to a boil inside him. This ugly, awful thing.

"You would know about destruction." I swallow. "Considering all the times you've made people disappear."

"I've helped the police arrest criminals."

"You're the criminal," I spit.

He smiles, mocking. "Not everything's that black and white, kid. Right and wrong." He inches closer. "Sometimes heroes and villains are the same. What matters is your vantage point. Who's telling the story." He holds out the match, flame dancing. "And this...this ending will make for one hell of a story."

The terror is a ball of electricity at the base of my stomach.

"A fire's a little old-fashioned, but there's something about the spectacle." He marvels at the small flame. "You see, a fire's something you never forget. This hungry thing, so hot it burns white. So wild that all you can do is stand back and watch."

I taste bile. Because that's exactly what he wants the people in this neighborhood to do.

To keep our mouths shut. To run. To hide.

To just stand back and watch while he devours everything that matters.

"You're fine with rotting in prison as long as you can make a point? As long as you can destroy as many people's lives as possible along the way?"

He looks me dead in the eye. "I won't rot."

"I'll tell them it was you."

He blows out the match, flicks it at me. "Your word against mine." He scrapes another match against the box, flame snapping to life. "Unless, of course, you can't give your testimony"—he presses me against the wall, flame grazing my chin—"because...you're dead."

In one swift motion he lights another match, the stick tumbling end over end before igniting a blue wave at my feet. I recoil from the heat, J. P. vanishing behind the rising flames. Everything hurts, my insides boiling. I gasp for air, choking on the heat.

I can't see. I can't breathe.

And all I can think about is Pen standing in the ashes.

I reach for her, trying to stay whole.

But it hurts.

It hurts....

It...

29

Pen

THE CREDITS ARE ROLLING on *The Princess Bride* by the time Chloe finally decides to change out of her date-night clothes and into her pajamas.

"I'm sorry my brother's a dick."

She slumps back down on the couch. "It's not your fault. I mean, you did warn me about him. I should have listened."

"At least now you don't have to wonder...."

"If there could have been something?"

"Yeah."

She pulls her knees to her chest. "I know this is going to make me sound like an idiot...but I still think there could be. Just not now. He's not ready."

"And he might never be."

"You're right." She chips at her toenail polish. "Which is why I'm done waiting." She falls into my lap. "Instead,

I'm going to focus on things that are actually important. Like my best friend and her new business and graduating and—"

"Maybe meeting someone new?"

"Or maybe learning to enjoy being alone." She sits up, lowers her voice. "My mom doesn't know how to be alone. That's why she jumps from guy to guy, every single one of them Prince Charming until he's not."

"You're nothing like your mom, Chloe."

"I know." She pulls her hair back. "But I am in love with someone who doesn't love me back. That's the story of her life."

"But it won't be yours. You'll get over him eventually."

"That might be hard to do since he's sort of my manager." She's quiet, staring out the window, the truck so massive it blocks out everything else. "What if I came to work for you instead?"

"Work for me?"

"I could cut my hours at Nacho's, maybe work mornings before Angel gets there. Then I could work with you in the afternoons. You know, in between classes and stuff."

I picture every day being like today—Chloe dealing with the customers while I cook. At Nacho's she was always stepping in when the situation called for compromise or a friendly face—two things that are necessary in the customer service business and which I lack the ability to muster. She's my other half for a reason, and I can't imagine taking this next step without her.

"Let's do it," I say.

She hugs me. "Thank you! It'll be so much fun. Just like old times." She yawns, curling into a ball. "Are you thinking of meeting up with Xander?"

I narrow my eyes at her. "How'd you know?"

"Because you've been gripping your keys since the movie ended."

"I'm sorry." I stare down at the new addition to my key ring. "I just don't think he realized that the second I drove out of Mr. Daly's yard, we'd be open for business. A lot of things happened today. A lot of good things. I just can't wait to tell him about it."

"Is he off work?"

"Should be soon. He texted me and said my dad asked him to take over closing tonight."

Her face falls again as she realizes that Angel did in fact take off work...just not to be with her.

"But I can stay if you want."

"No..." She forces a tired smile. "You go. I'm exhausted anyway."

"See you tomorrow?"

She walks me to the door. "Absolutely. And our first order of business? Matching T-shirts."

"I like it."

My car is still parked in front of Mr. Daly's house. As I pass through Xander's front yard, the folder Detective Freeman gave me clutched to my chest, a light buzzes on behind me. I look back and spot Xander's abuelo sitting on the porch. He's holding a small pipe, the tobacco long burned out. I lift a hand but the rest of me can't move. Because seeing him only reminds me of what's missing, the answers to Xander's questions, and maybe some of his abuelo's too, currently gripped in my fist.

The pages flutter in the breeze and I think about hiding them, throwing them away.

I could keep the secret.

I could keep Xander safe.

I'm on the front steps before I even realize I've moved, the folder at my side.

Xander's abuelo smiles. "The famous Pen."

I smile back. "The famous Abuelo."

He laughs. "If only fame meant something at this age." He chews on his pipe, thumb brushing his lighter. "I was just waiting up for Xander."

"My father asked him to close the restaurant tonight, so he'll probably be running a little late."

He nods, relieved. "Well, as long as he's with your father then I know he's okay."

I ease myself into the chair next to him, still clutching the folder, still not sure what I'm going to do with it. I feel compelled to ask, "Do you worry about him?"

He stares at the end of the street. "I always worry about him." He loads some more tobacco into his pipe, lights it. "Sometimes I'll wake up in the middle of the night and sit out here until I see his headlights turn the corner."

I stare down at the folder, wind still trying to tug the pages free. Xander wasn't the only one who lost someone he loved, but I can see in his abuelo's eyes, I can hear it in his voice that Xander has mended something broken inside him. How does it feel knowing that he hasn't been able to fill the same void for Xander?

"How do you like the truck?" he asks.

"I love it."

"I'm glad. He worked hard on it. It was a good distraction for him."

I look down. "You mean from finding his father?"

He puffs on his pipe, igniting the scent of vanilla. He exhales. "I mean from feeling like a disappointment."

Xander's been trying to redeem himself ever since he was a confused little boy who could only make sense of things if he was the one who'd done something wrong. So that's what he's always believed. That's why confronting his father is so terrifying. Because meeting him in a state of imperfection is too much of a risk. As if he could become the type of son a father would never leave. As if any of it was his fault. But...

"It wasn't his fault." Xander's abuelo rests his pipe on his knee, still waiting for his grandson's headlights to come up the road. "But until he believes that... he's not ready."

My stomach knots, my knuckles blanched around the folder.

"I just want him to be strong enough."

"You don't think he is?"

He grips his knees, staring into the dark. "Or maybe I'm the one who's not." He hangs his head. "Maybe that's a selfish reason to stand in his way."

Smoke swirls between us, the thin veil making it feel safe to ask, "What are you afraid of?"

He barely moves. "The past."

I pick at the pages, edges now damp from my hands and the heat. "But... if you could change it..."

He meets my eyes. "I hope I wouldn't be too much of a coward to try."

Slowly, I hold the folder out to him. He examines it, confused.

"Xander spoke with a private investigator," I finally say. "This is what he found."

He scans the pages, breathless when he comes to the names of the granddaughters he's never met. "He has a family."

"You and Xander are a part of that."

Suddenly, there's a sadness in his eyes. "Does Xander know about this?"

I shake my head. "And he won't unless you want him to."

He closes the folder, squeezes my hand. "Thank you."

"You're welcome."

The scent of something burning tickles my nose and as I follow Xander's abuelo's eyes back down to the end of the street, the night is gray, something thick moving over the tops of the trees. It rises into the sky just over the restaurant. Smoke.

The sound of sirens sets my teeth. Lights swirl up the road, a fire truck zooming down the next street. I think I hear him ask where they might be going and then I'm moving just as fast, racing to my car and jumping in the front seat. I catch up to the truck just as my cell phone rings. It's Angel.

He's standing on the edge of Monte Vista Boulevard when the truck finally comes to a stop. But I barely notice him.

It looks like morning and everything is cracking.

And screaming.

And *burning*.

I step out of the car, the heat steeling me back. Angel runs over, gripping my arms, speaking words I don't understand.

I don't understand.

I don't understand.

I see my mother, her arms around my father. He's so still. Just staring.

I run to him, my mother grabbing my face, her voice just as foreign as Angel's. She's trying to get me to look at her, to make sure I'm all right.

But I'm not all right.

Looking at my father—*destroyed*—I will never be all right.

But then I look closer. I stare at him as he stares at the flames, and for the first time he's not impossible to read. He's not a statue or a god or my enemy. He's a man, the faintest flicker in his eyes. And I know that he isn't mourning. He's free.

30

Xander

MY SKIN WAKES UP first.

It's screaming in a language the rest of my senses can't understand. So then they start screaming back, and suddenly I'm on fire again and... *Fire... the fire...*

Oh God. The restaurant.

"I think he's waking up."

"I pressed his morphine button."

"That's just gonna knock him out again."

"He's in pain, Lucas."

I hold tight to the voices, trying to make out each one.

"Yeah, and what about me?"

"You're a fucking hero." *Angel.* "Is that what you want to hear?"

"You think I'm that selfish? So, I do a good deed by dragging Xander out of a burning building. I don't need a medal or anything."

"No." *Pen.* "You just need to remind everyone a thousand times."

I reach for her, straining to open my eyes. I blink, the room bright, her face coming within inches of mine.

"Xander? We're here. We're all here. You're okay."

Lucas crosses his arms, mumbles, "Yeah, thanks to me."

Angel punches him in the arm, and that's when I notice Lucas's bandages. I stretch, stiff as I realize I'm covered in them too.

"How long have I been at the hospital?" I ask.

"Since last night," Angel says. "Pain meds have had you in and out of sleep for the past twelve hours."

Pen finally takes her eyes off me, looking to Angel and then Lucas. "Can I have a minute?"

"Sure, we'll be right outside." Angel looks down at me. "I'm sure it goes without saying, but I'll be doing the closing from now on."

This time Lucas punches him in the arm. "Dude, too soon!"

"What?" Angel shrugs. "You're the one who asked if that assistant manager position was up for grabs."

Lucas smacks him again. "Don't say that in front of him. That's my best friend!"

"Best friend? Really? Because a best friend wouldn't—"

"Get the hell out of here!" Pen shoves them toward the door.

A small, tight laugh tries to escape, and it's torture.

Pen slumps down on the edge of my bed. "I'm glad to see your sense of humor's still intact."

I look down, absorbing myself in pieces. My right arm

is covered in gauze and I can feel it taut beneath my gown. But the longer I sit in my skin, the more I sense the pain is only on the surface.

Pen registers my relief, her own forcing her to fall on top of me, face wet. "I can't believe you were inside."

"I'm so glad you weren't." My heart pounds against my chest, every detail sharpening until I'm pricked full of holes. "I'm so sorry, Pen."

"It wasn't your fault."

I squeeze my eyes shut again. "But I'm so—"

She presses her lips to mine, shoving the words back down.

"I love you," she breathes.

"I love you too."

She rests her head on my chest, both of us quiet for a long time—Pen probably trying to picture me in the middle of those flames while I try not to imagine the damage they must have done. I don't know if the restaurant is still standing or if anyone else got hurt. I don't know what happened to J. P. or how Lucas managed to drag me out alive.

I want to ask Pen, but I'm afraid the answers would wedge themselves between us, and I need her close.

Angel pokes his head in. "Dad just called to make sure we can still pick up Lola and Hugo from Mrs. Nguyen's."

She sits up, not letting go of me yet.

I swallow. "Is he...?"

They both look down.

"He doesn't blame you," Angel says.

Pen squeezes my hand. "No one does." She stands, kissing me on the forehead. "I'll be back in a couple of hours."

"Is my abuelo here?" I ask before they leave.

Pen stops, hesitant. "He was here earlier. I'll ask Officer Solis to give him a call and tell him you're awake."

In the quiet after they leave, I replay every second. J. P. toying with the matches, beaming with pride about the people he's made disappear. And then he set the place on fire and left me there to die.

But I didn't.

There's a light knock on the hospital door. Officer Solis pushes it open. "How are you feeling?" he asks.

I shove aside the pain, trying to get at the knot in my stomach. "Confused."

"How much do you remember?" he asks.

J. P.'s voice is in my head again. I pinch my eyes shut.

"How did I get out?"

Officer Solis sits by my bed. "Lucas. He smelled the gasoline and then he heard J. P.'s voice behind the door. Police showed up a few minutes later." There's something in Officer Solis's eyes that looks like defeat.

"And the restaurant?"

He hangs his head.

"It's gone?"

He just nods.

I feel the panic of a soldier whose last line of defense has just crumbled. Where will people go when they want to feel safe?

Officer Solis's expression changes, his voice strange. "They found J. P."

"And he's in jail?"

He looks from my bed to the window, avoiding my

eyes. "The police chief's a friend of his, and he's not the only one."

"But Lucas identified him. I'm a witness too." I try to sit up. "They can't just let him go."

Officer Solis grits his teeth, his voice almost gone. "I thought things were different. I . . . wanted them to be."

"But they're not," I finish for him. "They never will be."

"Not never." Officer Solis snaps out of his anger for a second, desperation in his eyes instead. "Not right now. But not never. We *never* say never, you understand?" He senses my doubt and lowers his voice. "You're alive, Xander. You won."

I want it to feel like all of the other times Officer Solis has rescued me . . . but it doesn't.

"I didn't. Not if it means he didn't lose."

"Maybe people like that never will." He looks me in the eye. "But surviving in spite of all he's tried to tear down, that's a victory. It has to be. Resiliency is its own reward, and it's something no one can take from us."

I don't argue. I'm too exhausted. But all I can think about is that if resiliency was worth something, I would be the one with all the power and people like J. P. wouldn't run the world. But even with blood on his hands, with hate in his heart, it turns when he tells it to. And I don't even want to tell the world when to turn. I just want the strength to tilt it a little more in our favor. To balance the scales. To make things right.

But it'll have to wait.

Because people like J. P. make those decisions too.

Or maybe that's the brokenness talking. Maybe when

the wounds have healed, I'll forget about the pain. Maybe resiliency doesn't work without a little amnesia.

———

After Officer Solis leaves, I tense at every sound—the shuffle of footsteps, hushed voices of the nurses, the whirring of the machines—waiting for someone else to come in and tell me something awful. Hours pass, and in the quiet, I tell myself stories instead, picturing the restaurant in flames, everything turned to ash and dust. It feels like I'm still choking on it.

But fixing what's broken doesn't feel so impossible anymore. That's all Pen and I have been doing since we met. Maybe that's the reason we did. To mend each other. To make each other better. What if the restaurant can be mended too? What if, just like Pen's truck, I can use my hands and my heart to put it back together? And not just for the Prados, but for all of us. Because we're a family.

I have a family.

The sun is beginning to set when the door finally pushes open again, Abuelo stepping inside. He looks exhausted, eyes ringed red. But he's not alone.

Behind him is a man I can barely remember in three-dimension. The giant is gone, what's left—a shell that shares my father's voice. *My father.*

I'm dreaming again.

I know I'm dreaming because this isn't the man who walked out our front door when I was four years old. This isn't the man whose crackling voice on the other side of a pay phone used to sing me to sleep. This man is weathered and graying and someone else's father.

"Xander...there's someone here to see you."

Abuelo speaks to me, low by my ear. But I'm not listening. I'm staring...searching for that thing I've been looking for since my father left. And then the stranger takes my hand, and there's a pang...like I've found it.

Or maybe he's found me.

Maybe that's how it was supposed to happen.

"Alejandro?" His voice hangs between us, the gravel, the tenor making the hairs on my arms stand on end. "Do you remember me?"

I find my reflection in his eyes, the boy in me staring back.

"Your abuelo called me last night." He sits, hands retreating like he's not sure where to put them. "I got on the first plane." His hands inch toward the hospital bed. "I'm so glad you're all right."

I'm too quiet and it makes him nervous, his eyes glistening like he's holding back tears. Mine are all over my cheeks, the rush making it impossible to breathe.

"I always wondered..." He marvels at my face, at my body stretched under the blankets. "You looked so much like her when you were little." He shakes his head, eyes smiling, still taking me in. "But now..."

Abuelo grips his shoulder. "He looks like you."

He leans into Abuelo's touch, his eyes closed like he's forgotten the way it feels. To have a father. To have a son. And I wonder if there's a hole in him too, one he never quite figured out how to fill.

"My little boy..." He can barely get the words out and I can barely see him behind the sting of tears.

"I looked for you." The tears spill into my mouth. "I waited for you."

He crumbles, taking my hand.

"He's here now." Abuelo squeezes him. "You're here now."

"I should have come for you...." My father chokes. "I should have..." He pinches his eyes shut. "I didn't know how." He presses my hands to his face, letting me feel the time that's passed all over again.

"I'm sorry, Alejandro."

I had forgotten what my name was supposed to sound like. The way it bends into a sigh. The way it curls and loosens. He says it over and over, like something sacred, and suddenly, I miss that little boy almost as much as I missed him.

Alejandro.

The tears don't stop.

I'm drowning in them.

"I'm sorry."

He's drowning in them.

And I don't care that he's too late. That I've become a man without him.

He's here. Now. And this close, I can see that familiar gleam in his eyes, the one my laughter used to ignite. I can see the truth. That it wasn't all in my head. That he loved me.

He loves me.

31

Pen

FROM THE CORNER OF Monte Vista Boulevard I can almost pretend that it's still intact, that my brother's inside behind the grill and my father's in his office thumbing through receipts; that Chloe's at the hostess stand swatting at rowdy customers and my mother is chatting with one of the regulars on the patio. I close my eyes, just for a second, imagining the clink of forks on plates and the buzz of music coming from the kitchen.

But then something catches in Angel's throat, shattering the memory.

That's all we have now. Memories.

We trek through the debris, cars pulling to the side of the road as people call out questions and condolences. My father just waves, busy listing the damages while the insurance adjuster scribbles them onto a notepad.

"What do you think he's going to do?" Angel's voice is practically a whisper.

My voice is just as low. "I don't know." I examine our father more closely, trying to sense the relief I noticed last night. I didn't just imagine it. As he stood before the flames, my mother weeping in the crook of his arm, he wasn't cursing fate, he was saying goodbye.

Angel shifts a chunk of concrete with his shoe. "I didn't think I wanted it...."

I know he's not just talking about the manager position or even the restaurant. He's talking about our father's legacy.

"But now?"

"I still don't think it's meant for me." He stares at the charred brick. "But I can't imagine life without it."

I can feel more eyes, more hushed voices as people approach the police lines to take a closer look. "You're not the only one."

"It's where we grew up."

Where we're still *growing up*, I think.

"He'll listen to you," Angel says.

"What do you mean?"

He sighs. "I can't ask him to rebuild the restaurant for me. But for you..."

"I think you're forgetting that I'm technically still fired."

"And I think you're forgetting that we're currently standing in the ashes of our father's dream."

He's wrong. We're not standing in the ashes of our father's dream. We're standing in the ashes of the dreams of this neighborhood, every single person who's eaten my father's food leaving behind this invisible hope—that's all that's left. But I don't know if it's enough for my father to rebuild.

"He needs you, Pen." Angel squeezes my shoulder.

I shrug out of his grasp. "Fine."

"I believe in you." He pulls me into a hug. "Always have. Always will."

I look up at him. "And I believe in you."

He rolls his eyes and I thump him in the chest.

"Ouch!"

"I believe in you," I say again.

"I heard you, all right?"

"Did you?" I hang an arm around his waist. "You'll figure it out, Angel."

He frowns. "When?"

"When the time is right."

"Like when I'm thirty?"

"When you're ready."

His voice drops again. "What if I'm never ready?"

It's exactly what I told Chloe—that my brother might never be ready for a serious relationship, that he might never be ready to grow up. Seeing him now, how scared he is to fail, to even try, I realize how unfair it was to judge him. My father's not the only one who needs me. Angel needs me too.

"Look at me." I wait for him to meet my eyes. "You'll figure it out. I promise."

He shrugs, still not sure.

"You said you believe in me, right? Then believe me when I say that you'll figure it out."

He squeezes me a little tighter. "Thanks."

"And you can start with calling Chloe. She was pretty upset last night. . . ."

"Obviously I was a little busy."

"And obviously she knows that and she understands. I'm just warning you that if you're actually interested, you have to make an effort. A real one." I pull out my cell phone, punch in her number. "Call her."

"All right, all right." He snatches it, saunters off.

"What are you and your brother up to?" My father's more amused than worried. Despite the destruction we're currently standing in, everything he's worked to build resolved to rubble.

"Just . . . helping Angel with some girl problems."

He shakes his head. "Of course that's where his mind's at right now."

After a beat of silence, the words form on my lips before I can stop them. "Where's yours?"

He glances at me, sensing that I'm asking about much more than just how he feels. I'm asking what he's going to do about how he feels.

He tests one of the exposed beams, leans against it. But he doesn't answer; just stares at the emptiness.

"Dad . . . ?"

"They need it."

"The neighborhood . . ."

"And your mother and your siblings . . . and you."

I take a step closer to him, daring to ask, "But what about you? Does the restaurant make you happy?"

He pulls me against his chest. "*You* make me happy."

I don't know how long I cry into his shirt. Until I'm not sure if I'll ever be able to stop. Until I feel him quaking too.

"We don't get to give up." He brushes my hair back. "You taught me that, Penelope."

I look up at him. "Because you taught me first."

We cling to each other in the middle of all that brokenness, forgetting every fight and finding strength in all the ways we're the same. I want to tell him again how sorry I am for lying, for thinking for even a second that he didn't care. But I can feel in his embrace that I don't have to say a word. It's done, the past swallowed up by those flames, along with everything else.

Now it's time to build something new.

He takes my hand. "I have a few ideas I need your opinion on. From one chef to another."

"I like the sound of that." I let him lead me back around to the front. "Show me the way."

He constructs our new home right before my eyes until I can see his vision past the tears. He shifts my gaze to the entrance, talking about moving the hostess stand and giving Chloe a taller stool. He walks me over to the bar, picking up a broken stick to map out a new configuration. He sifts through the dust, pulling out ticket stubs and scraps of magazines, handing me the pieces until I'm not such a wreck anymore.

"And I was thinking of widening the order window so the runners have more room. Maybe shifting everything this way…" He walks across the dining room. "We could use some more square footage here."

"And the patio?" I walk over to him. "Maybe we could

add a pergola and some lights." I take the stick from him, drawing it out. "We could have someone in this corner playing music for the people eating outside."

He smiles, coming to the edge of the patio area. "And what about here?"

I shrug. "More parking spaces?"

His eyes crinkle. "No." He takes the stick from me and carves into the dirt: *Pen's Pastelería*. He nods. "That's where you belong."

I can see it: the lights strung between the two buildings, people spilling in and out, my father just a few feet away, the music and laughter suturing us together.

My eyes well up again. Not just because it's perfect and everything I've always wanted, but because I know that some days I'll wake up and not be able to see any of it. Because that voice in my head will be louder than the one in my heart, and no amount of medication, no amount of distraction or even love will be able to quiet the fear.

But maybe I don't need to quiet it. Maybe I just need to learn to recognize the voice buried underneath. Until her whispers are more like shouts, the sound a tether to that moment just on the other side of my depression. The one I always know is coming even when it feels like the pain is all there is.

Before I can say anything, the insurance adjuster makes his way over, holding out some paperwork for my father to sign.

My father tips his chin. "You got your first customer."

I turn and see Xander.

"What are you doing here?"

He's frozen, taking it all in.

"Xander...?"

"Abuelo told me what you did...." His eyes settle on my face. "You found him."

"I'm—" I don't know if I owe him an apology, if seeing his father was even more painful than what El Martillo put him through.

"Thank you." He rests his lips against my forehead.

"Is he—?" Words fail me again. How do I ask Xander if his father is sorry? If he still loves him? If he even bothered to try to explain why the hell he left?

"Talking has been hard." Xander looks down. "There's just so much...."

"I know."

"But it's good. Seeing him...it's been good." He winces.

"You should be resting."

He shakes his head. "I needed to see it."

I let him look, knowing that he's reliving that night. He shudders, angry again.

"I have to fix this."

I squeeze his hand. "We will."

He looks down at me. "Together?"

"Together."

And even though there's almost nothing left, no clear way out or place to begin, I know we *will* fix this. Because we can. Because in life, sometimes the only way to move forward is to do the scary thing. Especially when it's the right thing.

That's what I've learned about fear. Courage isn't a currency, and claiming it isn't a game. The things that scare us aren't roadblocks but mirrors, and bravery isn't about shattering our reflection, it's about having the strength to look.

"What do you see?" Xander asks.

I sense the smile on my face and realize how strange it must seem. "Let me show you." Then I take his hand, leading him back to the entrance where my father and I started.

When we make it back around to the edge of the patio, *Pen's Pastelería* scratched in the dirt, Xander kneels, brushing the letters with his hand.

He looks up at me. "You're coming home."

Suddenly, I'm struck by the fact that Xander loves my father's restaurant almost as much as I do. That maybe he found something here he'd been looking for in all those old photographs and envelopes stamped RETURN TO SENDER. But I can also tell that a part of him is still searching. For answers to all of those questions about what happens next.

I don't know if justice will win out. If J. P. will never step foot in this neighborhood again. I don't know if getting answers to those questions will actually put anything to rest.

What I do know is that home isn't as fragile a place as Xander thinks it is. Home was never these four walls. It wasn't my grandfather's murals or that old prayer card. It wasn't even the food. When my mother made me leave home, I thought I'd lost that too. But her love followed me. Insistent. Just like Xander's love for his father carried him to the United States. Like his abuelo's love was a refuge.

Because the truth is, home is not a place. It's a heartbeat. A living thing made up of every person who has ever left a mark on us.

But maybe Xander needs to see that mark, to see that he is home to me as much as my father's restaurant is. That we can be his home too.

I take the stick my father used to map out our future, answering the only question I can as I draw a giant X in the rubble right next to my name. Then I look to Xander and say, "We both are."

ACKNOWLEDGMENTS

I'd like to start by thanking the people who are grievously underappreciated but who are so incredibly near and dear to my heart—teachers.

Mrs. Perry, thank you for always making me think I was special. To Mrs. Cox, thank you for letting me hang out in the library all summer even though the school was supposed to be closed. And to every other teacher I had who nurtured my creativity and encouraged me to keep writing, thank you for noticing what mattered to me.

Today, I continue to be surrounded by incredible teachers. I want to thank my mentor teacher, Jennifer Hoober, for modeling how to love kids, how to be strong in my convictions, and how to practice self-love. Thank you, Stephany Gaines, my work mom, for showing me how to set boundaries and how to stay laser focused on what matters—doing the right thing for kids, always. Both of you embody everything I adored about my favorite teachers growing up, and I'm so grateful to have you cheering me on now.

And if you are a teacher who is currently holding this

book in your hands or you're considering getting copies for your classroom library, thank you. While I had some amazing teachers growing up, none of them ever gave me a book like this. I wasn't assigned to read a book with POC characters until my senior year of high school, and I often wonder what would have happened if I'd been given those stories sooner. Would I have struggled less with my own identity? Would I have felt less pressure to fit in?

Knowing my book could be a powerful mirror for students who need one makes every hard day of writing and every rejection I've experienced along this publishing journey so incredibly worth it. Thank you so much for the work you do to get these books into the hands of kids. It means the world.

Next, and most important, are my students. I write books for teens for the same reason I teach teens. Because they are incredible. Because they are steadfast in their convictions. They're passionate. They're courageous. They're honest. They are everything we should strive to be.

I want to thank my students for letting me into your lives, for trusting me with your stories, and for letting me be myself. I feel safe and loved when I'm in my classroom, and I hope you do too. These stories about beautiful brown kids navigating the big scary world are for you.

None of this would be possible without the love and support of my family. I want to thank my parents for giving me the safest and most loving environment in which to explore my creativity. Thank you for always praising my brain above all else and being so easily impressed by any and all of my accomplishments, big and small.

I'm a storyteller because you read to me constantly, and because you let me eavesdrop while you talked about adult things in the living room, and because you let me watch R-rated movies as long as I covered my ears and eyes when you told me to, and because I was allowed to read whatever I could reach, nothing censored or denied.

You gave me so much freedom, so many colors to paint with now that I'm making my own art. I hope you know everything I make is to honor you.

To JD: You and I don't do Valentine's Day or anniversaries. Love letters aren't really our thing. But when I look at this book in its final form, I can see so clearly that that's exactly what it is. This story is my love letter to you. You may not have renovated a food truck for me, but you have made space for my dreams in so many other ways.

Thank you for always making me do the scary thing. So many people helped bring this book to life, but you're the one who lay awake with me at night when I wasn't sure how to be brave. You're the one who told me to try, who made me feel safe enough to fail. You're the one who knew I wouldn't. Not if I never gave up. Thank you for not letting me give up.

Nacho's Tacos was inspired by all your crazy stories from years spent working in food service, so it's only right that I also thank the 2005–2011 employees of Cagle's Steakhouse in Lubbock, TX, for inspiring many of the funniest scenes in this book.

I also want to thank my first storytelling partner and childhood best friend, Jamie Adam, for your willingness to play any ridiculous character I could come up with in our amateur movies (and for supplying the video camera and most other props). Telling stories with you was such a blast, but I hope you'll find after reading this book that my abilities are much improved.

To my fellow Musas, thank you for the advice, emotional support, and endless inspiration. I am honored to be part of this community of fierce and passionate women, and I'm so grateful to have any part in helping and guiding other musas and hermanas who are just beginning their journey.

I must also bow down to the marvelous Beth Phelan, champion of diverse voices and DVpit founder, for creating a space for marginalized creators to shine. Participating in DVpit completely changed my life. It brought me to my wonderful agent, Andrea Morrison, and my amazing editor, Sam Gentry, who are both the kindest and most incredible advocates for my work. I'd like to take a moment to thank them both for holding my hand through this life-changing process and making all of my dreams come true.

Moreover, I must thank the entire Little, Brown Books for Young Readers team for the time and effort they spent to make this little book shine. You took this dream of mine and turned it into something I can actually hold in my hands, which is so beautifully mind-blowing.

Lastly, I want to thank all the readers who have taken a chance on one of my books over the years. Almost a decade ago I chose self-publishing because I didn't know where else my Latina heroines would fit. You were the first to embrace those stories and give them a home.

So thank you, not only to every reader who has supported my work but also to every reader who so selflessly and enthusiastically helps spread the word about books that would otherwise stay invisible. Thank you for making it possible for me to do what I love.

LAEKAN ZEA KEMP

is a writer living in Austin, Texas. She has three objectives when it comes to storytelling: to make people laugh, cry, and crave Mexican food. Her work celebrates Chicanx grit, resilience, creativity, and joy while exploring themes of identity and mental health. *Somewhere Between Bitter and Sweet* is her debut YA contemporary novel. She invites you to visit her online at laekanzeakemp.com or follow her at @LaekanZeaKemp.